THE PHARISEE'S WIFE

THE PHARISEE'S WIFE

the PHARISEE'S WIFE

JANETTE OKE

Tyndale House Publishers
Carol Stream, Illinois

Visit Tyndale online at tyndale.com.

The Pharisee's Wife

Cover designed by Sarah Susan Richardson

Edited by Kathryn S. Olson

For information about special discounts for bulk purchases, please contact Tyndale House Publishers at csresponse@tyndale.com, or call 1-855-277-9400.

Library of Congress Cataloging-in-Publication Data

A catalog record for this book is available from the Library of Congress.

ISBN 979-8-4005-0588-1 (HC)
ISBN 979-8-4005-0589-8 (SC)
ISBN 979-8-4005-0590-4 (Large Print)

Printed in the United States of America

31 30 29 28 27 26 25
7 6 5 4 3 2 1

To you who hold this book in your hands, no matter the time or your circumstances, may you know that I have prayed for you, that in some way, as only God through his Spirit can do, your heart may be touched to meet whatever is your present, personal need.

What is the price of five sparrows—two copper coins? Yet God does not forget a single one of them. And the very hairs on your head are all numbered. So don't be afraid; you are more valuable to God than a whole flock of sparrows.

LUKE 12:6-7

CHAPTER ONE

The Market

THE SUN HAD NOT YET RISEN above the horizon and already the day felt stuffy from the heat. The market stalls were in full voice, sellers calling out their wares with loud and irritatingly harsh shouts that they hoped would outdo their competition. Bodies, already oily with sweat, pressed against one another as they forced their way past, sharing the same limited space, breathing the same limited air. Smells from the area where the camels and donkeys were tethered were heavy with familiar but offensive odors on the stifling, breezeless air. The young woman wending her way cautiously in and out among the harried and hurried crowd of shoppers lifted a corner of her shawl to her nose.

The nearest vendor did not miss her approach. It was obvious that this girl was not familiar with her surroundings. Perhaps she was not even familiar with markets in general. She looked lost and confused. The vendor felt not only a curiosity but also an interest. She had never seen the young woman before. Was she new to the area—or new to her circumstances? She certainly did not look like someone's servant out to purchase kitchen supplies for the day. The shawl she was wearing looked to be of finer material than any servant girl would wear. Yet she wore it casually, or carelessly, not draped carefully over her head and shoulders as a woman of means would wear it.

But this girl could not be classed as one of the wealthy either. Her clothes were not elegant, her manner not haughty. And she walked with an even full stride—not with carefully placed mincing steps.

It made the elderly stall owner curious enough to pause, still holding the fish she had been about to place in the cooler air beneath her table. Suddenly remembering the fish, she leaned over and tucked it in a shaded spot. She hoped for a buyer soon or the fish would be past its freshness.

When she straightened, the young woman was still standing there, her hand lifted to shade her eyes as she scanned the market before her. She was obviously looking for something. It brought the vendor back to her purpose. She straightened to full height and began to call, "Fish! Fresh fish from the Jordan! Fresh fish! Only one left! Get it now! Fish!"

She watched the girl turn and look toward her. "Fresh fish!" she cried again.

The girl changed direction and was now moving closer. The elderly woman reached under the counter platform and drew out the same lone fish so she could display it before her. Perhaps the sale had come in time.

As the girl drew closer, she still wore a frown of confusion. As soon as she got near enough, the woman spoke again. "Fresh fish!" she reminded the girl. "Caught with last night's catch. Ready for the—"

But the girl was shaking her head. "No," she timidly interrupted.

Then she caught herself. "No . . ." and she scanned the market around her again. "I do not . . . I did not come for fish." She looked even more confused.

For some reason impossible to explain, the vendor had a strange wish to help—to protect the girl. For the moment, she forgot about the fish she still held in her hand. "What did you come for?" she asked, but her voice was much lower, softer than the voice she normally used to sell her wares.

"Mother sent me for olive oil. Fresh. She said to be sure it is fresh. And spice. And—and any vegetable that I can find. As long as it is fresh."

The woman felt disappointment—surprisingly not because the young woman would not be buying her last fish. No, her disappointment came because she would not be able to help the potential customer.

She studied her more closely. She was young. Perhaps no more than fifteen. Her skin was soft and, though tanned from the summer sun, still pleasing. It was obvious that she was not a kitchen servant or a field worker. And she was pretty. More than pretty. Her eyes were big and sharing. If one had the time and the patience, the woman was sure those dark, almost violet, eyes could tell many stories. As she watched, the shawl carelessly slipped away, exposing the full face.

She was not pretty. She was beautiful!

The woman looked around quickly to see if others had noticed the delinquent shawl. To her left stood two men, their gazes passing over the entire market crowd. Pharisees! Why were they here? They certainly never shopped at the market.

Then she noticed that the younger one, likely an apprentice, turned his gaze their way. He was looking directly at the young woman, whose face was totally exposed. What would he think of the young woman's carelessness?

"Pull up your shawl," the elder woman hissed in warning.

The girl just looked at her.

"Pull up your shawl," she said with more force. "The Pharisees are here."

With one quick jerk the shawl covered the girl's entire face. Momentarily, even the beautiful eyes, large with alarm, had been hidden. She reached up hesitantly to pull the shawl slightly to one side so she could peer out. Eyes, still dark with fright, glanced around her and spotted the two men off to the side. They had not moved. The older one was continuing to scan the market before him, but the younger one was still looking at her. She pulled her shawl closer again.

"Come in," said the woman. She reached out a hand and urged the girl to move toward the simple tent that provided a bit of shade. "You never know when they might decide to arrest . . ." She let the words trail away. She sheltered the girl with a gentle arm as they moved quickly toward her tent.

The young woman's eyes darted around. The tent had room for very little. She looked around for a clear space where she could withdraw. *Arrest.* Would they really do that? Over a slipped shawl?

The older woman spoke again. "I need to get back to the stall. You stay here for a few minutes. Maybe they will go away without . . ." The shopkeeper did not finish.

She was about to lift the flap of the tent when a grizzled man ducked in the opening. He was shaking his head even as he entered. He nodded briefly toward the unexpected guest, then turned back to the older woman.

She spoke. "There are a couple Pharisees out there. Noticed this girl here with her face uncovered. I brought her in—"

But he interrupted. "I think they got more on their minds on this day than a young woman's misplaced shawl. Don't know why they feel they have to go snooping around—"

She stopped him. "What do you mean *more on their minds*?"

"Didn't you see him?"

"See who?"

"That teacher—Jesus—from Nazareth."

"He's here?"

"Don't know if he's still out there or not, but he and a few of his followers appeared to be shopping for some victuals."

The older woman seemed uncertain whether to retreat farther from the unwelcome Pharisees or run back out to check if the teacher still remained. Which would prove greater? Her fear of the Pharisees, or her curiosity concerning Jesus the Nazarene?

"Wish I had known." She opted to remain. "I've been wanting to see him. See if he is as they say he is. Or if it's just stories. Wish I'd spotted him. Did you see him?"

"Plain as day. Looked like an ordinary man to me."

She moved toward the tent opening, then turned back. Her eyes flashed with anger.

"So that's why they sent their spies! They learned he was here. I heard he can't go anywhere without some Pharisees—or Sadducees, or both—showing up to watch and question him."

The man chuckled. He brushed a gnarled hand over his greyed beard, then lowered himself to the room's only stool, running the hand over his sweaty face. "Hear they weren't successful in trapping him yet. They say he twists their questions right around to make them look a bit foolish. Bright, they say. Bet that's hard on their pride! Mere carpenter knowing more about the prophets and the Holy Scriptures than any of them do." He chuckled again.

"Hullo," a voice called from outside. "Anyone here?"

The shopkeeper ducked through the tent opening and hurried out to answer the call. The girl could hear the bargaining from where she stood. It seemed that the woman was trying hard to sell the last fish.

The man turned to her. "You seen him?" he surprised her by asking.

She shook her head. "I—I do not have any idea of whom you speak," she replied, her voice still shaky. She personally knew nothing of this teacher. She had heard plenty of stories about Pharisees and their strict code of conduct. There had not been Pharisees to bother them in her little village. But the stories concerning them often reached the villagers' ears—enough for her to fear their presence.

Her thoughts suddenly shifted. The man—the other man they were watching. The teacher. Why was he being watched? And why were the Pharisees so interested in him?

Then her thinking did an about-turn. Was this possibly the man of whom her father had spoken? Was he the reason they had left their village to travel to Jerusalem? Her father had referred to him as a prophet. Or was it a rabbi her father wished to see, as his eyes lighted with some unknown hope? No, she was quite sure her father had said *prophet* because her mother had sharply declared that prophets were a thing of the past. Was it possible he was here—now—instead of in the ancient city that was still some miles away?

Her mother had scoffed. Why were they taking this fool's journey away from their safe home just because her crippled father had heard some nonsensical gossip from someone about a strange prophet who could heal? With just his words. "Foolishness!" her mother had ranted.

The debate had been going on for months. The young woman was more than tired of it. She hated the spats, the tension, and even more, the long, hot, dusty trip by caravan to get to the city that was said to have had visits from this magical rabbi-prophet who claimed to have some kind of authority and power. She was weary of the entire mess and its disruption of her life. But she would not have dared to say so.

She jerked suddenly back to attention. She needed to get back to the rented room where she and her parents had resided for the night. But she still had not found the items her mother had sent her to purchase. And her mother was not a patient woman.

She shook her head and moved toward the door of the small tent. Just as she reached for the flap, the older woman's hands brushed it aside.

"Well, that is that," she said with satisfaction. "Finally sold that fish. I'm done for the day." She sighed deeply as though the thought brought great relief.

Then she turned to the girl. "And you? You said your mother needs olive oil."

"And fresh vegetables and—"

"I can take you right to the stall for that. Ruth has the best goods, and her prices are fair. She has all the things you need. Come. I see she hasn't closed up yet. Still a few customers there."

The shopkeeper led the way from the comparable coolness of the protecting tent out into the glare of the fully risen sun. The girl followed, lifting her shawl over her face so high that she almost covered her eyes.

The woman nodded toward the scattered vendors still at the market tables. Then her eyes traveled around the area. "I think the Pharisees have finally left. Everyone is breathing a bit easier."

It was true. Many of the stalls had already closed. But there were still a few shoppers who moved about, now with seeming freedom.

"What did you say your name was?" The question was direct and unexpected.

The girl knew that she had not said. She did so now. "Mary."

"Mary." The name was accepted without further comment.

"It's okay now," the woman assured her. "No need for worries now. If they were about to arrest you, they would have done so while they were here. Just noticed you as a stranger and were curious, I think. But remember—always keep your shawl in its proper place. You never know . . ." Her voice trailed off. When she spoke again, she was muttering to herself. "So—looking for the teacher, were they? Sure wish that I could'a seen him. Been hoping . . ." Her voice silenced as though she realized that her thoughts had been spoken aloud. She shook her head. "Just wish . . ."

They reached the woman with the olive oil, and without a word the older vendor gave Mary a friendly nod of parting, then turned away, still shaking her head and muttering to herself about her deep disappointment. Mary was not even sure if the older woman had heard her simple words of thanks.

CHAPTER TWO

The Family

RETURNING TO HER FAMILY'S overnight lodging place, Mary had not even opened the door before she heard her mother's voice. ". . . and you would believe any story you hear! Here we sit in this dirty little—" The voice stopped, as if searching for words degrading enough to describe their present rented abode. "And still you insist that we go on to Jerusalem because someone said he sometimes . . ."

The voice went on but Mary pressed her shawl against her ears. She did not wish to hear it. If her mother was already angry, would her daughter's lateness from the market just add fuel to the flames? Mary looked about, wishing there was another door to enter the small dwelling. She saw none. Slowly she pushed the door open and stepped in silently. If her mother's back was turned, maybe she . . .

But it wasn't. Mary looked straight into the flashing, angry eyes.

Her father spoke first—even daring to interrupt what her mother was about to say. "And here is our daughter with our meal," he said in an unusually loud, yet pleasant, voice.

For some reason her mother did not respond. She looked flushed—and drained. Mercifully, she merely nodded toward the kitchen space at the back of the quarters and Mary understood that was where she was to take the few purchases.

"And how was the market? You found your way around okay?" her father asked.

"Crowded! Hot! And smelly!" She heard his chuckle as she walked toward the kitchen. "And frightening!" she said over her shoulder.

"Frightening? How so?" Her mother's voice. Perhaps this would give her another argument to use in her bid to go back home.

Mary hesitated. She felt again the fright of the young man looking directly at her. "Pharisees," she said with a shiver.

"Pharisees?" Now it was her father's voice that shared concern. "So they monitor the market here?"

"Not usually, I think. The woman—the vendor—she said—well, it was her husband really—he said they were just there looking for . . . the teacher. The rabbi."

Her father instantly pushed himself upright on his mat. "The one they call Jesus? The Prophet? Here? The Prophet from Nazareth?"

She shrugged. "Well, I do not know who he was. I did not see him. They just said he had been there—shopping—and the Pharisees came to—to watch him or something." Mary reached a hand up to remove her shawl, tossing it carelessly toward a low table. "I am so glad to get that off my head. It is stifling!"

"Let me understand. You say some Pharisees were at the market—just—just looking for someone?"

She nodded.

"But you did not see who?"

A shake of her head.

"But they called him a prophet?"

"Yes. I think. Or a teacher. I think they said his name was Jesus."

"From Nazareth? The Pharisees said he was from Nazareth?"

"It was not the Pharisees who called him that. I did not talk to the Pharisees." She felt another shiver of fear pass through her as she thought of them and the bold eyes of the one who had stared at her. "It was the woman. The vendor whose tent . . ." She bit her lip. How was she to explain why she ended up in a vendor's tent?

"The woman," she went on, carefully selecting her words, and hoping they made some kind of sense to her two parents who were both staring at her, waiting, "she was kind to me. But she worried about the Pharisees who were—were watching me—so she took me into her tent until they went away. But—but her husband came back and said folks at the market had seen the teacher. And he had seen him, too—just an ordinary man, he said—but he was angry that the Pharisees had been there looking for him."

"But you did not see him?"

Again, she shook her head, then held up her shopping basket to indicate that she wished to be rid of it.

"It must have been him," she heard her father say as she moved away. "Right here in this very village. It must have been him. And I missed him."

Her father sounded so sad, so defeated. Mary wondered if he was about to weep.

Her mother's voice had gone soft. "You still think . . . ?"

"I do. I do! And I missed him."

Her mother's quiet reply surprised Mary. "He cannot have gone far." It sounded like a promise.

Mary's father hired two scouts to seek information concerning the Prophet, Jesus of Nazareth. Had he really been in their area? Which direction did he take when he left the village? He wished for news, any news at all that would give him a lead as to what he should do, where he should go to find this man with godly powers.

But the hired scouts returned with very little information. All they knew for sure was that a visiting group of unknown men had been in their village that morning, at their market, and many folks agreed that, yes, it could have been the one who claimed to be a prophet. Their shopping time had been cut short by the appearance of the Pharisees.

As to which way they had gone when they left their village, no one seemed to have noticed. Everyone had been far too distracted. The strange visit from Pharisees had unsettled them all.

The results of the search had only led to further quarreling between Mary's parents. Her mother's brief softness was forgotten. When her father had suggested that they should travel on to Jerusalem as planned because the Prophet had been known to visit the city from time to time, she loudly resisted. Again, she picked up the argument that her husband was following foolish dreams if he thought there was any help to be had from some unknown man who claimed to be a prophet with healing ability.

Without too much resistance, but grave disappointment, the man gave in and announced that come the morrow they would pack up their cart and head home.

It nearly broke Mary's heart to see her father crawl across the mat-floor and pull himself up onto a small stool, his dark eyes wet with his tears of disappointment.

With just a touch from the Prophet with the healing power—or even a word from him—Mary knew her father was sure he could have lived as a whole man once again, able to resume work in his shop that had always produced well enough to care for his family. He had clung to such hopes in traveling to try to find this man of power. And the Prophet had been here. Right at the same time they, too, had been in the village. And they had missed him.

Even as her heart celebrated the fact that they would be going home, she shared the grief of her father. He had always been so strong. So fervent in his care. He wished for healing only so he could continue to meet their needs.

The family consisted of only the three of them now. Her older brother had left the home because of her mother's harsh criticisms. Had her brother still been home at the time of her father's accident, he would have been able to keep the family business operating. But no one knew where he was. Their mother was still too angry with him for leaving to spend any time or money looking for him—and her father was too broken and proud to seek him for his help.

Mary grieved, though she dared not voice it. She missed her older brother. And she knew her father did as well. But any speaking of his name sent her mother into a long, angry tirade. So his name was not spoken. It was as though they had placed him in the burial tomb. Cold and distant and forgotten.

CHAPTER THREE

The Sanctuary

THIS WAS A ROOM OF QUIETNESS. One could not call it solitude, because it was shared by a number of silent members. They were scattered about in various positions—postured in silent prayer, bent over scrolls in concentrated silent study, or even walking about on silent soft-padded feet, their folded hands before them, their eyes on the ceiling or the floor, their lips slightly moving. No words would be spoken aloud here. No hymns of praise lifted heavenward. No signal of greeting passed from one to another. Even glances shared between its residents were forbidden. Private thoughts needed to be instantly checked and focused back on their purpose of being.

This was a study sanctuary, where young men with interest in their faith learned what it meant to be disconnected from the world and focused on the Divine.

Enos was one of the many spending his morning separate, yet surrounded. On any given day he was the most intent, the most focused, of any of the young men, but today he struggled. He fought against it, disappointment and guilt bringing a frown to his normally smooth brow. *"You must stop!"* he demanded his own scattered thoughts. *"You must concentrate! Concentrate!"*

He thought he had mastered the discipline. The strict structure of keeping one's thoughts controlled, one's focus on the demands of the community he served—but today his thoughts kept slipping from confinement and going back to the previous day.

Simon had chosen him, of all the students, to accompany him on a very important scouting trip to a village market. Rumor had reached the ranks of the Pharisees that the would-be prophet had finally dared to show his face in their small village. Enos had felt pleased and overly proud of the honor. Surely it said to the others that he was quickly moving up the ranks ahead of his peers.

But the market had not been what Enos had expected or desired. The day was already hot, exaggerating the unpleasant smells of the place. The voices of the sellers were loud and irritating and the crowd pushed its way forward with rudeness and hurry. Even the fact that he and Simon wore the garments of the elevated Pharisees did not keep them from getting an occasional brush or even a bump from some scurrying person of lesser class. Enos didn't care for the market. And by the look on the face of the senior Pharisee, Simon had enjoyed it even less. He could not wait to get home for "cleansing," Simon had muttered under his breath.

But even though they strained their eyes against the rising sun and scanned the bustling crowd of common people, they did not spot the man they had been looking for. Enos had so hoped that he would be the one who saw him first. He had pictured himself leading Simon to the very spot where the wanted self-proclaimed rabbi could be confronted. But that had not happened. It seemed that someone had sent warning of their coming to the wily man.

Enos had heard enough reports to realize that the Pharisees considered this man to be a threat. An imposter? Yes, but more than that. He was a dangerous false prophet who dared to put himself forward as the one the Israelite priesthood had been promised by long-ago prophets of their race and religion. Like those with whom he shared his life, Enos reasoned it to be a false claim. The unknown rabbi could not be the one. According to their records, he was not of the priesthood—or even the priestly line—and he was from the Galilee.

And to make them even more certain, they were not waiting for a new prophet, but a king. A king who would be their deliverer. A king to follow in the line of the great King David. And some even dared to hope that the one sent from God would also be their savior. Their Messiah! A holy one.

This man—this lowly son of a carpenter, with followers who came from the shores of the Galilee, mere laborers over boats and nets—the Promised One? Impossible!

Regularly the trainees of his community of Pharisees received reports and admonishments and stern lectures concerning this evil man. Not only did the Pharisees fear him, but they also hated him for the sense of insecurity he had brought to their safe and secure beliefs. The repeated lectures of caution had the whole community on edge. Whenever this strange man's name was spoken, Enos felt a chill. He had never tasted such venomous hatred before—and he had not yet met the man. But he had been schooled day by day to despise the very words *Jesus of Nazareth*.

And this man, who claimed such honor, certainly was not a prophet. He had no credentials. Had not studied the Law. Was not schooled by any of their recognized leaders of the Faith. A prophet from Nazareth? Ridiculous!

What legitimate prophet would ever come from a place like Nazareth? No one of worth had ever traced his roots to the ranks of the lowly laborers or fishermen of that area. Not a one of the Pharisees planted a foot in that Gentile-infested place if it could be avoided. To do so left one feeling unclean and degraded. It took many baths to erase the feeling of defilement.

But Enos had to admit that even though he had been schooled to loathe the man, he, like many others, still felt a measure of curiosity. Why this man was so hated, yet so loved, was a mystery.

Enos forced his attention back to the present. His normally focused thoughts were too scattered, too uncontrolled. He must get them under his command again. Why did he feel so totally distracted?

Well, certainly the news—or lack thereof—regarding the Nazarene had upset the entire residence. Yet, if he was honest with himself, his unrest was not as much about the man as it was about the strange girl he had spotted.

He was sure that she did not belong to this small village within a day's journey from Jerusalem. If she did, surely, he would have heard of her. But she was such a contradiction. Her dress, her manner, and especially her careless shawl, were all signs of humble birth, but her beauty spoke of kings' palaces. Honor. Prestige. He had never seen such a beautiful woman. Was it simply because he had rarely seen the full face of any young woman? No, he was sure that was not so. He remembered the local girls from his youth. None of them had the potential for such beauty. Just the thought of being the husband of such a beautiful woman made him tremble. He would be the envy of every man in Jerusalem.

Enos shook his head. He could not be in this confined space with such troubling thoughts. He needed solitude in order to properly work his way through this new circumstance.

He moved on silent feet toward the exit. Though none of his fellow students stirred a limb, he still felt their eyes upon him. He was leaving before putting in the required time. Would there be discipline? For the moment he could not care. He needed the air, the space. He must be off by himself where he could think.

After a long struggle in the garden, Enos reached a decision. It might be a costly one, but there was no other choice. He must somehow possess the beautiful young woman he had seen at the market. Having seen her, he would never be satisfied with a less beautiful wife.

It was true that she was from a lower class, but he could fix that. After he had made the arrangement with her parents, he would seek someone to provide tutoring in social propriety. He knew of a few higher-ranked Pharisees who used such training for the women they had chosen—though it was all very hush-hush.

The first thing he did was to sit down at his desk, take out a particularly long papyrus page, and make a list of the steps that must be taken. When he felt satisfied with his plan, he sounded the soft gong that called for his carefully chosen servant. He had complete confidence that this man could follow explicit orders without sharing any information with any curious outsiders. After all, the man was well aware that his very life depended on it.

The gong had no sooner stilled its soft echoes when he heard a stir behind the doorway curtains. The servant known as Ira moved in silently, bowed deeply, and stood with hands folded submissively in front of him. He did not speak, but waited to be spoken to.

The very sight of the man's complete and instant submission always brought pleasure to the heart of Enos. To have such power, such prestige, such control, was the answer to all he had ever dreamed.

He did not speak immediately. Let the man wait for his bidding. He could hold him there in this pose all day, if he wished, and the man would not stir.

But Enos's eagerness led him to cut the time short. "I have a task for you," he began. "Yesterday I was called to go to the market in the small village across the east valley. I do not even recall the name—it is of no consequence—but you will know it. There was a young girl there, shopping for wares. I have interest in her for personal reasons, but little information. And I do need some information. You can begin by speaking with a vendor at a fish market there. Her stall is at the southeast corner of the square. She has a striped tent, of poor quality, just behind her table."

In spite of his intense search of his own memory, that was all Enos could remember of the vendor's stall. His attention had been totally taken with the girl. He could have added that her shawl had slipped, revealing her beautiful face, but how would that help? Nor was he ready yet to reveal why he was interested in the young girl. Servants were trained to obey, not question.

The servant had not lifted his eyes, but Enos knew he had been listening and memorizing every word.

"Speak with the woman vendor." His voice became more firm, more commanding. "She is to understand that this inquiry comes from a Pharisee and she is to cooperate fully."

There was just the slightest nod from the man who stood before him.

"I wish the girl's name. Her family name and where she resides. And if the vendor has further knowledge, she is to share it. All of it. Understood?"

Another nod and the man disappeared as silently as he had entered, seeming to fade into the curtain.

Once Enos was sure the man was no longer nearby he leaned back in his chair, a smug smile of contentment on his face. The plan was in motion.

CHAPTER FOUR

The Reversal

It was not a happy party that began preparations early the next morning. Mary already felt her young shoulders drooping from the unpleasant task of packing the few belongings they had brought with them. It had been a long, dusty, hot trip to come to this small village. It was bound to be just as long, as dusty, and as hot to travel the long road back home. She could feel the sweat making her cotton garment stick to her arms and her back and they had not yet taken one step toward home.

She could see the pain in her father's eyes each time she looked his way. He sorrowed deeply that he had failed in his attempt to find the Prophet of Nazareth. If only . . . if only his dream had come true. If only the Prophet had been found. Their lives would have been so changed. Healed! It would have been healing for all of them, not just her father. Things would have returned to the way they had been before his accident.

Mary sighed deeply and brushed at her tears. Her father had always been the most important person in her world.

When she was young she would run to greet him at the end of his busy day in his shop. He used to reach down and lift her to his broad shoulder and carry her home amid laughter and teasing. It did not seem to bother him that her mother would scold about his improper manner in front of the nearby neighbors. He would merely laugh and swing his young daughter down to the ground with one great sweep of his arms. Mary would gleefully squeal and laugh along with him.

She missed being his little girl, the one who could be lifted up high on his shoulder, way above the ground where he walked. Up close to the branches of the olive trees along the path, high enough to reach to the very top of the door as they entered their home.

But he had other ways of expressing his pleasure with her now that she was grown. She saw the shine in his eyes when she walked sedately down the cobblestone path to meet him at the end of the day. And on the occasions when she was sent the short distance to his shop to carry some message from her mother, he looked so pleased as he introduced her to his workers.

"My daughter, Mary," he would say with pride in his voice. "She is my sunshine and my joy. She nourishes my heart each day with her smile." And he would place his big hand on her slim shoulder, and his smile would, in turn, nourish her young heart.

She was only eight when she began to go to the shop with him. She soon learned to keep the records of customer accounts for him. Before too many years had passed, she was quite proficient and had even added her own adjustments, making the records more informational.

But all of those happy memories seemed so far in the past. Since the accident, sorrows and worries troubled his days, gradually taking possession of the fun-loving father she had cherished.

Who would keep his shop producing? Who would supply the needs for his family?

Her mother, who had always had an inclination toward a toxic tongue, now became cruel with her cutting words and unchecked criticism. The happy home had turned into a dark place. Mary often wished she could spend her days in a corner of her father's shop. Then she would remind herself that the feel at the workplace had changed, also. Even though he now hired a young man with a donkey to take him to and from the shop each day, it was most difficult for Father to accomplish a day's work as he had always done in the past.

CHAPTER FIVE

The Search

Enos paced his small quarters, door to window, window to desk, back to the window, then to the door. It had been three days and still the two men his servant Ira had hired to go to the nearby village and market had not returned. His impatience made him sharp and curt with the servant. Had Ira selected men who were competent and efficient? What was taking so long? They should have been there and back by now.

His servant had replied in a calm, reasonable manner. "My lord," he said, "I did tell them that should they find some promising leads they were to follow them to conclusion. All available information is to be gathered."

His reply should have been an encouragement to Enos. Perhaps he would have all the information that he needed when the two men who had been sent on the quest returned.

But it did not calm him. What if someone else had seen her?

What if, even now, some other man were making an offer to the father?

Perhaps he should send out another man, one with the promise of added money as an incentive when he was successful. Perhaps he should go and talk to the vendor himself—but such an idea was offensive. It did not fit well with his position as a Pharisee.

He was not in a pleasant mood when the two men finally returned on the fifth day. He was tempted to be vindictive even as his servant showed them into the room, but he tried to swallow his anger in the hope that they had some good news.

It did not help that after their low bow they both stood in silent obeisance, their hands hidden in their coarse woolen garments. He waved aside their pretense. He knew without asking that neither of the pair had any loyalty to a Pharisee.

"Well?" he finally asked when they remained mute. "Did you earn your pay?"

The rougher of the two moved closer. Enos could smell his unwashed garments from where he stood. He deliberately took a step backward, causing the man to risk a cocky half-smile.

"My lord," he finally said. "We have come with our report." He stopped there and Enos felt a strong urge to reach out and slap him. Instead, he took another step backward and stared at the vulgar man.

He did not miss the twinkle in the man's eye. Enos could almost read his mind. He was probably delighted at having irritated a Pharisee. Yet he knew he would not be dismissed until the report had been given.

Enos could feel those taunting eyes glimpse down to the hem of his robe as if hoping to glimpse his footwear. Some claimed that many a Pharisee walked on built-up footwear so that he could artificially tower over other men.

For one brief moment Enos was tempted to expose a sandaled

foot to prove that he did not need the false boost to give him his height, but he dismissed the thought with an angry flip of his long, draped shawl.

"You were to be paid to gather some needed information. Either you have been successful, or you have not. If you have anything to report, report. If not, leave my presence. There is the door." Enos pointed toward the exit.

The response was not what he had hoped. The man before him did not cower. In fact, his chin lifted slightly. However, the second man, who was still standing near the doorway, frowned, clearly worried that the pay would not be forthcoming if his partner did not get on with the task of reporting.

"We do have a report, master." The man still did not appear submissive but he seemed ready to fulfill his mission. "We went to the village and to the market as requested. We found the vendor, as requested, and asked concerning the young lady who had visited her stall on the date given." He stopped, not even lifting his eyes from the piece of rumpled cloth he had pulled from somewhere within his sleeve. It seemed he'd used a cheap, makeshift papyrus to record their findings.

"And . . . ?" Enos prompted, rejecting the silence.

"The vendor is not well acquainted with the young woman in question. Furthermore, she was reluctant to answer any questions concerning her. *A stranger. Just passing through,* she said."

"Did you tell her that the request came from a Pharisee?" cut in Enos.

"Yes, my lord. That is the reason she did not wish to speak."

Enos whirled away. He took a deep breath to calm himself and asked as quietly as he could manage. "Did you get *any* information?"

"Her name is Mary," the man said as though that was enough.

"Mary! Mary?"

"You do not like the name Mary, my lord?" the man dared to ask.

"It is of no help at all. Every second woman on the street is named Mary. Mary! Common! Totally . . ." Enos stopped, unable to express his anger and disappointment.

But the unnerving man stated very calmly, "That is what we thought, my lord. That is why we spent another two days to see if we could find out *which* Mary she might be."

Enos whirled back to the man. He dared not even pose the question that clamored to be asked.

The annoying man looked back at his linen scrap, his eyes not even lifting to Enos. Then he took a breath and began, his words coming fast upon one another. "The girl is from a village near the Galilee, close by Jabesh-Gilead. Her father is a millwright. Or at least he was, until an unfortunate accident made him a cripple. His name is Amos ben Simeon, but he is known as Amos the Millwright."

A self-satisfied smile curled the man's lips but he continued. "He was commended for his good work and his shop did well until an accident took the use of both his legs. The girl has one brother, Benjamin, but no one knows his whereabouts at present. Her mother, Hulda, is a woman with a sharp tongue. Their reason for being in the village was just an overnight stop for rest. They were headed for Jerusalem—in search of the Prophet Jesus, from Nazareth. It seems that Amos the Millwright wished for a miracle to restore the use of his legs. They learned that the Prophet had been in the village, but when he found that two Pharisees were seeking him for unknown reasons, the Prophet and his followers left secretly. No one knows which way they traveled, though it was judged that they were *not* heading to Jerusalem. So Amos and his family decided to go home. Perhaps they heard, or hoped, that the Prophet was going their way."

The man shrugged a careless shoulder but did not slow his flow of words. “Mary, whose beauty is spoken of by all who know her, will be fifteen on her next birthday. She is obedient to her parents and respected by her neighbors and friends. She reads. And does sums. Unusual for a girl from a village but it seems her father taught her. She has helped him with his shop. Her favorite sweet is ripe figs. She does not care much for olives even though they are a staple for the villagers. She likes living by the lake and even rows their simple boat and occasionally catches a fish. She gardens and cares for the coop of chickens . . .”

“Enough!” shouted Enos, his hand coming up to halt the man. It was far too hard for him to keep up with the rapid flow of information. Besides he felt that the account was getting too personal. He wished to discover some of those things about the girl himself.

The rough man, who had not even stopped for a breath during his discourse, tucked away his rumpled notes, a cocky shrug to his shoulders.

“I trust we have fulfilled all requirements, master,” he dared to suggest. “We now wish to claim the bonus that your honored servant, Ira, has promised.”

“Yes. Yes, of course.” Enos agreed. He was not going to say one word of praise for the successful job the man and his partner had done. After all, they had only done what they had been hired to do. Still, he could not help but wonder how they had managed to gather so much information.

Enos was most anxious to be rid of this overly confident informer and his partner “My servant will give you the arranged payment.” He was about to say more when he noticed that his trusted servant had silently entered the room and with a formal bow to his master was ready to escort the two men from the residence.

But just before the cheeky man left the room he turned, and with a knowing nod, he said, “One more thing, my lord. At the present time the father is in deep financial need. A more affordable bride price might be accepted and still do much to relieve the family's debt. I feel assured that any reasonable offer would be very hard to turn down." He even dared to wink before he moved toward the curtain.

"One moment," Enos called to stop him.

He turned.

"Your notes—from your sleeve. They are not to be made public. Leave them with me."

The man grinned, pulled the folded linen from inside his sleeve, and tossed it carelessly on the floor. Without further acknowledgment, he turned and was gone.

Anger filled the young Pharisee. So, all the time the man had been gathering his facts he had known why Enos wanted the information. Had the hired spy shared his errand with anyone else? The vendor at the market? The village where he had researched the family? Anyone along the trail? It left Enos feeling naked and exposed to have people reading his mind and knowing his wishes. He deserved his privacy. He was a Pharisee. A Pharisee!

His hand was shaking with fury as he reached down and picked up the crumpled scrap of linen on which the man had detailed his report, turning it first one way and then the other. There were no markings on the cloth at all. He crumpled the sheet in an angry fist and threw it back to the floor. The man from the streets had been faking reading from his notes.

He banged the gong for Ira, who appeared immediately as if by some kind of magic. The servant stopped and bowed, hands hidden in his ample sleeves, then dipped his head to wait silently for his master's orders.

"I wish to make arrangements for a woman as my wife." He stopped and frowned slightly. Was that how one said it?

Ira seemed to get the message. He nodded.

"The family is from a village near Jabesh-Gilead. Father Amos the Millwright. Mother Hulda. The daughter is presently known as Mary. That will change. But for now, that will be the name on the contract."

Enos had some worries about the name situation. He had no intention of leaving her with such a common name as Mary. Yet he was sure he would not be able to make the legal change until she was his. He wished it was possible to have that arrangement made before their wedding. He hoped that once the bride price was offered and accepted he could proceed directly with the change of name. But, he reasoned, one step at a time. The courts could get quite testy if one tried to do things out of proper order.

"Do you wish me to procure a lawyer, master?"

Enos had not thought of that. Acting through an expert in the Law would give him standing he would not have on his own.

"Yes—yes, of course."

"When would you like to see him, Lord?"

"Well, I—I . . . As soon as he is available, of course. I wish to get the proceedings started as soon as possible."

Ira nodded. Before he could turn to leave the room, Enos spoke again. "Does this man—the lawyer—does he have other duties? I mean, is he able to do other tasks than the—the—the bridal arrangement—the bride price—with the father?"

There was a moment of silence. When Ira spoke again it was not an answer, but a question. "What did you have in mind, master?"

Enos felt a twinge of embarrassment, which was a rare feeling for him. He was used to being in control, not feeling his way through a circumstance. "Well, the young lady—she will be in need of a change of name. Does the lawyer—can he care for that, as well?"

Ira hesitated. "I have no knowledge of that, master, but I assume such tasks are within his power."

Ira had barely left the room when Enos had another thought. He thumped the gong with impatient knuckles rather than the implement made for the purpose. The servant was quick to respond.

"I wish you to have a list made up for my consideration of pleasing names—for a woman. A young woman. Of society. I wish to have it prior to the lawyer's visit so that I may study it and choose."

Ira stood in thought for a moment. "Pleasing names?"

"Yes. Is that so difficult?"

"From which languages, master?"

"Hebrew, of course. Only Hebrew."

"Yes, my lord."

Enos gave a curt nod that the servant understood as a dismissal. He was just disappearing behind the curtain when Enos called after him. "And do not bother putting Mary—or any of the other common names on the list. Understand?"

Ira turned enough so that he could nod in obedience, then he was gone.

CHAPTER SIX

The Lawyer

THE LIST WAS PRESENTED just after Ira had cleared away the remains from the evening meal. A number of the names Enos had not heard before. That fact pleased him. He wished the name to be different. Exclusive. And melodic.

Many of the names were quickly discarded. Still too common. No magic. Not suitable for the one that they would serve.

Abigal. Pretty—but used. *Amaris.* Nice. *Ardith.* Unusual. *Daniela.* The name brought up visions of a lion's den. *Dara.* Too short. *Davida.* He let it roll off his tongue a few times. He pictured King David. Too masculine. *Deborah.* He had heard it before. *Dinah.* No. *Edena.* Edena! Rather interesting but perhaps not as elegant as he would like. *Elizabeth.* Already taken. *Gabriella.* Pleasant. *Johanna.*

His eyes skipped a few more lines.

Keturah. It sounded a bit too familiar. *Lewanna.* Lewanna! He was quite sure he had never heard the name before.

He skipped quickly over a few more.

Manuela. Too much like Manuel, making him think of Emmanuel. Masculine. *Mara.* Short—but it had a rather nice ring. *Mara.*

He skipped a few more. They sounded familiar.

Simona. That caught his eye. It was nice.

He reviewed them all again. The list was narrowed down to two: Lewanna and Simona. He listened to the sound as he pronounced them, one after the other. Which would be better—making her distinctive, yet approachable? Desirable, yet morally grounded.

He retired with the two names still on his lips. Surely by morning, in time to meet with the lawyer, he would know which best suited his young bride-to-be. He wished for a name that would complement her youth and yet leave her room to mature to be a woman of strength and beauty.

The lawyer whom the servant Ira ushered in was tall and almost skeletally thin, with black piercing eyes that seemed to take in the entire room and its resident with one full sweep and no hint of a smile.

His first question was blunt and spoken without offering any greeting first. "Do you wish to move to a private room or remain here?"

Enos was taken aback. Surely the man could see for himself that the only other rooms were his living quarters, including his bed chamber. This was as private as he wished to be. He was thankful that he had at least cleared the surface of his desk, which was stationed beneath the room's largest window. He did not answer, merely nodded toward it. He was pleased with Ira's foresight in moving a second chair into the room.

The man followed the nod and settled himself in what Enos considered his own chair. Begrudgingly, he moved to take the borrowed seat.

The lawyer began by opening his cloth sack and spreading its contents across the limited desk surface: reed pen, ink, pumice stone, and rolls of papyrus—some already written upon.

"Your servant has informed me that you wish to offer a bridal price for a young woman who lives in a distant village." Enos opened his mouth to respond, but the man continued. "I understand there is also the matter of a name change. Has the young maiden asked for a change of name?"

"No—but . . ."

"I see," said the lawyer. "You have taken it upon yourself to make the change. Without her knowledge, perhaps?"

For the first time in his life Enos felt challenged in his own home by someone with authority above his own. He shifted uncomfortably. Then indignation seized him.

"My servant was to arrange for me a lawyer who would come to my home to serve me—to follow my bidding. Not one to—to question my intent." Enos stood to his full height and glared at the man.

The lawyer did not even raise his eyes. His gaze remained on a length of papyrus he was unrolling over the too-small desktop.

"And since my time is limited—and costly—I suggest we get at the task," he said calmly and with practiced authority. "The first order of business is to have a clear understanding. When you make any statement it must be truthful and direct. If it is found not to be so, my reputation will be called into question and you—you may end up lying under a heap of stones. Clear?"

It was clear who was in charge here. Enos could not even utter a sound in response. The man seemed to take the silence as consent.

He gave his reed pen a few quick strokes with the pumice stone in order to sharpen its tip and cleared his throat. Enos would have had the man thrown from the room, but he needed him.

"You wish to make an offer to one Amos ben Simeon, a millwright, for his daughter, Mary, as your bride. But you also wish to, without the girl's or her parents' knowledge or permission, change the name of said maiden. Correct?"

Enos almost choked on the word. "Correct." He could not wait for the day when he had full authority as a Pharisee to put this loathsome man in prison for his superior manner.

But the man, his eyes firmly fixed on the document before him, went on. "And your offer? What are you promising Amos ben Simeon in exchange for his daughter in marriage?"

Enos had no answer. "I have not—this is—" He felt like a foolish schoolboy. "I expected that you would be familiar—"

The man cut in. "You wish me to make a suggestion? I understand the young maid is of unusual beauty." He said the words with no emotion but, Enos felt, with considerable understanding of the implications. "Where did you meet?"

Enos felt his temper rise again. Was this really necessary, or was the man just being difficult—and nosy?

"In a market," he finally managed to say, hoping that would end this part of their conversation.

But it did not even slow the man down. "Why were you at the market?"

Enos took a deep breath. "I was sent with another of my order to check out a report that—that the man they call Jesus of Nazareth was there."

For the first time the man turned to look fully at him. "And was he?"

Enos sighed. It felt like he was admitting yet another failure. "We did not find him," he said.

The man could not hide his look of disappointment before he

turned back and dipped his reed pen once more. "I have always wished to see him," he admitted as though to himself. His pen tapped against the rim of the jar to rid itself of extra ink.

"And the girl?"

Enos brushed at his hair with a nervous hand. He stood up and crossed to a window to look at another sultry day. Even the village dogs were stretched out in the shade, ignoring all action in the streets.

"She was there—buying from a stall, I presume. When I sent men to find her, they discovered that she was just passing through with her family and had stopped for the night."

The man put down his quill and turned in his chair to face Enos. "You asked for my advice regarding the bride price. Here is what I would suggest and how I have come to my conclusion." He stood and pinned Enos in place with dark, sharp eyes. "You are an impulsive young man. And ambitious. You are most anxious to reach the highest ranks of the Pharisees. You like to impress others with knowledge, power, and position. It is important for you to have the best available. You have seen a young woman. I would count her a child were she my daughter. I've been told she is not yet fifteen."

His words continued like a series of blows. "You conclude her beautiful enough to tempt others to jealousy. So, you want her. You have not met her, nor she you. She is of, shall we say, lower status. But you feel you have ways to correct that. First of all, you will change her name. Mary is too common. I would guess that you will also engage some training—some upgrading. You are even willing to pay a bride price that is considered . . . impressive. And you wish me to tell you what that price should be."

It all sounded so ugly. The man had made it sound demeaning and sordid, even to the ears of Enos. But he did not speak. Nor did he hang his head in shame. He had rights. Other men in his position would do the same thing. He stood his ground in silence.

The man of law took his seat again and lifted his pen. "I will need the name."

Enos blinked. He was not following.

"The name," prompted the lawyer. "You wish to discard the name of Mary. What do you wish to put in its place?"

Oh, *that* name! For a moment Enos felt his mind go blank. What was it he had chosen? "Oh, the—the new name. Yes, it is . . ." It came to him. "It is Simona."

The man wrote the new name carefully onto his page. Then he reached for another scrap of papyrus, dipped his pen once more and wrote a number—then another number—as Enos watched him silently. "Here is my suggestion for the bride price," he said. "And here is the fee for my services."

Both numbers were shocking. Enos stared at them dumbly. He'd had no idea it would cost so much. It would consume almost his entire inheritance. He would need to figure some way to increase his income—and quickly.

But the lawyer rose and looked directly into the eyes of the younger man. "For this amount I will write the proposal that will be delivered to the girl's father. I will word it in a way that will promote you and that will make him welcome it. I have a solid reputation for successful propositions. And I understand he is in great need through no fault of his own."

A hint of frustration appeared in the man's eyes. "And the young woman's name will be officially changed on the documents sent along with the proposal of the bride price offer. If her father disagrees with any part of the contract, name change, or money offered, my price still stands for my services. It does not depend on his agreement. I will be paid in full before the courier leaves to present the offer to the millwright."

Enos swallowed. "Agreed," he managed to say.

"I will have your copy of the agreement ready for you by noon tomorrow. Ira knows where to find me. You can send the two payments with him."

The lawyer gathered all of his scrolls and supplies from the desktop and bundled them back into the sack that he carried. He gave Enos a curt nod, flipped his shawl back over his shoulder, and stepped toward the curtain that hung by the door to the entry. Before he even reached it, a hand swept it aside and there stood Ira ready to show him out.

There was no exchange of pleasantries as Enos watched the curtain fall back into place. Never had he been happier to have a guest take his leave. He had loathed the man. His arrogance. His cockiness. His stark honesty.

On the other hand, he had just won a victory. He would soon have his bride. He had been given no reason to think that the millwright would reject his generous offer.

CHAPTER SEVEN

The Proposal

THE CALL FROM the small outer court was such a surprise that Hulda, who was busy dressing pieces of lamb to place on the roasting spit, took a nip from her own finger with the sharp blade. Anger more than pain made her desire to curse whoever was making the clamoring noise at her front door. She was already constructing the words she would use in response as she wrapped the injured finger in a corner of her apron and headed toward the unexpected call.

Before she reached the door a second shout came. This time it was addressed to her husband the millwright. That fact had her frown with concern. Who would want something of her husband and why? Did their family not already have enough distress?

"Mary," she called in a loud voice. "We have some trouble out front. Come quickly." Even as she spoke she jerked open the rickety wooden door that led to the street.

But what met her eyes was nothing like she had expected.

Before her rose a pair of impatient grey horses hitched to a small chariot. The driver was dressed in finery with a red cloak wrapped over his shoulders, attached with some kind of insignia. He wore a helmet with a huge feather that fluttered with each movement of his head.

Hulda stood transfixed until a voice spoke, coming from just next to her ear, causing her to jump. She had not seen this second man, who stood next to the wall holding out some kind of document. He, too, was dressed in a manner that Hulda had never seen before on her quiet street.

Her prepared rebuke was totally forgotten. She stood staring instead, trying to sort out in her mind why they were standing before her simple abode. Obviously, there was some mistake. She heard a gasp behind her and realized that Mary had joined her.

The man with his official-looking script stepped forward. "You are the woman Hulda, wife of Amos the Millwright?"

Hulda could not speak to answer. Quickly her mind switched directions. What could this man possibly want with them? Had something bad happened to her husband? Was there trouble at his place of business? Or was it their son, Benjamin?

Then her thoughts shifted again. Whatever this was it was not meant for them. For this humble house—unless—unless it was some trick. Some false claim from somewhere. She stiffened and anger took over once more. "Why do you ask? Where did you come from and why are you here?"

The man before her straightened to his full height and returned her scowl with one of his own. "We have come with authority from an honorable Pharisee of Jerusalem, Enos ben Elias, to present a message to Amos the Millwright. Is he at hand?"

Hulda began to tremble. Surely it must be something about Benjamin. What had the boy done that the Pharisees were after their family? She turned back to the messenger. "There is no reason for any Pharisee to be seeking my husband. He has done nothing against the Law—neither the laws of our Faith nor of our nation—nor of the occupying army," she stated boldly.

She heard a sharp intake of breath behind her. No one dared to speak to a messenger from a Pharisee in such a manner. Hulda reminded herself too late that they could all be thrown in jail—or worse—if she did not recant her harsh words.

But the man had stepped closer. "This is not a matter of unbroken law," he said firmly. "This is a legal matter to be presented to Amos the Millwright in person. Is he here?"

Mary, flipping a shawl over her face as she moved forward, brushed past her mother. It had happened. It was the Pharisee from the market. He had tracked her down for not keeping her shawl properly in place. It was all her fault. She would accept the blame, take the punishment, and free her parents of the consequences.

She dipped her head, acknowledging the authority of the man before her. "It is I with whom you need to speak. My father is a man who honors the Law and adheres to the guidelines of the Temple. He would—"

But the man cut in. "Then you should know that it is to your father we must speak. You are not yet of age. And you . . ." He hesitated, then turned to Hulda and continued, "You are *women*."

His stern voice and even sterner expression caused Mary to take a sharp breath and step back.

"Is your father here?" the man almost barked. Mary noticed a third man, holding the shifting team of horses, shake his head in warning as he looked to the courier, still holding out the official-looking wrapped parchment. He seemed to fear that the outspoken man would be jeopardizing their mission.

"Your father. Is he here?"

"He is not," Mary answered, her head still down. "He is at his shop."

"When will he be home?"

"He—he arrives about sunset."

The man looked past Mary to Hulda, who still stood mutely next to the door. "You will tell your husband that we will be back tomorrow as the third hour of the day begins. He would be advised to be here to meet us."

As sunset neared, Hulda met her husband at the gate to the courtyard, where she had kept watch. "What have you done?" were her first words, even before the youth who was hired to transport her husband had lifted him down from his cart.

In answer there was only a surprised frown. Then the hired courier placed her father on the mat inside the entrance and turned to leave.

Already Hulda was talking. "So, who surprised us with a visit today? Pharisees! That's who. And they would not speak to a *woman.* Oh no. They had to speak to the *master* of the house. What have you done that the Pharisees have come?"

Mary stepped forward, her voice shaking. "It is my fault. I am so sorry. It was the market. The one I visited. I—I let my shawl slip down from my face. The woman—she tried to protect me from them but they . . . they must have tracked me somehow. I am so sorry, Father." Tears were sliding unrestrained down the girl's cheeks.

Her father reached up a hand to her and Mary sank into his waiting arms, curling herself beside him on his rough reed mat. His legs stretched out before them, angled and motionless. "I am so sorry. I . . ."

"Shh," he said, his hand going up to brush at her hair. "Surely it will not be so bad. A warning, maybe, for a first offense and a promise—and maybe a few coins. Surely it will not be . . ." His words trailed off. In truth no one could predict what the Pharisees might demand.

"They will be back in the morning, at the third hour. You are to be here," Hulda informed him firmly, a sense of envy rising as she watched the two of them exchange affection while she stood apart. "First our son runs off and then our daughter gets sought by the Pharisees. What will—?"

But Amos cut in. "It is not the girl's fault. Perhaps our honored Pharisees would be wiser to spend their time tending to more important infractions."

Mary stirred in her father's arms. Her eyes rose to meet his in fear and she whispered, "It *is* my fault. I was careless. I didn't realize the difference in the laws between our village and the larger towns near Jerusalem."

Hulda spoke again at full volume. "None of this would have happened had we not gone off to Jerusalem to try to find the Prophet you were seeking, and all for naught. And now this."

Mary's father gently released her. "I think your mother needs your help with the evening meal. We will get all this sorted out in the morning. It cannot be too serious." But a bit of a sigh escaped from his lips as he struggled to smile. "I had a good day today. Got two more orders for millwork. Zedec came to pick up his purchase and was pleased with it, so the money is now mine to pay for needed supplies. But it has been a long day and I am anxious for my supper. Let us have no more talk of Pharisees this night."

It was seldom that Hulda heard her husband give an order—for that was exactly what the carefully spoken words were. She and her daughter both knew it. There would be no more discussion of their problem this night. There would be nothing more mentioned about the situation until the Pharisee's courier arrived the next morning.

The whole house held tension as the sun rose. As instructed, no one spoke of it, but it was there, thick and oppressive. What would this day hold?

Mary had thoughts of running away. But where would she go? If she had known where Benjamin had gone, she would have tried to find him.

Her father would be struggling with much the same thoughts, she was certain. What could he do to try to hide her from the Pharisees? Who could help them? But surely there would be dire consequences if he tried to protect her. She was grateful he had made no suggestion of escape.

Mother walked about with her stubborn chin jutted forward. Her lips said nothing, but her attitude broadcast angry defiance. Mary wondered who she was most angry with—the Pharisees, her husband, or her daughter. Again, she felt the anguish of the trouble she had brought to her parents.

At precisely the beginning of the third hour there was a loud call from the courtyard entrance. "Amos ben Simeon!"

Mary's father had instructed her to stay in her room unless she was called, but she could picture again the impressive cart, the flashy uniforms and fancy headwear. Here they were, and there was no way to avoid them.

Mary was relieved that she would not need to face the man. However, she felt like a coward as she left her parents to deal with the consequences of her actions. She heard the gate rattling open and her mother say in a stiff voice, "You may enter. My husband will see you now." He had positioned himself on a stool at the outdoor worktable.

Mary knelt beside her bed, her silent prayer causing her lips to tremble. "Please, Lord God, please," was all she could pray.

In the open courtyard beyond the simple wall, she heard her father greet the man.

He responded in a very official tone. "You are Amos ben Simeon, the Millwright?"

"I am he."

"Your wife is Hulda, daughter of Hiram of Kerak."

"She is."

"You have a daughter Mary?"

"We do."

"It is concerning your daughter that we have been sent by Enos ben Elias, a member of the order of the Pharisees of Jerusalem."

Mary heard her father clear his throat, but before he could utter a word, the courier went on.

"The honorable Enos requests to receive your daughter Mary in marriage."

"What?" Mary heard her father cut in.

"He wishes her to be his bride," the man repeated as though the millwright was slow in thinking or perhaps hard of hearing.

Mary froze in place. Her mind refused to comprehend this shocking turn of events.

"She is only a child," her father responded.

Unbelievably, Mary's mother had said nothing. Mary could not help but wonder what thoughts were going through her head, what expression had flashed across her face.

"How long does this man plan to wait?" her father asked.

"He will arrange for some—introductions regarding the role of a woman in such an honored position as the wife of a respected member of the order. Then he wishes for things to move forward without delay."

"Do I have any say in this matter?" Her father's voice was tight.

"I would strongly advise you not to deny the request. It would not be wise on your part, should the honorable Pharisee need to take this request before the courts—when it could be dealt with amicably."

Silence.

"I may add that the man has honored you with a very sizable dowry for your daughter as his bride. Very sizable! You should be flattered that a girl from this humble village has so impressed him."

"How sizable?" It was her mother's voice that Mary heard, the first that she had spoken.

There was a pause before the sound of a purse of coins dropping to the table.

At length her father spoke again. A bit of irritation edged his voice though Mary could tell he was trying to remain patient. "A daughter is not . . . not chattel—to be sold off to the highest bidder."

But the man cut in, "You could not ask for a higher honor for your daughter than to be wedded to a Pharisee. Surely, you understand . . ."

"What I understand," said her father, his voice tight with emotion, "is that you are asking me to give my daughter to a man I do not know. He may be a Pharisee—he is also a man. And a stranger. Her life will totally change—"

"For the better, sir. She will be a lady of high standing. She will live in dignity and comfort, be honored and envied."

A long pause.

The man changed tack. "Every father in the nation would be honored to have such a price paid for his daughter. I would think that you—in your present circumstances—would feel that God had granted you a gift in offering such an opportunity. The heavy burden of debt can be lifted from your shoulders. You will never need to work again."

"My needs are not my consideration. My daughter is of more worth to me than anything the bride price could buy."

Mary heard her mother quickly cut into the conversation, even though a woman had no right to do so. "I think we need a few minutes to discuss—"

"There should be no need for discussion. It is not wise to treat a Pharisee with contempt."

Mary felt a shiver go all through her body. This was real. And that was not an idle threat.

"We will discuss it, and pray for God's leading," her father said. "May he grant wisdom."

"Indeed!" said the man. "I will be back in the morning, at the second hour. We have a long journey back to Jerusalem and the master will be anxious for our return."

There was no reply from her father, but Mary heard a shuffle of movement and then the gate closed.

Mary sank down onto her low bed, struggling to catch her breath. Her mother's voice was heard the instant the horses pulled away. Mary knew she would have much to say.

CHAPTER EIGHT

The Agreement

As promised, the man was back the next morning as the shadow in their courtyard reached the second hour. Mary's father, who had positioned his stool directly in front of the entrance from the street, opened the gate to him but made no invitation to enter. This time, Mary watched through the small window.

Two copies of the legal document that would seal her destiny were passed from one set of hands to the other and signed. The courier was wise enough to make no comment. He had already been informed how Mary's father felt about the exchange.

After the man had left them the day before, her mother had been quick and forceful in offering her arguments. They had always known that their daughter would need to marry and leave their home—someday. This was earlier than they had supposed, but it would undoubtedly have been no more than a year or two longer. Would he rather see her joined with some poor man from the village than to an honorable member of the Pharisees? They would be wrong to deny her such a life.

She was young, yes, but she was astute. And she was beautiful of face. Such a woman was considered of much worth in the home of a man of means. What more could they wish for their only daughter?

And besides all this, the man had been right. This was a gift from God. What future did they have if they refused this generous offer? Because of the accident that had robbed him of his legs, they were getting further and further behind in what was owed to their creditors. Their son was not there to help them. Who knew where he had gone and why he had left. Mary deserved this opportunity. They would be selfish to think of their wants, rather than the honor . . .

Round and round the arguments had gone, making Mary's head ache. She had tried to block out her mother's voice by placing her hands over her ears, but the thin wall offered no help.

Mary failed to see this marriage as an honor. Again, she envisioned the face of the man who had stared at her. She did not like that face. She would not feel safe with that face. There was something wrong in the way he had looked at her. Like an animal sizing up its prey before pouncing.

But she would never say that to her father. Never. She'd heard him weeping after her mother had finally felt she had won with her repeated arguments and retired to her bed.

Mary's father did not come to her—but she knew that he wished he could. Could one more time hold his little girl and assure her he would never stop loving her. She would always be the nourisher of his heart. She could feel his love in each muffled sob that reached her.

There was to be some reprieve. The wedding ceremony would not take place until Mary had been given some preparatory training for the life she would live as a Pharisee's wife. The Pharisee himself would make the arrangements. A suitable woman would be chosen to be her mentor. A cart would be sent for the girl once the arrangements had been finalized. Her residence would henceforth be in Jerusalem. She was not to be concerned about bringing her garments with her. Her wardrobe would be supplied to suit her new role.

Her father had delivered the news, head down, pausing now and then to seek control. The arrangements were straightforward, all-inclusive, and demanding. Mary's life would no longer be her own. Yet oddly, when Mary heard the words, she felt a measure of relief. At least she had a little time to prepare her thinking—to be ready, as much as possible mentally and physically, for such a confined and controlled life. And with the money her parents had received, her father had some possibility for doctors, for healing.

Amos had stopped and taken a deep breath, then stated with emphasis a strange addition. All the legal work had been done in order that she would no longer be known as Mary, but Simona.

What? Why? She tested the new name on her tongue. *Simona.* She did not like it.

But her mother beamed and sent a silent message her father's way. She seemed pleased with the new name. She even dared to say so. "That sounds so—so regal—like a queen. Already it is starting—the honor to our daughter."

Her father did not even lift his head in response.

Each day Mary faced the fear that today would be the day. That this day a cart or a coach, or some other type of conveyance, would pull up to the door and summon her, and she would need to say goodbye to the village she knew, the friends from her childhood, her simple little room tucked at the back of their dwelling, and the father she loved so much. She was totally unconscious of the fact that when she made the mental count of her upcoming losses, her mother was not included on her list. Mary had never understood the woman she called mother.

She did think of her older brother. They had shared the home for many years. He had been a good brother. She had looked up to him. He was gentle and caring and had often acted as the buffer between her mother's sharp tongue and the young girl's confusion and sense of fear.

But where was Benjamin now? Would he know where to find her? Then, with thankfulness, she realized that if her brother ever again came back home to reconnect with their father, the news of her going would be shared. She would be living in Jerusalem—somewhere.

She knew nothing about her future abode. Where did Pharisees live? What part of the city? Did they all live together? In a commune? Or did they have separate houses? Would she be the one to care for a home of her own? She could do it, of course. She knew how to proceed with each of the household chores. But would it be different in a Pharisee's house? Did they have rules that she would need to learn?

And then she relaxed. There was to be training. She was hopeful that each of her duties would be carefully explained. That was one worry she could lay aside.

Mary did not count off many days before a small coach drawn by a pair of prancing horses pulled up to their door. There had been no warning or message for her to be ready. She was in her mother's small garden, pulling the last of the summer growth, when her mother rushed out, waving a towel and in such a state of excitement that she could not even talk properly. The normally contented chickens in the nearby coop squawked and scrambled, feathers flying and the rooster scolding.

Mary stood up from her kneeling position and brushed at the garden dirt on her hands.

"Look at you! Just look at you! Do not let them see you like this!"

All the time her mother spoke, she was using the towel to brush at Mary's disheveled state. "Your hair is a mess and there is dirt on your chin. And oh, my—your dress—it's your oldest—and so worn—how will we ever get you ready without them seeing—oh, my . . ."

As she fussed, the towel was being flicked and rubbed and swiped at Mary's face and clothes.

Mary took the towel from her mother's hand and began to wipe her own brow. At least she could get rid of some of the sweat from the heat of the sun. Perhaps some of the garden dust would wipe off with it.

Her mother turned and headed back around the courtyard again, still wringing her hands and muttering. Mary continued to wipe at her hands and clothes.

It was not long until her mother was back. "I told them you were at a neighbor's," she said with some satisfaction. "I requested they come back in half an hour." She reached for Mary's arm and pulled her toward the dimness of their dwelling. "Your father should be here—but maybe this is best. You get out of those messy clothes and I'll bring a pitcher of water for you to wash."

Mary had little time to remove her clothes. She could hear her mother coming with the water. It was freshly drawn from the town well and cool. So cool it made her shiver as her mother pushed her head into the basin and began to scrub her hair. Another towel was waiting.

"You finish up here while I get your clothes."

Mary continued the scrubbing as her mother went through the scant wardrobe that hung on the hooks of her wall.

"There is nothing fit for . . . Why didn't they give us notice of their coming? We could have . . ." Her mother's words were mumbled. Mary was glad for the towel over her head as she attempted to dry her hair. She really did not want to listen to the words. She wished with all her heart that her father were home.

Mary dutifully dressed in the garments her mother tossed to her and realized that her mother had been quite right. Her garments were in poor shape. All except the head shawl. It had been brought back by her father from one of his business trips to Capernaum before he had the accident that had made him an invalid. Mary cherished that shawl. It was beautiful and represented so much love. She pulled it close around her face and felt unbidden tears spill into its rich fabric.

Her mother was still bustling.

"They will soon be back. We need to pack." Then she caught herself. "Oh, no. They said there was no need to bring your wardrobe. There will be a full set of clothing at the home where you will be staying. They said you will first go to stay with an elderly widow connected in some way with the Temple courts. When you have finished your—your lessons, then the wedding will be celebrated."

Mary again felt great relief to be reminded that the wedding would not be soon.

"Now come. They will be back any moment."

Mary looked at her mother. How would they say goodbye? Would there be tears? Would there be words of sorrow? Or promises from her mother that she, her only daughter, would be in her prayers?

But no. There was only excitement in her mother's eyes. Her cheeks were flushed, her hands fluttering in anticipation. "Just think, my daughter, married to a Pharisee! And they promised that once they pick you up, the money will be handed over." It was obvious that her mother had great plans for the sizable payment.

There was a *hullo* called from outside the house and Mary knew that the time had come. She heard her mother at the door, speaking to someone. Then all went quiet.

Soon her mother stood at her door, totally silenced in awe. "They gave me this case of clothes. He said you are to wear them. Already. To leave your old things here. Imagine! Isn't it . . ." Her mother could not come up with a proper word, but looking at her face, Mary knew that she was flushed with excitement.

The new garments were nothing like anything Mary had worn before. Some things were a puzzle. How did one wear them? Did this piece go over that? Was this to be under or on its own? What were these ties meant for? She was thankful that her mother had left her and she had quietness to figure it out herself. It would have been awkward to show her ignorance in front of her mother.

Everything was new—and expensive looking. She had been bidden to wear it all and to leave her old things behind. She did not particularly like the new things, but she was at peace with following the instructions—until she came to the new shawl. It was colorful and soft to the touch and felt pleasing against her skin. But she laid it aside. She could not wear it. She much preferred the shawl her father had given her. She placed the familiar shawl over her head just as her mother entered the room.

"What are you doing?" the woman fairly hissed when she saw Mary wearing the familiar gift from her father and the new shawl lying on the bed.

"You must wear this." She picked up the shawl and shook it toward her daughter.

"I—I cannot wear two," Mary responded.

"Of course—of course you cannot—but it must be this one." Mother shook it again.

Mary wished to argue further, but she knew she must obey. She removed her father's shawl and accepted the new one from the outstretched hand.

The woman, satisfied, bustled from the room. The main door opened and closed. Mary could hear her speaking to someone in the courtyard. "She is almost ready. You can wait outside the gate if you wish and I will bring her out to you."

With one quick grasp of her hand, Mary grabbed her father's shawl and stuffed it down the front of her gown. She prayed that her sash would keep it from sliding farther. Then she carefully arranged the generous new shawl in thick folds around her front, hoping to conceal her secret. She took a deep breath, wiped once more to remove the tears, and with head held high left her simple little room for the last time.

Her mother was already busily counting out the prearranged payment to be sure the bride price had been paid in full. When she looked up, her face glowed. Mary understood. It must have all been there as promised.

Her mother tucked the money back into the plush sack that had contained it but did not lay it aside. Holding it close as though she feared the man might try to reclaim it, she hustled her daughter toward the rickety gate from the courtyard to the street and out to the waiting men and their conveyance—this time a luxurious covered cart meant for passengers rather than the chariot meant for speed.

This would be their goodbye. Perhaps the last time they would ever see one another. If only Father . . .

Then her mother stepped forward and surprised Mary by pulling her close. Mary accepted the embrace. This was something new coming from her mother. She felt the tears rising again. She would cherish this moment in her memory.

As her mother drew her close, she whispered in a stern

voice. "Remember, you are not Mary now, but Simona. *Simona.* Remember!"

Mary swallowed away the tears. It hurt deeply that the embrace her mother had given was not an indication of her love but an opportunity to give a warning. To secretly remind her that she no longer belonged in any measure to the simple home that she was leaving behind, nor to the people she had known as her father and mother.

Mary—Simona—moved away, drawing the strange shawl more closely around her face, and climbed up the two steps to take her place on the seat inside the covered cart. As she settled on the rich padding, she heard the two men take their places on the outside bench at the front of the small cart. There was a bit of a jerk, and they began to move.

CHAPTER NINE

The Decision

It was already getting dark when they stopped at a small village. It seemed to Mary—Simona— that they had been traveling forever. The padded seat that had felt overly plump when she had first settled upon it had grown uncomfortable and given her an aching back for the lack of a firm support. She wondered if she would even be able to walk properly.

Before she could test her legs by standing erect, the one officious-looking man was drawing aside the door curtain and motioning her to exit from her seclusion. With no greeting or preamble, he spoke. "We stay at this inn tonight. The innkeeper will give you all your directions. This bag holds all you will need for the night."

Simona accepted the bag with a nod of agreement. She lifted her shawl and tucked it more closely about her face and took the two steps to the ground.

The man began walking and Simona supposed she was to follow him. They entered the dimness of the simple traveler's refuge. Immediately the guide turned to her and with a nod of his head handed her over to the care of the innkeeper.

The man was old and stooped and seemed to struggle with a vision problem.

"You are the lady Simona? Your private room is ready for you. My wife will show you to your chamber. Your evening meal will be brought to your room as soon as you desire it. What time do you wish to be wakened? Do you wish your morning meal before or after you are dressed for the day?"

Whatever does he mean? Simona puzzled. *Who would not be dressed before partaking of breakfast?* She was not sure how to answer but tried to be clear. "I will be dressed and ready for my breakfast to be served at sunrise."

"Very well, my lady. Breakfast will be served in your chamber at sunrise, one hour before you are to leave."

An equally elderly woman entered the room. Simona could read the unspoken message on her lips. *A child?*

The man sent her a silent signal of caution. She nodded her head in a curt bow, then spoke rather loudly for the size of their confined space. "Your chamber is ready, Lady Simona. There is a basin of water for your refreshment. Do you wish a time of rest before partaking of your evening meal?"

Again, Simona was puzzled. Why would she need rest? She had done nothing all day except to sit on her cushioned seat in the traveling conveyance.

"My supper can be served at your convenience," she answered.

Now it was the elderly woman who looked puzzled.

Simona studied the faces of the couple before her. How should she have responded?

"As soon as it is ready I—I would have my—I will be ready for some refreshment as soon as it is ready." She attempted a smile. "It has been a long, wearying day. I will wish to retire early."

The woman nodded and picked up a small oil lamp. She cupped her hand to protect the little flame, nodded her head again and began to lead the way down a narrow passage. They did not walk far. The inn was small and simple, and soon the woman was opening a low door that led into a chamber. She placed the lamp on a wooden table near the door, nodded to Simona, and left with the promise that she would soon be back with her meal.

The room was small and sparsely furnished. Still, the small lamp had little power to light it. Simona could not hide a smile. It suited her, this unadorned space. It almost felt like home. At least it would be private.

In spite of her inactive day, she felt weary. Weary all the way to her very soul. She could not wait to have a quick meal, peel away the layers of pricey garments, and bury her head in her pillow so her sobs would not be heard. She was so tired—and so lonesome for her father.

Simona tossed her heavy shawl onto the cot and went to the table that held the lamp, a jar of water, and a basin. A plain cotton towel hung on a hook nearby. She was surprised at how good it felt to wash her hands, her face, her arms.

Her thoughts went home. Her father would have returned from his work to find his wife excited with the money that had been duly delivered in its fancy, official bag. Simona wondered if her mother had put it down or if she'd carried it with her all day.

But she, her father's little girl, his heart-nourisher, would be gone. Gone forever.

Thinking of her father, Simona remembered the shawl she had tucked in the bodice of her fancy garment. She reached in to retrieve it and a few more tears escaped as she pressed it close to her cheek. She must stop weeping with every memory of home. She must. She carefully folded and placed her father's shawl on the cot beside where the other had been dropped in a pile.

She reached again for the towel, and as she wiped it over her wet cheeks, she spoke firmly to herself. "No more of this. You are no longer a child. You are soon to be wed. Put aside the childish tears and learn to be an adult. Make your father proud—even if he cannot see you. Choose to feel his presence. His encouragement. His love."

A few more tears, in spite of her resolve, had to be wiped away with the towel before she hung it back on its hook. She shifted back her shoulders. She would not weep again.

She had just replaced the towel when there was a tap on the door. Simona reached to open it and found a young girl with a small tray holding a simple meal and a steaming cup. She was not quite sure what to say. How was one to address a servant girl if one was representing the home of a Pharisee? She opted to stand back and nodded toward the other small table in the room.

Without a word the girl walked toward it and set down her tray. She looked shyly at Simona, cast one glance at the two shawls lying on the cot and turned to go. But Simona could not yet let her leave.

"Do you live here?" she asked, in a surprisingly loud voice.

The girl swung around to look at her, her eyes revealing fear.

"I am sorry. I did not mean to startle you. I—I just wanted—I wondered if I might see you again. If you would be bringing my breakfast in the morning?"

"I only work in the day," she answered shyly.

"Do you live here?"

There was only a shake of the head.

"Where do you live?" Simona went on.

"I live over there," she pointed to the north. "It's just my grandparents who live here at the inn."

"So, you help your grandparents?"

She nodded.

Simona saw the girl's eyes take in the small room in one quick sweep. They came to rest on the cot where Simona had placed her two shawls and widened in surprise. Simona could almost read her thoughts. Two shawls? The girl quickly checked herself and looked back to the floor, shifting lightly from one foot to the other.

"Do you like pretty things?" Simona asked.

Another silent nod.

Simona took the short step to the cot and picked up a shawl in each hand. "This one," she said, "is brand new. I just got it. But this one . . ." She held up the other hand. ". . . I have had since I was a little girl. My father gave it to me. It is my favorite. Feel how soft it is?"

She held out the shawl but the young girl was hesitant. "It's okay. I have touched it many times—and laughed into it, and cried into it—and covered my ears with it. It always washes up very nicely."

Timidly the child reached out a hand and touched the softness of the shawl. Her eyes lifted to Simona. "It is the prettiest one," she said in a near-whisper.

"I think so, too," agreed Simona.

Suddenly the girl seemed to remember she had been sent on an errand.

"I—I must go." She apologized as she waved her hand toward the door. "The men need their supper, too. You came first." She showed a hint of a smile.

"Thank you." Simona smiled in return. She wrinkled up her nose and tried to answer lightly. "It is nice to be first."

The young girl did return the smile and left the room to complete her deliveries.

I did not even ask her name, Simona regretted as the door closed softly.

She lowered herself to a seat on the cot and lifted her father's gift to her cheek again. There were many things that might soon be lost to her, but she knew that her father's love was not one of them. This time, she did not weep. She smiled.

Simona was up and dressed again in time for the breakfast delivery the next morning . . . though she chided herself for asking for it so early. What was she to do with her time until they would be continuing their journey? She paced the small room and fidgeted the long minutes away.

Unbidden, her thoughts turned to the young Pharisee who was to be her husband. What could she do to prepare herself for the coming marriage? She would need to be obedient—pleasant—and agreeable. How could she do it when her heart, her soul, felt only fear toward the man? Had she given him a fair chance? A minute of eye contact across a crowded marketplace was hardly enough opportunity to make a sound judgment of another person.

She must not be so quick to judge. She must keep an open mind. She would try. With all of her heart, she would try. But she knew she was going to need the help of the God of heaven. The God her father clung to as he traveled his difficult path as a handicapped laborer. She must cling to her father's God.

Her ponderings were cut short by a rap on her door. Once again, they were ready for travel. She answered the knock with the reply that she would be right out and reached for the new shawl, which she wrapped over her head and arranged to hide most of her face. Then she picked up the overnight bag and the second shawl and, casting one last look about the room, left with a feeling of no longer being a child. She had battled through the fears and loneliness and with God's help felt prepared for what lay ahead. She still did not like it. But she was ready to face it.

She made one brief stop at the desk where the older woman was taking her turn at the duties of innkeeper.

Simona smiled. "Your granddaughter—the one who served my meal last evening—she is very sweet."

"Sarah," said the woman.

"Yes, Sarah. I would like to give her this shawl. As my thank-you. As a gift. My father gave it to me when I was about Sarah's age."

She ran her hand over the softness one last time.

"I—I will not need it—where I am going, and I would like Sarah to have it. Tell her . . . Please tell her that there is love that comes with the gift. Much love!" She nodded a farewell to the woman who now held what had been her most priceless possession.

It had been the right decision.

Simona turned and, as she went out to take her place in the richly decorated cart, pulled the new shawl more closely over her face. She was ready now—ready to learn how to face life without the comforting presence of her father's much-loved gift. The knowledge of his constant love was enough.

CHAPTER TEN

The Arrival

Simona felt sure she would not be able to make her numb legs work to leave the small conveyance that had held her captive for these long days of travel. Coming from a humble home where many tasks awaited her each day, she was not used to inactivity for such a long period of time, and it was almost impossible to keep her mind from belaboring the unknowns of her fate.

At last they arrived in Jerusalem, a city she had visited only a handful of times. This was where her father had hoped to meet the Prophet—Jesus of Nazareth. Simona was told to close the cart's curtains, not peer out at the city's streets. That would be most unbecoming for a lady of her position, she was firmly informed. But the girl inside her had been so tempted. She could hear all sorts of strange sounds and even smelled unfamiliar smells, with no opportunity for exploring this new world that she had been forced to enter.

But now—now she would be allowed her first look at the place that was to be her temporary home. The cart door opened, the curtain was pushed away by the man with the stern face, and she was motioned to descend.

Gingerly she took the first step, one hand holding the side of the cart, her other hand pressing her shawl close to her face.

It was a quiet street. The line of wooden courtyard doors that curved into the distance as far as her eyes could see had an oddly regal bearing, tidy and well maintained. The towering stone walls crowded tightly together, just wide enough to allow the cart to pass between them.

As her eyes lifted to the nearest thick wooden door, she saw that the one opposite looked much the same. Rows of doorways, differing little in their outward appearance. A strange thought went through her mind. *How do they ever sort out which one is theirs when they come from the market or the Temple?*

The man interrupted her pondering. "This is the home of the widow Mary."

It seemed a mockery that the lady who was to school her also shared her real name. But if this widow could live here in the capital city—and could be accepted as Mary—why hadn't Simona been allowed to keep her own name?

She quickly brought her attention back to the man, who had continued with instructions. "She will be your mentor during your training period. It would be prudent for you to listen well to her instruction that you might shorten the days to the wedding ceremony."

His voice was so stern, his face so void of compassion, that Simona found it hard to respond. He continued to stare until she found her voice and whispered, "I understand."

He stepped back a pace. "Leave your belongings. I will see they are delivered to the back door. I shall escort you in."

Simona felt her stomach go into a tight knot. "Oh, God," was her quick prayer, "please be here with me. Please."

It was not the widow Mary who answered the summons at the gate, but a young woman, looking as serious and uncomfortable as Simona felt. She did not speak a welcome, so the man again took charge.

"The lady Simona. I trust the widow Mary is prepared to give her residence as arranged."

The servant clenched her hands in front of her nervously.

"The widow Mary extends her deepest regrets, master, but she has taken to her bed with a fever. She accepts the lady Simona, who will be looked after until the widow Mary is up and about once more."

"This is most disappointing," the man grumbled. "I had strict orders to deliver the lady to the widow Mary, *only*."

"A messenger was sent to the honorable Pharisee. He gives his permission for the lady to take up residence here as planned."

Simona thought the woman still sounded nervous. She wondered if the Pharisee Enos had been gracious in his response.

"Very well," said the man, and he stepped aside. "You may enter."

She was not sorry that there were no words of farewell. She had felt him more like a guard than a guide. She would not be sorry to leave his stiff and formal care.

With the closing of the gate, Simona stopped and waited for the woman behind her. The servant looked unsure as to what procedure to follow.

Then the sound of the cart moving away down the street echoed over the wall. Without thought, Simona released the breath she had been holding. She reached up and pushed the heavy shawl back from her face and dared to turn to the still-flustered servant with a bit of a smile. "Do you mind," she asked softly, "if I remove my shawl? It seems so long since I've had a full breath of air."

The woman seemed to relax a bit. "My apologies, my lady. I am—so sorry for this unexpected—the illness of my mistress was most unexpected. We were completely unprepared . . . Everything has been upset today. Please come in. I will show you to your room and you may remove your shawl and—and wash after your journey. Your meal has been prepared. I—I am so sorry—this—this is not my usual duty. I am simply in charge of the laundry—I do not know—but . . ."

Simona was bold enough to reach out and place a hand on the woman's arm. "Then we are both suffering a new circumstance. I do not yet know how to be what is expected of me today, either. I was born in a small northern village and am more used to working in the garden or the kitchen than I am to riding in a cart. We will learn together." So saying, she reached up and pulled the shawl from her head and took a deeper breath.

The tension seemed to leave the yard, just as it left Simona's shoulders. Maybe they would be able to relax and be of help to one another.

They ate together in the kitchen. The young woman, Amaris, was shocked at the suggestion. But Simona insisted that she would be most comfortable there near the fire.

It was a simple meal, but familiar, and Simona enjoyed the stew and hot cup of tea. The meal tasted much like home.

They chatted. Comfortably. Amaris shared that she had been widowed, just like the widow Mary, though not through the same circumstances.

Amaris had lost her husband to army duty, his life taken in battle. They had only been married for two short years. She could have asked for a home with her husband's brother's family, had she consented to be a second wife. There had even been pressure for her to fulfill such a role.

But she had chosen, instead, to become part of the staff that served the Temple in various ways. She had now been with the widow Mary for almost twelve years. The elderly woman was dear to her. Almost like the mother she had lost when she was very young.

Simona, too, shared a bit about her life: her father's accident, her simple duties in the village home, her love of being able to help her father in his place of business, and her concern for her brother who had left home and not been in contact since.

There was silence while both sorted through their thoughts and their circumstances.

"You've been brought to a good place," Amaris went on. "The widow Mary takes her role very seriously, but she is filled with love. She teaches with patience and devotion." Then she added, seeming to carefully choose her words, "But she can be firm. She abides no opposition—or neglect. She . . . she understands—life. One must be prepared to face it."

Simona listened carefully. She had just been lovingly issued a warning. She did not respond but sat in silence, letting the words caution her very soul.

"Mary!" mused Simona into the silence. "That was my name."

"Your name?"

Simona nodded.

"But why did it change?"

"Enos the Pharisee declared it to be too common, I've been told."

"So you changed it?"

"He changed it."

Amaris looked surprised but made no further comment. She sat quietly for a few minutes, then stirred.

"Forgive me. You must be very weary and I've kept you from your bed." She stood. "Everything you need has been delivered to your chamber. This is a simple place. But it is a place for learning. I hope you find it sufficient."

She took a deep breath, then went on. "Esther will be your maid. She was called home unexpectedly because her mother's health was failing. But she is to be back again tomorrow."

"Her mother is well again?"

The woman's eyes began to shine. "It was another miracle. Of the rabbi Jesus. He visited her town and she was healed in an instant. A miracle!"

Simona's breath caught in her throat. "Then it is true? He really can bring healing?"

"Oh, yes. He has healed many. Haven't you heard—?"

Simona interrupted. "My father—he is crippled from his accident, as I said. Not long ago we tried to get him to this Jesus but we did not know where to find him. Is he here?"

"He has been here, a number of times, but he is not here now. He went back to the Galilee. But many expect him to be back for Passover in the spring. He comes each year, faithfully."

Simona could not believe what she had just heard. It might be possible to contact the man her father had long tried to see. What if she could find him? Was that why God had sent her here?

"I must find a way to get word to my father." Simona stood and paced to the covered window and back. "How can I do that?"

"Perhaps you could get a courier . . . But as a woman . . . I don't know."

"Oh—I hope . . . It would mean so much if my father could be healed. His life—it all would be normal again. He has not even been able to make it back to Jerusalem for the Holy Feasts since . . . since he cannot move on his own. That has been a deep concern for him."

"I could ask Esther—my friend—she might know." There seemed to be a profound reluctance on Amaris's part.

"Would you? Please—please ask. My father—he needs help. If the rabbi could but touch him . . ." Simona could not keep the tears from coming. But tears of desperation were strangely mixed with tears of hope. She felt suddenly very weary after her long days of travel.

Amaris led the way to Simona's room by the light of an oil lamp. It was a short and silent walk. She opened the door and motioned Simona in.

"In the morning, there will be three knocks on your door. The first will be to let you know it is time to rise. The second knock will usher in the time of devotion. With the third knock you are to prepare yourself for the first meal of the day—unless you have chosen a day of fasting. The meal will be served in your room. You will be sent for when the widow Mary is ready for you."

Amaris was turning to go when she spoke again. Her voice was hushed as though she did not wish to be heard. "There is one thing you must know. Though perhaps I am wrong in sharing it." She stopped and seemed to feel her way forward, to search for the right words. "I spoke of feeling like . . . like a daughter here—and I do—but that is . . . that was—the way it used to be. There is conflict now. You see—the widow Mary is of a very strict group of the Jews. Her father was a Levite who served in the Temple. As was her own husband. That is why she is allowed this place of refuge. She keeps me now as a servant—but her heart is not with me any longer. It cannot be."

The anxious woman seemed to have returned, casting a shadow over the face Simona had become familiar with.

"I tell you this because—because—had not Esther been away, I would not have been allowed to speak with you. You will be strictly kept away from me because of my—my—sinfulness. If I were a man I would have been put out of the synagogue and sent away from the true followers. As a widow"—she shrugged—"I really had no place, except to serve. I must keep to the laundry tubs and the back garden. Even Esther cannot speak with me.

That is why I was so afraid when I had to face the envoy from the Pharisee Enos. But circumstances dictated that there was no one else to let you in. You do understand that we are not to speak of eating together in the kitchen. Nor will we speak to one another from now on. You are to be the wife of a Pharisee. You must keep yourself from the pollution of the world. And you must be very careful. Do not ask anyone—*anyone*—questions about . . . well, anything. It could cost you—everything. Even—no, *especially*—about Jesus of Nazareth."

So saying, she slipped from the room, pulling the door closed behind her.

Simona stood confused. The words had made no sense to her. What kind of world had she entered?

CHAPTER ELEVEN

The Mentor

SIMONA FELT STIFF AND SORE the next morning when she awakened. She rolled over and rose to a sitting position, then stretched her feet toward the floor. With a push on the side of the oversoft, cushiony bed, she lifted herself and began to pace back and forth, swinging her arms in gentle arcs and stretching out her shoulders.

She had not been out of bed long before the first knock came. It was not a loud nor harsh sound. She wondered if a person who slept soundly would even hear it.

She accepted it as her opportunity to dress for the day. Several new garments lined the wall hooks. Her glance went from gown to gown and then repeated the study. At length she picked the least fussy one.

Carefully she removed her sleeping shift and began to dress. Some of the items were strange and she had to sort out how one was to wear them. When she deemed herself ready for the day, she opened her door and was about to head to the kitchen when she remembered and quickly closed it again softly. That was not correct. She was to be served in her room—but first . . . ? For the moment she could not remember what was to come next.

The second knock made her jump. Oh, yes. This was the silent time between rising and partaking of the day's first meal. She was to spend it praying and meditating. She had never practiced such a discipline. She lowered herself to a seated position on the bed, tucking her feet up under her. What should she pray?

In the village this was the hour when she had many chores to care for. Chores that would help her father begin his day. Other things to give aid to her mother. Simona pictured what would be happening at home if she were there.

The morning meal itself would not be prepared and served until the servant returned from the market. And this servant was now shared with a family who lived close to them.

It had been different before her father's accident. In fact, there had been two servants for their household then. She made a mental list of things that had changed for the family. The shared woman for the morning trip to the market was all the help Simona and her mother had for their busy days.

And then a new thought. Now Mother would make do alone. No, that was unlikely. Simona wondered how many servants had been hired already to take her place.

The third knock came softly and Simona realized that she had neither prayed nor meditated. But before leaving the room Simona did pray. A simple, quick prayer that God would be with her through whatever lay ahead.

She was about to open her door when she heard a scuffing sound and the door opened of its own accord. *Oh, yes,* she remembered, *I am to be served in my room.*

A girl, younger than herself by a few years, came in with a tray. When she saw Simona, she stopped short, then nodded at the tray she carried. "Your breaking of the fast," she almost whispered.

She placed the tray on the small table and turned to go, but Simona stopped her.

"If I am not to leave the room," she questioned, "what am I to do?"

The girl turned. She blinked a couple of times, then shook her head. "Wait. Until you are summoned."

"What am I to do here, while I wait?"

The girl looked toward the tray with its simple breakfast. It seemed to be her only answer.

Simona dared to press further. "What am I to do after I finish eating?"

The girl was already turning toward the door. She answered as she left the room. "Wait." Then she was gone and the door closed quietly.

Simona felt frustration stiffen her entire body. Wait! Just sit in her one chair, in the small room, and wait. Surely there was something productive that she could be doing. She turned from the closed door and was reminded of the tray that had been delivered. Oh, yes, she was to eat. That would take a few minutes from the day.

But the tray really held nothing that appealed to her. Some type of curds. A piece of bread and a cup of a hot liquid. And then she spotted ripe figs. She reached for them and then remembered that she should sit properly to eat her meal. She went for the one chair and pulled it up to the table.

She did not have to wait long after she had finished her meal before there was a knock on her door. It was the girl again. She wasted no time in announcing her mission. "I am to take you to Widow Mary."

Simona sighed her relief. She would not need to spend the

day locked away after all. Gladly she followed the young girl through the hall to an almost-barren room. All the furnishings it had were a desk, two chairs, and a cabinet that held some scrolls and tablets.

Seated at the desk was the oldest woman Simona ever remembered seeing. She was slightly slumped in her chair, a heavy shawl about her shoulders and one thin-skinned hand resting on the surface before her.

When Simona entered the room she stirred slightly, her wrinkled face showing no greeting or smile. Her eyes looked deep and watery and Simona wondered if she had vision.

She did not wonder for long.

"You are Simona?" the woman asked and her voice was surprisingly strong.

Simona nodded.

"You must answer, child," said the voice.

Simona was quick to respond. "Yes, I am Simona—now."

"And what do you mean by *now*?"

"I . . . used to be known as—as Mary."

"And why did your father change your name?"

"He—he did not change it."

"Who did?"

Simona swallowed. "It—it was the—the Pharisee. The one I am to marry. He had it put into the contract with my father."

"He did not like the name Mary?"

"I do not know."

The widow humphed.

"Well, bring your chair and we will begin."

Simona lifted the chair and moved it closer as she was instructed. She was soon to discover that the elderly woman did not mince words.

"Do you know why you are here?"

"I—I was told it is to prepare me for being the wife of a Pharisee," she answered evenly.

"That is correct. The Pharisee Enos has judged that your life in the small village has not prepared you for such an honor. Do you agree?"

Simona did not know how to answer. "I suppose it did not. I . . . we did not have Pharisees in our village—nor did they visit."

"So, you have never heard of the Pharisees?"

How was she to answer that? She had heard plenty over her short years about the Pharisees. Enough to fear them. Enough even to resent them. "I have heard of them, yes."

"And what did you hear?"

Oh my. What could she say? Her father had taught her since she was very young that untruths were not acceptable. But . . . ? "It was not always . . . a good report," she dared to answer.

The widow Mary did not even blink her watery eyes. "Did you believe the reports?"

"I would suppose . . . I did not know their source. My father always said one should not judge." She stopped. "I am sure that there are—kind men among them" was her conclusion.

The widow finally did turn and look at Simona for the first time. She seemed to study the stranger in front of her for a moment before speaking. "You are very wise for your age" was her comment, "and perceptive. I think we will get along fine."

Simona had no idea how to interpret the words.

"Shall we begin?"

Simona nodded. She hoped the woman understood her silence as agreement.

"Let us start with your home. Tell me about it."

"I live—*lived* in a small village near the Galilee Sea. My father is a millwright but he was injured in an accident so it is difficult for him now."

She was stopped.

"Your father. Can you tell me about him? Both before and after his accident."

Simona felt the warmth rise all through her body. Her father. She loved her father. She had nourished his heart, he had said. "He was—*is*—a wonderful father. I used to go to the shop with him. I kept his accounts."

"You kept his accounts? How could you do that?"

"He taught me," she answered simply.

"But one would need to know numbers to do that."

"Yes," she agreed. "He taught me."

The woman shook her head but asked no further question about the arrangement.

"Does your father still have his business?"

"He does. But it is very hard for him since his accident. He has hired a man to take him on his cart each day, but he has no one now to help him at work."

"Who keeps his accounts now? Your mother?"

Simona was quick to shake her head. "She doesn't know numbers," she replied simply.

"But if your father taught you, could he not teach your mother?"

"She does not wish to learn how to be a servant," she replied with honesty. When she thought of how the words might sound, she was quick to add, "She is more . . . She prefers to keep the home."

"You said your father had an accident. Has there been no treatment for healing?"

Simona felt a wave of familiar sadness sweep through her. "We had hoped so. He was sure that if he could just get to the Prophet he could be healed."

"The prophet? Which prophet?"

The memory of Amaris's stern warning caused Simona to flush. She whispered, "The one from Nazareth."

A strange expression crossed the woman's face. "The carpenter?"

Is he a carpenter? My father just called him the Prophet—Jesus of Nazareth. But should I answer so frankly? Simona's habit of honesty worked against her efforts to restrain her words. "That was why we were in the village where the Pharisee Enos—" She stopped short once more and changed direction. "We had traveled from our village to try to find the Prophet who heals. My father was sure that if he could find him . . . But we missed him."

"Missed him?"

"Yes, we stayed in a village overnight—to rest. He was right there at the market. But when he heard that the Pharisees were coming, he left before we knew he was there. Then when my father heard about it and had men search for him, it was too late. He was gone."

"Your father thought he could be healed? By this man, this Jesus?"

"He was sure that—"

"What if he was a fraud? What if he had no power to heal?"

"But my father was convinced that he can. My father actually spoke with a man who had been healed by the Prophet."

"What if the man was just paid to say he had been healed?"

Simona was puzzled. "Why would he do that? It would be dishonest and against God's Law."

"Yes, it would be. Just as it would be against God's Law to say one could heal by one's own power."

Simona did not understand the words—or the woman's angry look. Had she said something wrong? Before she could sort it out in her mind the woman spoke again. "Let us continue." She nodded toward her desk with its assortment of scrolls, and Simona relaxed with the change of subject. "You have no siblings?"

"I have an older brother."

"Why did your father not teach him to keep the accounts?"

"Oh, he did teach him. He knew everything about the running of the shop. But . . . he is no longer . . . at home. He left just shortly before my father's accident. And we were never able to find where he is."

"And your mother takes care of your home?"

"Yes."

The woman shifted slightly in her chair. "Did your parents teach you about our Faith? Did they observe the Law?"

"Yes."

"You had a place of worship in your village?"

"Not really in our village—it was too small—but within a Sabbath-day's walk."

"You attended?"

"Yes, we went together."

"Did you *participate* in the lessons?"

"I—I did not get the lessons that my brother did. But I—I still learned some of the things. When he was memorizing and repeating, I listened. And learned. I liked the stories and the . . ." She stopped. Was she to be saying all this? Would this woman think her parents were wrong in letting their daughter learn from the Scriptures?

She waited for a reprimand, but none came. The elderly woman was already looking weary. Simona studied her for a moment and then asked quietly, "Would you wish me to get you a cool drink? It always refreshed my father . . ."

The woman looked surprised, and then smiled. "I think we have begun well. I will need to go over what we have discussed so that I am prepared to give you the lessons you will need to fit your new role. Enos the Pharisee is quite anxious to make you his wife." She rested her head on her hand and seemed to think deeply. "But he had not told me that you are so young," she continued after a moment. "How do you feel about this important and esteemed role? Do you wonder why you have been blessed to be chosen as the wife of an honored Pharisee?"

Simona fidgeted on her hard chair. Surely the woman did not expect her to answer that question. What could she say? "I had not desired to be the wife of a Pharisee. I was quite content to help my father."

"I see."

Simona shifted on the seat again.

"So your father wished you to go—?"

"Oh, no," cut in Simona. She stopped, flustered. She must not interrupt.

But the woman seemed to be waiting for her to go on.

"It was the bride price," she finally stated truthfully. "My father did not wish me to go—it was difficult for him—he wished me to stay. But my mother knew that the money would—would help them. Maybe even get a doctor for my father. And—and . . ." She faltered to a stop again. Then she decided that she might as well share the whole truth. "It was my fault. I—I let my shawl—slip away when I was in the market and the Pharisee saw me—and there was trouble—and . . ." She could not go on. She still did not understand why a slipped shawl should result in her needing to marry a Pharisee she did not even know. She shrugged. "I do not know why he chose someone like me," she finished simply.

The widow Mary frowned. Things were becoming all too clear to her. This very young bride had been selected because of her beautiful face. She was to be a trophy, presented with pride and ego, on display to the Pharisee's world of separation and distinction.

And now she, the widow Mary, had been selected as the mentor to lead this much-too-young bride, in her innocence, to the wedding bed. And on to her future position as the wife of a Pharisee, with all of the rules and regulations and honor-duties that went along with it.

Her role had suddenly become a painful duty.

CHAPTER TWELVE

The Tumult

Enos unrolled the small scroll that held his list of necessary steps. He smiled. Things were progressing well. Simona had arrived safely in Jerusalem. The widow Mary, from the Temple laity, had agreed to be her teacher and mentor. He could not have asked for anyone better. The widow was known for her solidity on the principles of the Faith, and for her ability to shape the chosen young virgins into pliable and dependable assets for the young men entering the calling of God in various positions of authority.

The next item on the list brought a frown. He still had not found a way to rebuild his assets. Between the bride price, the rental of a cart to deliver Simona to her present abode, and the cost of her training, his funds had seemed to trickle away. No, not trickle. It had seemed much more like a flood.

It had reached his ears that there was a duty ahead that would involve a promised payment. A sizable payment if his informer had been correct. He made a note to himself to inquire about the rumor. If there was truth to it, he would certainly apply. He had no concern about being able to meet any prerequisites. He had always maintained the position at the top of his class.

A deeper frown creased his brow. At least he *had* led his class until recently. As of late, that much-desired leading role was being challenged. A young man from the far-off city of Antioch had joined them. It was the thinking of Enos, and some of his classmates, that it was unwise and unfair to allow those from the *outside* to seek positions among the Pharisees. As far as Enos was concerned, the young man had no right to the training offered in Jerusalem.

It was true that they could not challenge the fellow's bloodline. He had the long line of genealogy to prove that he was of pure Jewish blood. But there were differences. Little things that kept being revealed.

The young man had passion for the Faith—yes. But not without some questions. And he dared to voice his questions with words like, "Do we know . . . ?" and "Could it be . . . ?" or "What if . . . ?"

He did not just ask the questions. He put time and effort into trying to find the answers. He was a true scholar and likely spent more time studying the sacred scrolls than any other student. Enos feared that the teachers of the Law would soon become aware of that fact. They seemed to favor diligence.

His name was Judah. It was a Jewish name, testifying to the fact that his parents professed the Faith, even though they lived in a Gentile city. *Judah of Antioch.* Every time Enos heard the name he felt the hair rise at the base of his neck.

Something had to be done about Judah. Enos had still not decided what that might be.

He shifted on his simple chair and forcefully pushed the matter of Judah aside. He had other plans to make. He would need to work on the problem of this competitor later.

The last meeting of the Sanhedrin had been worrisome. Enos had been told that it was filled with reports of the man from the Galilee whom the locals had known as Jesus of Nazareth, but who now dared to allow his followers to refer to him as Rabbi. The latest report was even more distressing. Some were calling him the Promised One and claimed that he was fulfilling the words of Isaiah, the prophet of old.

Of course, the whole thing was ridiculous. Should the promised Messiah ever show up, the religious hierarchy would be the first to know. After all, they were the ones who kept and protected the ancient Scriptures that held all such promises. They studied them daily. How would it be possible for such learned men to miss their fulfillment?

But even with that knowledge, Enos knew that his superiors were more than a little concerned. Daily they heard stories of false miracles and the gathering of large crowds being duped by this pretender. So many people were wavering in their devotion that those in the priesthood feared the Temple coffers would soon be feeling the results.

Enos stopped in his thinking. That was it! The priesthood was already expecting the giving to decrease. All he needed to do was to become involved in the gathering of the Temple gifts. The amounts were never counted and recorded until the bags were delivered to the priests who carried that responsibility. No one would ever know if some of the funds went missing in transit.

Enos pushed aside the list he had been working on. The long page curled itself up and rolled away from his hand. He had to think this through. Each step needed careful planning.

First of all, he would need a teammate. The Law required two men. Enos knew that he did not wish to work with another person who shared his plan. It was too risky. Should things become strained, or if the other person was careless, both might be exposed. Besides, he did not wish to share the proceeds.

A new thought suddenly made Enos lean forward in his chair. Perhaps Judah was exactly who he wanted. They were not known as friends. And if it were ever discovered that funds had been lost, he would manufacture some way to shift the blame to Judah. That should be simple enough. Everyone respected the name of Enos ben Elias. He had been at the school for much longer than the new young man from Antioch. He was sure that he had built sufficient trust among his teachers and his classmates.

The job was rather tiresome and unrewarding. Younger students, who were trying to earn favor with a teacher, were the ones who usually volunteered for menial tasks. Enos decided that he might earn some favor as well, by demonstrating to all that he, as a senior member of top standing, was not above giving his time and attention to the Temple courts. Then he would suggest that Judah would make an excellent workmate. He felt confident that Judah would accept the assignment. He always seemed to be looking for ways to be involved or lend a hand.

It would not take Enos long to find the name of the priest who was in charge of the offerings. Before asking for audience with the man, he rehearsed his speech. He had, for some time, been looking for a way to give back to his community in return for the wonderful training that they had freely been giving to him. To show his deep appreciation he was willing to spend some of his time aiding in the gathering of the daily Temple contributions. He felt that it was one way he could contribute without taking too much time from his important studies.

Enos played his little speech over and over in his mind, rewording it, enhancing it, until he was confident that it sounded natural and sincere. Then he went on to prepare his suggestion for his next step.

He had a rather new classmate in the young man from Antioch. He believed that Judah was his name. He would be happy to share the duties with Judah in the hope that it would make him feel more a part of their community. He thought it must be difficult to take up studies as a stranger when the rest of the class had been working together since the beginning of their training.

Sounded reasonable. He hoped with all his heart that his intentions would not be questioned. He had no idea what he could do if he were turned down. He needed funds.

Simona's class times with the widow Mary began. The primary focus was on societal conduct, both in and out of a Pharisee's home: how to walk, how to stand, how to sit, how to observe without staring, how to listen without responding, how to regard the leadership and authority of her husband without argument or contradiction.

She was also told that she must show *open* devotion and respect to her husband. *Open devotion? What does that mean?* she wondered but did not ask. She would wait for the woman to explain as the lessons went on.

The widow Mary also brought in a middle-aged woman who showed Simona the proper way for the wife of a Pharisee to dress, to do her hair, to use cosmetics, and to wear her various shawls in public and in the privacy of the home.

Simona had been raised to be obedient, so the lessons were not a struggle. The thing that did confuse and bother her was a seeming coldness on the part of the widow Mary. Simona's first impression had been of a warm, motherly woman willing to share her life's wisdom. Now the elderly woman appeared to find excuses to absent herself from the lessons and let someone else take her place as instructor. Simona wondered if she had done something to offend the older woman.

When the widow Mary did appear, she was stern and stiff and demanded full understanding and acceptance.

Another puzzle for Simona was that the woman seemed not to want Simona to interact with the household staff. Simona longed for companionship but there was none offered. Amaris had already informed her of the reason she was not allowed to build a friendship with her. The woman had confessed to being a sinner—though Simona had not been told her crime. But why not Esther or the young girl who served her breakfast? Were they sinners, too? Or was it her own fault? Simona did not know what she had done or said that caused the need for isolation.

Dared she ask? *No,* she decided. That would not be wise.

So how was she to fill her time? She asked for permission to work in the garden, but it was denied. They were using special oils to make her hands, darkened from her previous garden work, soft and smooth and lighter in color. And she must learn to keep them that way.

Could she do mending?

No, that might strain her eyes, making them look tired, which would be offensive to her future husband.

Other requests to help with things around the home were similarly dismissed. The wife of a Pharisee was to be concerned only with the happiness of her husband and the supervision of the household staff.

Staff? Simona had no idea what it would mean for her to have staff. But she trusted that future lessons would cover that.

Simona felt a shiver go through her body. She still felt confused regarding the workings of a home with staff. She would much prefer to do the work herself.

One morning, Simona arrived in the classroom for the day's instructions before the widow Mary had finished her daily devotions. Simona quickly voiced an apology and began to back out, but was surprised when the woman stopped her.

"Come take a chair," the woman said, rather sharply.

Simona moved forward and took her place in the room's second chair.

"I think we need to have a brief talk," the woman began.

Simona could only nod and wait.

"You spoke of your father trying to find the man Jesus."

Simona nodded again.

"Did your father really believe that this—this ordinary man could heal?"

Simona swallowed and tried to answer the question. "Yes, he did."

"Why?"

"He—he met a man who had been healed."

"Yes, you said that earlier. But what made your father think that man was telling the truth?"

"He said . . . he said his eyes shone with the miracle that—that it had really happened. To him."

"And your father thought that this—Jesus—could heal him as well?"

"He did, yes."

"Why? Why would he do that for a—a mere millwright?"

"It is said that Jesus loves all people—especially the poor. He wishes to help them."

"One must be cautious in believing what is *said*. Much untruth is passed from mouth to mouth."

Simona nodded. She knew that was true.

The woman shook her head and then went on. "Or perhaps," she said, "he does not love people but he is interested in trying to take over a kingdom."

Simona was puzzled. "Why would he do that?"

"For power. For glory."

"I—I think he already has that."

The woman looked shocked. "Why would you say that? Do you believe he is—is who he claims to be?"

Simona shrugged and turned her face to the floor. "I do not know. I have never seen him, nor heard him speak. But I would like to know."

"And if you saw him—heard him talk, saw a miracle—would you then believe?"

"I—I do not know. I would need to see—to understand. But if it was a . . . a *real* miracle . . . Yes. Yes, I think I would."

The lady raised her hands to her lips as though she were going to pray. "My dear child," she said. "You do realize why you are here? You are about to be married to a Pharisee. A very strict Pharisee, I understand. The Pharisees see this—this Jesus—as an imposter. The enemy. A false prophet who deceives people. Those who believe in his miracles are turned out of the synagogue. Sent away. Alienated. Persecuted."

She paused to let those powerful words sink in. "Do you think you would survive among them should you dare to claim allegiance to this—this self-proclaimed, yet false, Messiah?"

Simona froze. She did not understand all of the implications—did not know which side was right and which side was wrong. But there was something about the stories of this strange man from

Nazareth that drew her. Why, she did not know. But if her father thought that he could heal, then . . .

"I do not know," she replied softly, evenly. "All I know is, if he is as he says . . . If my eyes—and my heart—would tell me that he has come from God, then I would have to believe him."

The conversation left the widow Mary shaken. Simona seemed so innocent, so passionate in her stance. Yet she was a child—a child who had no idea of the tensions and unrest all around. One misspoken word could bring severe repercussions, even ostracism or death, especially now that she was to be claimed in marriage by a passionate Pharisee who was anxious to take a position with the elite of the ruling class.

The prophet from the Galilee—the man called Jesus—had the entire nation in confusion. Was he or was he not the person he claimed to be?

The widow had been taught that when the Messiah, who had been long expected, finally came as promised, they would *know*. It would not be misunderstood or doubted. The leaders of their faith had been watching. Waiting. They would inform the people. They would know.

This could not possibly be him, concluded the elderly woman. At the same time, she felt an involuntary shudder go through her entire body. What if she was wrong?

CHAPTER THIRTEEN

The Partnership

To say that Judah of Antioch was surprised when Enos approached him with the comment that he had long contemplated how he might show appreciation for the excellent training he had been receiving would be an understatement. The young man nodded his head in agreement. He was quick to affirm that he was enjoying the studies, as well.

"Well, after much thought," Enos went on, "I have decided to offer my services in gathering the daily Temple contributions and carrying them to the priests who count and record them. If you have any interest, we could work together. This is the one task I have thought of that we could do without it taking too much time from our lessons. Yet it does need to be done and those who have been doing it are elderly."

In actuality, he had no idea who had been doing it. Maybe he should have done a bit more investigating before coming to Judah.

He changed tack. "Look, I will go to the Temple and get some more information tomorrow."

Judah agreed with a nod, giving Enos a bit of confidence. He must be careful. He had been so excited with his plan that he could have derailed it.

When Enos walked through the looming gates and into the Court of Women, his eyes flashed around the extensive interior. He first felt panic. There was the familiar row of receptacles with their long narrow necks. He'd been here often to allow a handful of coins to clink and plunk noisily into the coffers. But he had never looked carefully enough to see how and when the coins were removed. Perhaps his plan would not work.

He decided to look for a priest. He knew that his garments identified him as a student of the Pharisees, which should stand him in good stead.

It took a while to find a priest who was not already occupied. He found an aged man sitting on a small bench near the Nicanor Gate, which led to the area where the animal sacrifices took place. The man was thin bearded and seemingly poor of sight. That pleased Enos. If anything ever did happen where questions would be asked by those in authority, this man would not be sought as a witness.

"Esteemed father," began Enos with what he felt to be a voice that held deep respect, "I am a novice of the Pharisees, seeking a way to serve our God in a practical way. I have noted, in the past, an elderly priest carrying heavy bags of the daily funds gathered from the giving receptacles."

He stopped. The man not only seemed to be poor of sight but also poor of hearing. He had a strange look of confusion, as though unable to follow the words Enos had just spoken.

Enos was about to turn away, when another priest appeared. He looked annoyed.

"Do not trouble him," he said quite sharply. "He no longer sees, hears, or understands."

Enos backed up a step. "My apologies," he declared quickly. "I am new here and was . . ." He looked down at his robe, which was easily identifiable. That was a mistake. The priest would be quick to recognize the color combination that said plainly *an underling of the Pharisees.* Such a one, if faithful, would have no excuse not to know his way around the Temple courts. And the garments also said that he was well along in his training—not *new.*

Enos could feel his cheeks redden as he saw the priest studying him closely. He did not turn away or point out the stupid mistake Enos had just made. Did he enjoy seeing the younger man squirm?

"You seem to be more confused than my brother," he said rather gruffly, helping the elderly man to his feet.

Enos fought to regain control of the awkward situation. "I do apologize," he said. "I did entangle myself. You see, I am here on a mission and—and very nervous to approach my—my revered superiors."

He took a deep breath and hurried on before he lost the priest's attention. "I wish—I wish to serve in the Temple—and because of my studies I have little time. So I am new to volunteering to serve here. You see how I merely misspoke. I thought of the daily offerings and the fact that at the end of the day they need to be taken to the treasury for counting and storing. I thought this might be one way that I could serve my God."

The priest had been listening, though his face showed no softening. When Enos stopped for breath, he cut in. "And you think we would allow a stranger to be trusted with the Temple coffers?"

"Not a stranger, my lord. I have been training for three years and have many reputable teachers and fellow classmates who would testify to my good report. And—"

The priest interrupted. "Why, of all forms of service, do you wish to collect the daily offerings? It seems a strange request for one who has no direct connection with the Temple."

"Hardly so, my lord. We feel very much a part of the foundation of our Faith. We should be doing more for one another—but the studies—they leave little time for other interests during the day. However, I felt that this is one way I could serve when our day is complete. I have a fellow classmate who would also like to serve in this way. We could work together."

"Two unknowns working together to handle the Temple funds? Give me a reason to believe this would be a good idea."

Enos felt the slump of his shoulders. "So there is no room for my service."

"Plenty of room for your service," the priest said. "You could start in the barns where the animals are kept. Or you could spend time watering the vines or hoeing the gardens. But, oh, no—you wish to start by handling the offerings. Curious."

Enos decided to try one more ploy.

"I have watched the elderly priests carry the heavy sacks. Coins can be weighty. I thought perhaps younger arms and backs would be more suitable for the task, my lord."

The priest cocked his head to the side and studied Enos. The anger seemed to drain from his face. Enos dared not speak for fear he would sabotage the moment.

"Come back tomorrow at this same time. We will discuss it and decide if we need help with carrying the heavy sacks you spoke of."

Enos could not believe the sharp change. "I do appreciate that, my lord."

The man was already turning away. "And bring the friend you spoke of. We work with two for security."

Enos exhaled. It had worked. He could not believe it. It had worked.

They arrived at precisely the requested time and were greeted promptly by the priest that Enos had met the day before, along with two others.

Enos introduced Judah, but the priests did not share their names. The youngest priest took charge.

"We visited your classroom today and found that you, Enos of Jerusalem, student of the third year, and you, Judah of Antioch, beginning scholar only recently joining the local school, are as you say. Both of you are known as good students, no demerits toward your names, and in good health."

He paused and looked directly at Enos. "Considered to be quite capable of carrying the heavy bags that our elderly priests have been carrying for years."

Enos felt his face heat. *Was that sarcasm?*

"The puzzle to your teachers is why? Why would you wish to offer yourselves for such a menial task? And why the very two students who are at the top of the class? The credit—if credit for service is what you seek—will be equally divided, giving neither of you the advantage." He looked from one young man to the other, his gaze cold and searching.

Enos realized that this would, indeed, look strange in the eyes of the Temple priests. He did not fault them for questioning the reason behind such an offer.

The plot was not going to work.

"But," the man continued, "why do we not give the plan a try in another area? You see, though we have never allowed outside help with the offerings here, perhaps there is one way that the laity could serve and feel more a part of the functions of our Temple and our Faith. Meet us in the outer court just before the closing of the Temple gates tomorrow. Both of you.

There was a mumble of farewells as the three priests took turns offering their blessings to the two young men but Enos scarcely heard the words. It had worked. Or at least it seemed to have moved a step forward. Now he had to carefully maneuver the priests so that the rest of the venture would produce the return he hoped for.

The activity in the outer courtyard was dwindling by the time Enos and Judah entered cautiously through the southern gate. Crated doves were being carried away, feathers flying in all directions. Two sheep, apparently not required by any out-of-town visitor for this day's sacrifice, were being led away toward a side gate.

Only the youngest of the priests they'd met the day before was there, waiting near the tables used by the money changers. His chin was raised high as if it could elevate him above the activity around him. His arms were crossed beneath his outer robe. He kept his voice low as he explained, "As you were told yesterday, collections within the Temple are gathered by Levites. This is the Law. However, the fees due from the vendors and money changers in the outer court—this Court of Gentiles—" The priest as much as spat out the word. "The collection of these fees is an odious task to many who work in the Temple. Because of this, we have agreed to allow you to serve as our agents in gathering these funds on a trial basis."

Slowly the implications began to dawn on Enos. This was even better than he'd hoped. These would not even be Temple offerings. They would be monies obtained from Gentiles. And Enos was well aware that an astute Jew could require a little extra with any fee he collected. There would be no consequence to him for cheating here. He hid a quiet chuckle of delight behind a feigned cough.

It was not difficult to learn the simple procedure. They were supervised for the first three days and then on their own. They had to wait until the last Jewish visitor had left the Temple and until the gates leading farther into the Temple, into the Court of Women and beyond, had been securely locked. This left only the Gentiles who were packing up for the day. He and Judah worked in tandem, hurrying from one vendor or money changer to the next, collecting the fees required for them to use the space within the Temple court for their business.

After the first day, he spent some time sewing a small pouch to the inner side of his sash. It would only take a small movement to separate one coin from the others and, concealed in his palm, slip it into the pouch. He practiced in the confines of his own room and got adept at disguising his movement.

There were things to watch. He could not be clumsy. He could not let the coins clink against one another within his clothing. He must be sure to have Judah's eyes turned elsewhere for two brief seconds. And above all, he must not become greedy. Should the amount of fees diminish too quickly, the priests charged with the task of counting and recording might be alerted.

CHAPTER FOURTEEN

The Preparation

THE NEWS CAME via a servant. Tomorrow was to be her wedding day. Simona was informed by a member of the kitchen staff, whom the widow Mary had sent to tell her. She was to meet the elderly woman in her office room as soon as she had finished her breakfast.

Simona pushed aside the tray that had been placed on the small table. She had no desire for food. The dreaded day had come, far too soon, to her thinking.

For the first time she could remember she longed for her mother. Her father she had missed daily ever since she had been taken from her home. But today, with the news of her upcoming wedding the next day, it only seemed right that her mother should be with her.

The familiar steps to the office room were far too short. Before she was able to quiet her rapidly beating heart she was at the door. She took another deep breath before she reached out her hand to knock softly.

She was bid to come in. The widow Mary was in her regular place before her desk.

Simona felt the lady's eyes study her with one long sweep of her glance. There was kindness in the motion—a kindness Simona had not noted before. It made her wish to weep, to share aloud all of her confusion, her anguish, her dread. But she did not permit herself to step forward and claim the sudden compassion that she had felt from the elderly woman.

The woman nodded to the familiar chair. Simona moved forward and took the seat, her hands tucked beneath her shawl, tightly clasped together.

"The Pharisee Enos has named the morrow as the day you will be wed," the woman said, neither looking at Simona nor giving her time to respond. "You are to be ready by the eighth hour for the cart that will come for you. Your wedding garments have already been delivered. They are in the chest across the room. The Pharisee Enos will send help in the morning to aid in your preparations. This means that we have only this short day to review everything that you have been taught while here. So we must get started."

Simona felt the groan that was not allowed to escape. She did not enjoy the long, long list of rules and regulations. It had been grueling work to learn them all and she dreaded the thought of the review and quizzing that she knew was about to come. Suddenly she wished that she had eaten at least some of her morning meal. Even if she had taken some liquid her stomach might have felt better. Instead, her mouth went dry.

"Could I—could I have some water please, before we begin?"

The woman looked at her and seemed to understand. She reached forward and shook the bell before her. The kitchen help arrived so quickly that Simona wondered if they had been lurking at the door. Widow Mary placed the order: water with a touch of citron. Two cups.

Simona felt that water had never tasted so refreshing.

And they began. But the questions were formed in a different way. How would you respond in this circumstance . . . ? Who would you contact if . . . ? What would be your reply to such a request as . . . ? If the maid were negligent, how would you address it?

The questioning continued. What would you wear to such an occasion? What would be the proper order of addressing and seating this list of guests? If you felt ill, whom would you call? Which servant would be responsible to care for this, or that, situation?

On and on the questions went, until Simona felt her head begin to ache. She asked for more water and the widow Mary took a second cup as well.

Then they continued down the long list that the widow lady had prepared. At length the questions changed. What would you do if the Pharisee Enos, your husband, asked . . . ? If this happened or that happened? If he said this or that? If he is harsh? Demanding? If you have a child in your first year? What if he desires a second wife?

Then the conversation took yet another turn. This time there were no questions to answer—but cautions offered.

"It is most important that you adhere, fully, to the teachings of our Faith. The Pharisees are not delinquent in dealing with anyone who denies the truth as taught by our fathers."

"Do not let the unrest of our day sway you into believing any false teaching. Even if your heart longs to accept it—refuse to let your mind embrace it."

"Do not let the uninformed mob distract you from Truth. Hold steady to the fundamental beliefs that have been held for centuries by our people."

Simona felt drained. As the widow's voice droned on, there were questions to which Simona had no answers. There were rules and regulations that she had not yet confronted. There was a mindset that seemed to exclude her from seeking Truth on her own.

As a summation at the end of the long session, Simona, weary and benumbed, offered her response. "I can only say that I will, with God's help, try to be a good wife for Enos the Pharisee. I realize that I have much to learn. I cannot promise to be perfect. I will promise to try."

The widow Mary leaned back in her chair. She looked as exhausted as Simona felt.

"May God be with you, daughter," she said. "We have done our best to prepare you. Our prayers will go with you."

Simona felt comfort when the lady reached over and took her hand. She gave it a gentle squeeze and then looked away. Simona wondered if that was a tear she saw on her teacher's cheek.

Three women arrived the next morning. They informed the kitchen help who answered the door that they were sent by the Pharisee Enos to prepare his bride for her wedding day.

The widow Mary was consulted and came from her chamber to offer advice. Simona's room was much too small and poorly lit to have three people fussing over the bride-to-be. It was decided that they would move everything to the larger study room that was sparsely furnished.

The large desk was pushed up against one wall and the two chairs removed to the end of the hallway. Then the three women began to unpack their supplies of unguents, creams, and lotions. Various hair ornaments came next with decorative jewelry. Simona had never seen such a display. Once organized, they began applying layer upon layer.

Is this really necessary when one marries a Pharisee? Simona wondered. She had not known that such finery and fussiness existed.

All morning they rubbed and brushed and braided and coifed and fussed, then pulled things apart and started all over. When it was finally decided that the bride was ready for her wedding, Simona felt exhausted. The tallest of the trio pulled a polished mirror from one of her bags and held it so that Simona could see what they had done. She quickly closed her lips so that the comment that wished to be spoken would be held in check. She had never been one to study herself in a mirror, but once she had seen her own image when one of her childhood friends had shared the gift her father had brought from his travels. This person she beheld in the mirror now looked nothing like the young girl she had studied then. She could scarcely find her face amongst all the cosmetics and jewelry. Was this really what the young Pharisee would want his bride to look like?

But the three women seemed to be very proud of what their combined efforts had achieved. Their chattering grew louder and louder until Simona wished to cover her ears. A sound from the street signaled that the cart had arrived. The three women, still chattering, went to work once again arranging the bridal veil to hang in softly pleated folds covering her face. Simona felt it smothering and wished she could brush it aside for a breath of fresh air. The perfume that had been poured over her in abundance was almost suffocating.

The final event before Simona was allowed to move toward the door and the awaiting cart was for the cook, the woman who did the daily market purchases, and the widow Mary to be invited to see the final product. Simona was fussed over and praised—but not touched. There was not so much as a hand on her arm lest something be messed up.

This was her exit from the home she had shared for the last five months. She would miss it. They had been kind. She could not really claim them as family—not even as dear friends—but they had offered a safe place. She wished she had words to express her appreciation. Hiding behind her veil, trying to keep in check the tears that she had been strictly warned not to allow to fall lest they ruin the carefully applied cosmetics, she tried to express her thanks through the drape of the veil.

Then she stepped from the home, carefully followed the leading hand to the cart, and was moved inside, mindful of the bridal gown, the slippers, and the veil. This would be the beginning of a whole new world. If only she felt comfortable entering it.

CHAPTER FIFTEEN

The Wedding

THE ROOM SIMONA WAS USHERED INTO was large and filled with strangers, all dressed in finery that flashed and glittered. They were noisy in their chatter. Even though Simona heard much, she understood little.

She was escorted by two richly robed attendants. They led her in front of the entire roomful of people to a small raised and partially enclosed seat bedecked with flowers, ribbons, and silk cushions. Standing beside the two steps that lead up to the chamber stood a young man dressed in the most elaborate robe she had ever beheld. His beard was groomed and oiled with a fragrance that met her even before she neared him. Off to the side stood an older man, dressed in fine robes that distinguished him as a priest.

As she neared, the younger man in the colorful robes stepped forward and held out his hand. She almost shivered as she responded by offering her hand in return. He eased her up the two steps and seated her, then allowed one of the attendants to step up to rearrange her gown and her veil. As the attendant stepped back, he took the seat beside her.

The ceremony began when the priest stepped forward. Simona could not catch all of the rapidly flowing formal Hebrew. She was used to her village folk and the intermingled jargon of her people who had allowed several other dialects to contribute to their speech.

The ceremony seemed to go on and on and Simona felt trapped behind the heavy veil. She stopped listening to the droning voice and was caught off guard when he came to a place where he needed her response. Enos the Pharisee had to nudge her, making some of the crowd of observers chuckle softly.

Eventually the ceremony ended. The groom shared wine from a fine goblet with his new wife, and she was assisted from the raised platform and led to a private chamber that held the draped and decorated wedding bed.

Simona's thoughts went back to one of the afternoon lessons at the widow Mary's. It contained all of the rights and wrongs and the various rituals and happenings of the marriage bed. She reviewed them quickly as she was led forward amid cheers and calls and even whistles. She was thankful for the training. She would have been totally unprepared had she not had the instruction.

When they stepped inside Enos turned to his new bride and began to carefully remove her veil. He had not seen her face since the day in the market and he wondered if his recollection of that beautiful woman had been accurate. He was relieved to see that she was even more beautiful than his memories of her had been. And today, at the bridal feast, he would finally get to display her beauty before all his friends.

But looking at her, he was also reminded of how young she was. Just a girl. Was she prepared to be a wife? He hoped the widow Mary had done a proper job in her training.

When they returned to their guests, amid more cheers and clapping, Simona was no longer in her wedding gown but wearing an embroidered robe, lighter in both weight and color. Her veil had been changed as well to a half veil, much thinner, that she could drape in such a way to give her freer access to fresh air.

The music had already started and the line of male dancers was circling the floor, whirling and clapping and calling out hoots and good-natured challenges to other dancers. Simona felt that some of them evidenced the fact that the wine had already been liberally served.

She was led to the bridal table and seated with great ceremony. From the way the young man Enos glowed and smiled, Simona felt some relief. He seemed to be pleased with her.

He was not ugly. In fact Simona decided that under different circumstances she might have found him attractive. He did not seem evil, as she had feared he might. In fact, he seemed quite caring as he led her to their place at the table. He even ceremonially removed her veil and placed a kiss on her forehead—much to the delight of the young men in attendance. Simona felt her cheeks redden, and that had just seemed to draw more attention from the crowd.

She was well aware of the many staring eyes that continued to be turned upon her. The man beside her also seemed to be aware that she was being studied. It appeared that it brought him pleasure, rather than jealousy. He even pushed her veil farther from her face as they sat at the bridal table for the meal. She lost a little gasp that escaped her lips and was tempted to reach up and restore the veil to its customary place. He must have read her thoughts for he reached out and took her trembling hand in his.

It seemed very late when the meal and celebration finally ended. Simona was so weary she longed for the comfort of her own room and bed.

He surprised her when he whispered in her ear. "I know it is late and you are weary. I do wish some more time to celebrate with my friends. My servant Ira will see that you are taken home and the chambermaid Una will assist you there. Sleep well, my love. I will see you in the morning."

Simona had never heard more welcome words.

She was not awakened the next morning. It was later than normal when she roused and began to reconstruct where she was and why. She had been married. She was now at the home of her husband—the Pharisee Enos. But where was he?

She sat up and looked around her. The room she was in was not opulent, though it was far superior to the home she had grown up in. There were Grecian rugs on the floor and draperies at the lone window. The bed stood on a raised platform and had a billowy canopy that could be lifted or dropped at will. A small table stood beside the bed. It contained a simple lamp and a bronze bell. She did not remember a lesson that spoke of bells in bed chambers. What would happen if she shook it?

She hesitated. Was it really there for that purpose? Was this the way she was to communicate?

She shook the bell because she did not know what else to do. Almost immediately an older woman appeared whom Simona remembered as the servant who had assisted her the night before. She stopped and bowed, then stood silently waiting for Simona to speak.

When Simona just stared and said nothing, the woman became bolder. "You rang, Lady Simona. What can I do for you? Do you wish to take your meal in bed, or do you wish to be assisted in dressing for the day, and then to be served in the room for dining?"

Simona did not know how to answer her questions. She responded with the first thing that came to her mind. "Where—where is my husband?"

"The Pharisee Enos has left for his usual duties. He said not to waken you. He will see you when he gets home at the end of the day."

Simona threw back the bedcovers and almost stumbled from the bed. "Oh dear, I've missed him. And what am I to do?" she dared to ask.

For one moment the woman looked confused. Then she answered evenly, "Whatever you wish, my lady."

"But—but who is—is looking after the—the home?"

Another puzzled look from the woman. Then she seemed to stretch up to appear a bit taller, and answered evenly. "The household staff, my lady."

"Oh."

This life was going to be much different than she had supposed. Had not the widow Mary taught her that *she* was to be in charge of the Pharisee's home? What had she meant?

There was a chair nearby. She took it.

The first thing she did was to force a smile, directed right toward the stiff woman in the stiff wool tunic. "I guess you realize that this is all very strange for me. I grew up in a village where we—we looked after ourselves. We only had one servant."

There was no response.

"Would you lay out my proper clothes for this day? I will dress myself. Then you may bring me a light meal—with ripe figs if you have some—here will be fine. Then I will need to learn all about—about the—this household—so that I can make wise decisions—to please my husband."

Her smile had slipped some during her long speech. She attempted to bring it back again as she nodded toward the woman who had waited patiently for her words to end. The servant nodded and went to a small side room. She selected garments for the day, with no questions asked of Simona. Then she bowed herself from the room and Simona took a deep breath. For a moment she just sat where she was, blinking back tears that wished to come, even though she had no reason for them.

Then she roused herself. The woman would soon be back with her meal. She had to be dressed and ready.

The meal was delivered. It was more food than Simona needed. She did deplore waste. She was tempted to set it aside for her noon meal but decided that was neither wise nor necessary.

She finished her meal, tidied up the tray, and waited. Nothing happened.

She stirred about her room, restlessly tapping a foot and walking from window to door and back again. She spread her bed, making sure that each blanket hung evenly, each pillow was fluffed.

Still nothing.

Then her eyes fell on the bell. The bell? Was she to use the bell for each summons?

Frustrated and impatient, she reached for the bell and gave it one firm shake. It was too loud. It reverberated through the small room.

Almost immediately, the older woman appeared. Simona felt that she should apologize, but she was not sure what words to use. As the woman picked up the tray, she turned to Simona. "Is there anything else, Lady Simona?"

Simona took a deep breath. "Yes. Yes, there is. I—I need to talk to—to whomever is—is in charge here. I—I'm sorry, but I don't know the—the rules—the way things are run here. I need to talk to whomever . . ."

"That would be Hugo. He is the overseer."

"And how—how do I meet with Hugo?"

"He will meet with you, whenever you wish."

"And where do these meetings take place?"

"Normally it would be in the hall room."

"And where do I find the hall room?"

"I can take you there, my lady."

Simona nodded and the woman moved the few steps to the door and led the way to the hall room.

Simona, who still was not acquainted with the home, was surprised to see a small room directly off the entrance hall. It contained only two simple seats and a small table. Already flushed and nervous, she was glad to accept the seat that Una indicated.

Una had only just disappeared when a small man with a very serious expression walked into the room, bowing his way in with each step he took. Simona felt the need to stand to greet him with a nod.

"Please, let us sit at the table," she proposed.

He looked surprised but he did her bidding. She took her seat and turned to him.

"I want to be—honest and—and frank with you. I am not really a lady of standing. I am a simple girl from a small village near the lake of Galilee. My father is a millwright and my mother a housewife. I am used to doing my own chores. Gardening, cooking, laundry—you understand?"

The servant named Hugo nodded. But he still looked confused and uncomfortable. He sat patiently, listening but not looking at Simona.

"What I am trying to say," she went on, "is that I know how to do all of the household chores, but I do not know—have no practical experience in how to—how to work with servants. Will—will you teach me? Please?"

The kind man seemed to dismiss the line between mistress and servant and see instead a very young girl in need of gentle guidance. He nodded and moved his chair just a bit closer to the table. "This is not usual," were his first words, "and under normal circumstances I would not speak so boldly. But I see that you wish to please the master, as do I. As a Pharisee, the master is . . . young, though quickly making a name for himself. This household is small. Only a few servants are needed here. We have recently hired Una, who was engaged to meet the need as your chambermaid. Hiram runs the kitchen, and he has a helper, a young lad named Edim, who does some of the market chores. Then there is Ira, who is the personal servant of Master Enos."

"What do *I* do?" she asked, with a puzzled look.

He frowned. Then he dared a bit of a smile. "You tell us your wishes," he responded. "Nothing more."

"But that sounds so—so useless and—and selfish."

The servant shook his head and stood, looking ready to excuse himself. He tucked his hands back in the fold of his robe and took his normal posture of eyes to the floor. "I would think it will be a full-time job pleasing your new husband," he said. "He often comes home weary from his studies."

Simona nodded and rose to her feet. "Of course," she mumbled. "Yes, of course."

The man turned to go when Simona spoke again. "Excuse me, please, but one more thing."

He paused.

She fumbled, embarrassed. "When—when do I ring the bell?"

"You ring the bell whenever you wish assistance."

"But I—I do not wish to be a nuisance."

"We are here for *you*, Lady Simona."

"But there is so much I could do for myself."

He stepped forward, one hand coming out from under his robe to reach toward her. "Oh, my lady," he cautioned, "do not try to change our world. This is how it works best. Masters and servants, each living their role. You are now the esteemed lady of the house. We know how we are to care for you. If it were to change, we would all be confused."

Simona shook her head. It seemed she was the only one who was totally confused. "Thank you," she whispered. "Thank you for being patient with me."

The man nodded once more and silently slipped from the room. Una appeared at once to lead Simona back to her chambers. She followed silently, meekly—feeling like a child who had been scolded and put in her place.

Little did she know that she had just endeared herself to the entire staff of the home of Enos. Though no one spoke of it, there was not one among them who would not have given their most devoted service for the young wife of the prideful Pharisee.

CHAPTER SIXTEEN

The Promotion

ENOS WAS FLUSHED WITH PRIDE when he entered the building where they were to gather to discuss the serious issue of the day. He knew he had impressed all of his fellow trainees who had been invited to the wedding. Indeed, his new bride had more than measured up to his expectations. The comments he had received were even more flattering than he'd hoped. He sensed envy in the voices of his classmates as they expressed their congratulations. She was indeed a beautiful woman.

However, she was young, even younger than he had expected. But he reasoned with himself that she may be the kind who blossomed with maturity. He tried to imagine what she might look like in another five or even ten years. It pleased him.

But as he entered the room, among smiles and nods and winks from the other young men, his pleasure was quickly replaced with more serious thoughts. Every face of the ten Pharisees who were seated at the long head table before the group looked angry or frightened—or perhaps both. He caught immediately that they had not been gathered for friendly chitchat.

One of the elderly leaders raised a hand, which indicated that all voices were to be silenced. There was an immediate hush and all eyes focused on the leaders at the front of the assembly room.

The man spoke from where he sat. Enos noted that his normally strong voice seemed broken. He stopped, cleared his throat, and started over.

"We have just received word that the man who calls himself Jesus of Nazareth, or the prophet of Galilee, or any of the various titles that he has bestowed upon himself, is getting bolder in his claims. People are gathering in ever-increasing numbers and many are falling into his trap and believing the nonsense he is teaching. We, as Pharisees, have decided that we can no longer sit back and let this charlatan lead our people from the Truth. He must be stopped."

Nods of agreement followed.

"At the same time, we are forced to keep peace with Rome. To cause a nationwide rebellion or conflict would only increase the Roman forces that already overrun our cities. Thus, we must proceed quickly, but cautiously. If we do not put a stop to this ranting man, we could lose our positions—and even our nation."

A second leader spoke. "We have been in discussion for most of the night. There were varied positions expressed, but we did come to a unanimous conclusion. This man must be stopped. Immediately!"

There was an undertone of voices. Rumblings could be heard, gathering momentum until the man rapped on the table with heavy knuckles.

Again, silence settled.

"We will act immediately. It has been decided that we will send out a group of our own scholars to counter whatever this man is teaching, to challenge him at every turn. He is, after all, the son of a carpenter. From Nazareth, west of the Galilee. As far as we can gather, he has never been properly schooled in the Holy Scriptures."

Again, rumblings. Again, a call for silence.

"We will send some of our scholars of the Word and show the masses that he is simply a babbler with no basis to the lies he is presenting as truths."

Even a thumping fist could not quiet the shouts that filled the council room. Louder and louder the din grew as angry voices and hot blood stirred up the group of men who considered themselves to be the authorities and guardians of Truth.

The man relaxed his fist. *Let them roar,* he appeared to decide. And Enos agreed that it was good to stir them up and have them ready to defend their position. While they shouted and howled in protest, those at the head table appeared to watch the crowd, approving of those who were the most vocal, the most intense. And when they were spotted, it was clear that he told the recorder at his side to write down the names.

Enos rose from his chair and called out words of defiance, pumping his arms above his head. If a spectacle was what they seemed to be looking for, then he would be among the most outspoken.

"We will select a group for this important mission. It will be rigorous and without many of the comforts that you are used to. But we feel that the task will be a rewarding one for those who take part. Remember. You will be saving our freedoms, our Faith, and our future. It is a noble cause."

So saying, the elderly Pharisee gathered his robes and rose to his feet, with a bit of aid from supporting hands. His regal coat swished about his slender frame as he left the gathering.

Immediately there was a buzz. Finally—finally someone was

willing to take some much-needed action against this imposter. It had already gone on for far too long.

Simona had retired for the night when there was a knock on her door. It was followed by the entrance of Enos. He had already changed from his formal robes of the day. He crossed to her bed and sat down on the edge. She did not know what to say, so she remained silent.

"It has been a long day," he said. "Long and busy . . . and stimulating."

She still did not respond. She could tell by his face that he had some type of exciting news he wished to share.

He reached down and lifted a handful of her loose hair, exploring its texture and softness. He raised it to his lips, and then let it slip through his spread fingers. His eyes were shining.

"You would not believe what happened today. The leaders are finally going to take some action. We, my classmates and I, have been trying to push for action for some time and they kept saying not to worry, it would go away when the people realized that this imposter was not who he claimed to be. But it did not go away. It just got worse and worse. More and more people gather around him everywhere he goes. Well, they finally see that he is a danger—to all of us. And they are taking steps to put an end to his ravings. They are going to choose a team to follow him wherever he goes to expose him for the deceiver he is. And I am hoping that they will choose me as one of them. There is even payment for the duty."

He stopped and smiled and played with her hair again.

"They will post the names tomorrow. I cannot wait. It would be a dream come true—to expose him. To defeat him. To crush him."

The last words were said with such unchecked rage that it made Simona shiver.

And then he changed—totally.

He lifted her hair to his cheek and bent over her. "Did you miss me?" he asked softly but did not wait for her reply. "I missed you. Everywhere I went the young men were asking if you had a sister." He chuckled softly. "I told them, no, you were the one and only. And you are already mine."

He leaned over to kiss her temple.

He nudged her over slightly and lay down beside her, reaching out an arm to draw her close. She still had not spoken. Her mind was too busy trying to put together all the pieces. What was he talking about? Why was he so filled with hate toward someone? What had the unnamed person done? This unidentified enemy?

And, even more confusing, she could not understand how he could so quickly go from rage to romance.

But she dared not ask. Not now.

CHAPTER SEVENTEEN

The Assignment

There was an underlying current of wonder and excitement the next morning as the full group of the Pharisees congregated in the Temple court. The gates, which could not be closed during the day, were guarded to hold would-be worshippers at bay until Jewish Law decreed that they would need to give access to the faithful again for the next prayer session.

There was a hum in the air, low and controlled at first, but it grew as the gathering grew, until it became a tension-filled moan of both excitement and dread.

The false prophet, Jesus of Nazareth, had to be stopped. Reports kept coming in of healings and exorcisms and other strange miraculous occurrences. The people of lower class were quick to attribute these acts to the power of God, thus accepting the doer as being the long-awaited Messiah that God had promised in the prophetic writings of old.

Enos stood among the crowd, shoulder to shoulder with many

of his classmates. His pulse was racing, his anger intense. Why had they waited so long to act? If he had been in charge, this man would have been gone long ago.

He pushed forward, step by forced step, drawing closer to the makeshift platform on which the leaders sat. He wished them to see his intensity. His fervor. His dedication to the Faith of which he had long been a part.

And, besides all that, he was eager to partake of the remuneration that would be paid to those who were sent out to represent the position of the faithful. He still had plans that were not covered by his current resources.

By the time he had pushed his way to the front, someone had hammered a gong to indicate a call for silence. The response was immediate. The roar became a silence so intense he could almost feel it.

The spokesman stood and held out a hand for continued silence. "We all know why we are gathered this day. Our nation, our religion of Truth, our very existence, is being challenged."

With his words the crowd threatened to erupt, and the gong was sounded again with three loud bangs that reverberated throughout the entire gathering.

Enos felt his cry choke back into his throat. He trembled with the intensity of his rage. This man—this man called Jesus—had no right to try to claim that which had always belonged to them. They were the religious leaders of the people. They led the people in the Faith of their fathers. They were the ones with the gold-embroidered robes, the honored places of their towns and streets and gatherings. He had no right . . .

The man with the gong continued, "We met again last evening until late into the night and we have decided that we must not wait any longer. We have tried to expose his deceit through reason but the masses are too blind and too ignorant to see the Truth. We have looked for opportunities to catch him in the breaking of Roman law, giving reason for him to be charged in the courts of Caesar. So far, he has eluded such attempts.

"Now, we realize that we must take action. Under our law, the man is worthy of death—and we must see that he is destroyed before he does further harm to our Temple, our heritage, and the people of God."

Even the banging of the gong could not stop the roar.

The man conceded and took his seat. There was no use trying to speak against the heated blood of the gathered followers. They had become a fully enraged mob.

The Temple guards assisted the robed leaders from the platform and out the Temple gates, leaving behind the remaining mass, still cheering and milling, to disentangle itself and find its way home.

Once free of the congregants, the leaders looked at one another in satisfaction. They had clearly done what they had come to do. The energy of the crowd was enough to carry them forward. They, at the top, appeared quite confident that the angry masses would follow any future orders they were given. One of the lesser Pharisees was given the honor of posting the scrap of papyrus containing the names of those chosen to be agitators who would bring about the change.

Enos's was the first name on the list.

Enos did not even wait for his servant, Hugo, to bow him into his quarters. His excitement led him directly to the chamber of Simona. To his surprise, and annoyance, she was not there. For one terrible second, he had the thought that Simona might have found some reason to leave him. Surely not!

He fairly bellowed for Ira, who arrived so quickly he had no time for a bow.

"Where is my wife?"

"She is in the small court at the back. She enjoys . . ."

But Enos was already headed for the mentioned court.

He found Simona seated on the bench, a picked flower in her hand and her head bowed over it studying the colors of the petals. Near at hand a startled sparrow rose from the small fountain that spewed silvery water drops into the sultry afternoon air.

His anger was still hot. "What are you doing here?"

Her head jerked up and the flower fell from her fingers. Surprise—and fear—filled her eyes. She pushed herself to her feet, as if unsure whether she was really to answer his question.

He did not give her time to do so, but went on. "You are to be in your chamber to welcome me at the end of the day," he hissed.

She surprised him. Her head lifted, her eyes studied him thoughtfully, carefully, and then she said in a very controlled voice, "It is not the end of the day, my lord."

He was so thrown off-balance by her calm retort that he did not know what to say for a moment. "You are to be there whenever I come," he sputtered.

She dipped her head in submission. But she did not reply.

His anger began to slip away as he remembered the reason he had rushed home. He crossed the short distance and gathered her in his arms, excitement making his heart rate increase.

"They chose me," his voice squeaked with his excitement.

She shook her head in puzzlement.

He was crushing her against him so tightly that he was certain she could feel the wild beating of his heart. "They chose me," he said again, "as one of the men being sent to destroy the false prophet!"

She shook her head and tried to look up at his face.

"Do you not understand?" He gave her a little shake. "The prophet. The one from Nazareth. We are going after him."

"But why?" Her words were barely audible.

He pushed her back and looked at her, his eyes angry and glaring. "Did that widow woman from the Temple teach you nothing? Or are you just too dull to learn?"

Simona made no response. He gave her one more little push, then spun on his heel. "Go to your room," he hissed. "We will talk later."

He was gone, slamming the door as he went in.

Simona stared after her husband. Then she reached down and reclaimed her flower. It had been stepped on. Her fingers tenderly stroked the damaged petals, trying to make them whole again. She placed it on the edge of the fountain where the stem could reach into the cooling water.

Then she turned and walked slowly back to her chamber with its unwelcome isolation.

She had already retired for the night when he came to her room. His mood had changed, but there was no explanation or apology.

He sat on the edge of her bed and began to toy with the loose, dark tendrils of her hair. Simona said nothing. Nor did he.

When he did decide to talk his words surprised her. "This is the last evening I will see you for some time. It would be a shame to waste it."

When she made no response, nor asked any questions, he went on, his voice filling with excitement. "I will be leaving in the morning—early—before the day gets too hot for travel. There will be three of us going together. They wanted to make sure there would be enough for a valid statement and charge in court."

Simona's eyes widened and it seemed to make him more excited.

"It has been reported that the carpenter has last been seen in the Galilee. We are prepared to take as long as needed to bring him to justice."

She froze. Was he speaking of Jesus of Nazareth?

"I do not know when I will be home again." He ran his fingers through her hair as he spoke. He needed to boast a bit. "This is an important assignment. We are even to be paid for our part. I have been greatly honored in being selected to go."

He hesitated and Simona feared he was waiting for her words of praise. She could not speak them.

"We will be seeking the death penalty." His words were so calm and controlled he could have been speaking of the weather.

She turned her head, almost pulling the hair from his fingers.

He jerked it back again. "Listen to me!" he said firmly. "Don't you ever turn from me when I am speaking to you." His eyes were burning with anger.

She knew she had to speak. To say something that would cool his anger. "I am sorry, my lord," she managed to mumble. "The news of your long journey has troubled me."

She had told the truth. She was troubled. It was not right that the Pharisees had ordered this Jesus hunted down like a criminal. He was not a bad man deserving of death. And now her father would never have the opportunity for healing.

He misinterpreted her words. Pleased, he nudged her over so he could lay beside her. "It should not take long and I will be home to you again. But we must remember, every day I am gone means more money in my purse."

She sensed that he was smiling as he said the words.

When he left her room later, he turned at the door. "If you like," he said, "while I am away you have my permission to use the small court. I will inform Ira."

She did not respond.

CHAPTER EIGHTEEN

The Separation

Each day Simona checked with Ira and asked if he'd had any word from Enos. He had not. It had been almost three months since Enos had left them.

The use of the small court with its flowers and fountain was not the only thing that had changed. Though the staff still maintained their individual roles in an orderly and respectful manner, Simona noticed a sense of peace and freedom she had not felt before. The tensions began to relax.

Except for missing her family, she did not struggle against the imposed exile. Occasionally, she thought of Widow Mary. She wondered how the elderly woman was faring. In spite of the large chasm between teacher and student, she did have respect for the widow and would have liked to claim her as a friend.

Simona enjoyed the courtyard. Daily. If the sun was too hot during the day, she spent some time sitting in the softness of evening shadows, or arose early in the morning and enjoyed her breakfast as she shared her breadcrumbs with the bold sparrows. She even spoke to them—since there was really no one else with whom to communicate. But something had begun to concern Simona. Something had changed and she was not sure why. Dared she consult Una, her maid? Though Una was pleasant and helpful, she kept a firm line drawn between mistress and servant. Simona, who had never had the pleasure of having a sister or even a close friend, had rarely had opportunity to have chats with girls of her own age. But as the end of the third month approached, she felt the need to talk with another woman. It was a difficult decision. As she rang for Una, she wondered how she would approach the subject.

Una was quick to arrive at her door, the customary bow taken as soon as she entered.

"Yes, Lady Simona?"

"Would you have Hiram send tea, please—to the courtyard—and an extra cup. Then I wish you to have tea with me. And a . . . a chat."

"My lady?"

"Yes. Tea—a special tea—for two. In the courtyard. And make sure the pillows are fluffed up, with clean coverings."

"Tea—in the courtyard—for two. And clean coverings on the pillows?"

Simona nodded.

Una bowed herself out.

Simona arrived at the courtyard first and was there to welcome Una. The pillows had, indeed, had the coverings changed to fresh linens and looked full and soft for sitting.

Una placed the tea tray on the small table and stepped back to await her next order. The tray contained more than the ordered tea. Small pastries and fruit were also displayed.

"Would you pour, please?"

Una poured, but her hand was a bit shaky.

Simona indicated the seat beside her on the small bench. Una sat.

Simona took a sip of the aromatic tea that Hiram had prepared. It tasted as a flower garden smelled. "That's very nice. You must thank Hiram for me." Simona never went near the kitchen.

Una nodded.

Simona passed the tray of sweets and Una, haltingly, accepted a few fresh grapes. Simona helped herself to a handful of ripe figs. "Did you have sisters?"

Simona's sudden and direct question seemed to startle them both.

Una swallowed the grapes she had been chewing and replied, "Two."

"Were they older or younger than you?"

"One of each."

"Did either of them marry?"

Una nodded. "Yes. They both married."

"But you did not?"

Una looked uncomfortable. But she did answer, softly. "No."

Simona wished to stop her planned line of questioning so she might ask Una why she was the one to remain single. But Una went on to volunteer the answer.

"My family was poor. I was hired by the town's carpenter to help his wife who was with child."

Simona leaned forward, one hand going out to touch the arm of her servant. "You were there—with the woman when her time . . . ?"

Though Una looked surprised, both by the touch and the question, she answered evenly. "Yes, I was there."

She stopped and looked down at her cup, pain already showing in her eyes. When her eyes lifted again, Simona also saw tears. "We lost the baby."

Her voice was almost a whisper. Simona had not missed the word *we*.

Simona was so shaken by the response that she could not speak. Again, she reached out a hand to the grieving woman. She was surprised when Una accepted the offered hand and placed her own hand over it.

Simona took a deep breath. "I—I sent for you because I have been—been wondering . . . I know nothing, but I have been wondering if—if I might be with child."

Una's head jerked up and her face turned pale. "What makes you think . . . ?"

"I'm not sure. I—I just feel different somehow and—and I have not been needing the—the . . ." She could not go on but hoped her servant would understand.

Una did understand. In fact, she spoke. "I—I wondered. The laundry . . ."

"What do I do?"

Una stirred, then gave Simona's hand a squeeze. "You thank God. And ask for his help and protection. A child is a blessing that not all women share."

Simona nodded. It was affirmation that she had not dared to hope for.

"You still are very young," the woman went on, "but you are healthy and strong and will have all the food you need to nourish . . ."

"Food," repeated Simona, "I have been having a bit of trouble with food recently."

Una's eyes brightened. "Are you noticing any increase . . . ?" Una stopped and made a motion across her stomach.

Simona hesitated as she thought about the question. "Not—not really. But it would still be early."

"Of course."

There was silence. The older woman broke it. "When will your husband be home again?"

Simona could only shake her head. "I have no idea. I have heard nothing from him since he left."

Una stood. She took a deep breath, then managed a smile. "We will take good care of you. I will arrange with the kitchen for the proper foods you will be needing. Do try to eat. Babies need to be nourished long before they make their appearance. I will do some shopping so that you can begin to make small garments in preparation. It will give you something exciting to do with your many hours. The sparrows will miss you, but they can wait their turn. Perhaps, you will, one day soon, be able to introduce them to your child."

It was an exciting thought. Simona sat in silence as she watched Una gathering up the tea things to return the tray back to Hiram's kitchen.

Simona was so thankful that she had the older woman to help her through the emotional days ahead. If only her mother were close . . . But there was no use wishing for things that could not be. At least she had Una.

Gradually Simona's appetite returned. Food tasted good again, and Una and the kitchen servants made sure that the things on Simona's tray were not just tasty but nourishing.

But the days passed by and still Enos did not come. She was now past the dreadfully lonely time that she had endured for the first few months. The household staff no longer felt like strangers. The courtyard felt like her own comfortable place that she could claim whenever she wished the company of birds and flowers. And though she still missed her family, she felt she did have a home.

They were into the fifth month since the departure of Enos

when Ira tapped on her door, then stepped in when he was bidden to enter. He did not wait for ceremony but went directly to the message he held in his hand.

"Master Enos has sent word that he hopes to be home soon."

He bowed himself out and Simona held her breath. He was coming home—in a short time. He had been gone so long and they had spent such a short time together after their marriage that she wondered how they would respond to one another. She really felt that she did not know the man who was her husband. She and the servants had finally managed to work well together. Una now seemed more like a big sister—or even a mother—than a servant. How would Enos fit with the way things were done now—the easy communication between master and servant?

Then she thought of the coming baby. It, too, would make a big change to the home. She dared to hope that the child she carried would be a son for Enos. Every man hoped for a son to carry on the family name and heritage.

Her concerns quickly changed to exciting expectations. It would be good to have him home. They could begin their life together all over again. It would be different this time. The coming baby would draw them together in the bond of family.

CHAPTER NINETEEN

The Outrage

Each morning when Simona welcomed a new day she wondered if this would be the one when Enos would walk through the door and, after his long, long time of following the orders of his superiors, he'd be home once again. They had not parted on the best of terms but things would be different now. The coming baby would give them reason to look forward to the future. Daily her excitement grew just thinking of what it would be like to be a family.

But each day, as she watched the evening sun slip behind the distant hills, she had to hide her disappointment that he still had not come.

Her exciting secret was slightly evident now. Oh, as she dressed in loose garments and tucked a light shawl around her shoulders, it was still easy for her to hide the fact that she was to be a mother. But each night as she prepared for bed, the small roundness reminded her that she was not dreaming. It was true.

Since she had no one else with whom to share her excitement, she spoke to her unborn child. "Your father will soon be home. He has not heard about you yet. I cannot wait to tell him. He will be pleased to have a son. And if . . . If you are a daughter, he will love you just as much. My father—your grandfather—was very special to me. He was a wonderful father. I would wish you the same happy and close relationship with your father. There is nothing better than the strong bond between father and child—be it boy or girl. Just wait. You will see. The love is so strong. I can still sense my father's love all the way from the Galilee to Jerusalem. Even now."

Where before Simona had always chosen what she wished to wear for the day, she began consulting Una. She wanted to look prepared and properly groomed when Enos arrived home. She even had the maid do her hair in an appealing fashion. As she studied herself in the gilded mirror, she wondered if her appearance would please him. It had been so long. With the coming baby, she felt like an adult. She would be a much better companion now. The young girl that Enos had married had been shy and unsure of herself. And though her age had not changed but by a few months, Simona felt like a different person. She was ready for the adult world. Ready to be a true mate—and a mother. She was sure that Enos would be pleased with the maturity that she had gained.

The days crawled by, one by one—and still he did not come. Simona was about to lose heart when a courier came with the news that he was on his way. He first had to stop and share his report with the senior Pharisees. They were anxious for all the information of his time spent on the trail of the prophet.

Simona immediately rang for Una.

Should she change her gown for a fresh-looking one? Did her hair need a touch-up? Her cheeks need more color?

Una, in an effort to calm her, refreshed the gown, pampered her hair by adding a fresh sprig of citron blossom, and assured her that the gown hung graciously about her still-slim body. All the time that Una worked she talked. Simona began to relax.

The night's darkness had enfolded the household when Una tapped on the door and entered her room. "It appears he has been held up by some very important business, Lady Simona. Could I help you to prepare for retiring?"

Without waiting for the answer Una began to remove the pins from her carefully coifed hair. Simona did not argue. Soon she was tucked in for the night—alone, again.

"Good night, my lady," Una whispered softly as she stood at the door. Simona managed to express her thanks before the door closed.

When Simona was sure that Una had walked away, she turned her face into her pillow and wept.

Enos did come the next day. Simona had not fussed with her hair or her gown. She did not wish another disappointment.

She was seated in the outer courtyard, an uneaten tray of food before her, the sparrows getting bolder and bolder in their desire to rob from her tray, when Enos made his appearance. The first thing he did was to take off his cloak and, waving it wildly, scatter the sparrows.

"Why do you allow them such freedom?" he scolded. "They make a mess of everything they touch. They will be coming to the kitchen if you keep this up."

Simona had not yet caught her breath.

"Come in," he said nodding his head toward the door. "We need to talk."

Woodenly, Simona rose to her feet and moved toward the door. He was so angry. What had she done now?

"Go to your room," Enos ordered. "We'll talk later."

She went. Bewildered and hurt. She had hoped that things would change but apparently nothing had changed for Enos.

But she did not go to bed. She decided that when Enos came to her room—if he came to her room—she would not be lying there waiting for him to make the call. This time she would find her voice.

But it was not Enos who came to her room. It was Una who was sent with a message. "Your husband is weary from his travels. He wishes to wait until tomorrow to speak with you."

Simona nodded. She felt numb. What had happened to her dream of a happy reunion?

Una hesitated. "Would you wish help in preparing for bed, Lady Simona?"

Una seemed so formal and so back to the way things had been when Simona had first come to the home of Enos. What had happened? Where had the close connection—the ease with one another—gone?

"No—thank you—I will be fine." Simona managed.

Una turned to go but Simona did not miss the concerned look in her servant's eyes.

Simona ordered her breakfast in her room the next morning. She had no desire to join her husband in the small dinette. She had battled for most of the night with her disappointment and pain. *What kind of a world will I be bringing my baby into?* she asked herself.

She tried to pray but she felt no comfort or assurance from her prayer. It was as though the God of Heaven no longer had interest in her life. She cried for her father—and longed for her mother.

Her breakfast tray sat untouched. She had no appetite. She tried to tell herself that she should eat for her baby's sake, but she was afraid if she tried, she would just bring it up again. Her stomach had no desire for food. So she went back to her bed in spite of the fact that she had already dressed for the day. Her window informed her that it was almost noon when her door opened and Enos walked in unannounced.

There was no preamble. "I expect to leave again in the morning." He shook his head. "That false rabbi is as sneaky as a snake."

He was angry again. His face reddened and his body shook. "We just get him cornered and he disappears in the night. Even if we post guards, he gets by them. And it doesn't matter that our logic overrides his—he finds some Old Testament law that contravenes it."

He spit on the floor. Simona cringed.

He spun around and faced her. "And when I am out there drinking stale water and eating road dust, people like you lie around and do nothing—say nothing. And the hierarchy, what do they do? Nothing! That's what. We could have had this all over and done with if they had let us take action. But, oh no. It has to be done by the books."

He picked up a pillow and hurled it at the wall with all the strength he could put behind it, a string of curses accompanying its flight.

"Well, I am sick of it. So, who gets sent home to cool down? Me! The only one who has guts enough to take some action. 'I might stir up the Romans,' they say, or 'I might upset the people of the Law.' Well, it's about time someone got upset. I am sick of the whole mess, and he is making us look like a bunch of sissies—or fools. So now I get sent off for some fool's errand in the opposite direction."

He hurled another pillow at the wall. It missed and tipped over the pitcher of water that was sitting next to her washbasin.

Simona, white-faced, did not know how to react to his rant, so she said nothing.

"I am—"

There was a sharp knock on the door. Enos turned toward it. Simona was sure there would be another outburst of cursing. Ira dared to open the door, and without the bow said sternly, "There is a messenger from the High Priest. You are wanted immediately." He did not even bow his way out but retreated, leaving the door open behind him.

Enos cursed again, but he followed the man from the room.

Simona collapsed, the fear causing her shoulders to shake. A gentle hand touched her. Una was there. Her arms went around Simona, pulling her close.

"It is okay. He is gone. We are here. It is okay. Relax. Just relax. It is not good for the baby to feel such turmoil. Shh." It was some minutes before Simona could relax enough to be helped to bed.

Simona was surprised to be nudged over in the night. Enos was there. He made no comment about his earlier outrage. Simona knew the moment she felt his fingers entangle themselves in her loose hair that he would be staying. She said nothing. She was too frightened.

It wasn't until later that a hand reached out and fingers traced the outline of the child she carried. Enos lurched upright.

"What is this? Are you—?"

"Yes, my lord," she cut in quickly. "You are to be a father."

"Me? A father? Now how can that be? I have been away for—"

"I know, my lord. The baby was begun before you left."

"And how do I know . . . ?"

There was an accusation waiting on his tongue. "Ask your trusted staff. There have been no visitors here—and I have not left—"

"I *will* ask," he said, his voice loud and forceful. "I certainly will!"

Simona again cried herself to sleep. When Una brought her

tray the next morning, she also brought news. Enos was gone again. But sometime in the night he had visited an apothecary and he had left a small bottle of medicine. "For my wife," he had said, "to help with her condition."

Una smiled when she repeated the words. Simona was to take the medicine along with her morning meal.

Simona sighed in relief. It seemed that Enos was no longer angry, but pleased about the baby's coming.

It wasn't until late afternoon that Simona began to have stomach cramps. She tried to ignore them but they seemed to intensify as the day moved on. By bedtime she was in extreme pain. Ira was sent to find a physician. By the time the man arrived Simona was rolling on her bed in severe pain. Una was there, wiping away the perspiration with wet cloths and rubbing her back in between the cramps.

It was the physician who boldly made the announcement. Simona was losing her baby.

She cried aloud when she heard the words, but it wasn't long until her intense pain had her beyond tears. The physician knew that there was nothing he could do to save the child and his full attention was now on the young mother. Una was kept busy running errands and bringing fresh linens.

The tiny child arrived, already lifeless, and the doctor passed him to Una, who bundled the wee body in a linen wrap and laid it aside. They must now spend their efforts in trying to save the mother who was losing way too much blood.

At one point they were sure that they had lost her, but with a small shudder Simona fought for another breath. It was a long night and the outcome did not look promising. Not long after midnight the doctor stepped back and wiped his brow. Una feared that he was going to quit fighting.

"We must keep trying," Una urged.

When the sun announced that another day had begun, they were both exhausted but Simona was still drawing shallow breaths. Her face was white, her body cold to the touch, but she was breathing.

Ira came. Quietly. He offered morning refreshments from the kitchen. The staff was anxious for news. What they received was both sad—and hopeful. The baby had not survived, but Simona still fought for each breath.

"She is a brave fighter, this young woman," said the doctor with admiration in his voice.

"Indeed! Please, God, that it proves true!" agreed Ira. And he left to take the news back to the kitchen.

The doctor took a brief break and a breakfast tray, stepping out into the courtyard at the back of the home. He was exhausted. And touched. Never had he seen the household staff more concerned about their mistress. What was the story? She was so young?

Who was the father? Where was the father? And where had the strange empty medicine bottle come from? What was going on in this home of a Pharisee?

He rubbed his hand over his bearded face and longed for rest. It had been an exhausting night and the young woman was still in danger of losing her life. If she did survive it was going to take her a long time to regain her health.

He found himself cheering for her. By all appearances, she was deeply loved by those who cared for her daily.

CHAPTER TWENTY

The Healing

Simona spent many days in a pain-filled fog. She was aware of Una with her anytime she was awake. Gentle stirrings to freshen her bedgown or sponge her face, or coax her to swallow a spoonful of broth. Una seemed always to be there. At times Simona thought she heard the voice of Enos, but she was never aware of his being in the room.

One morning she was surprised to feel a bit more alert. When she stirred and opened her eyes, Una was immediately leaning over her. "Hello," she whispered. "Are you awake?"

Simona tried to lift herself but Una's gentle hand went to her shoulder, holding her in place.

"You must be sure you are ready. We will take it one step at a time. First, let me help you to sit up. I will tuck some pillows behind you."

Simona nodded in agreement.

"Do you mind if I ask for help?" were Una's next words.

Simona frowned. Who would help?

"I will lift you, and Ira will place the pillows. We will keep you fully covered. Only my hands will touch you."

Simona nodded. Her mind was still hazy but she saw no problem with the arrangement.

Una reached behind her and gave the bells a sharp shake. Ira was there immediately. Simona could feel his eyes pass over her face. She thought she saw pain in those dark eyes. *Do I really look that bad?* she wondered.

Ira made no comment, just reached for one of the pillows that were stacked on a nearby stool. It appeared the maneuver had been preplanned.

It was not at all difficult for Una to gently lift Simona by her shoulders until she was semi-sitting. Ira tucked in the pillows and was gone as silently as he had entered.

"It is good to see you sit up, my lady," Una said. "We will not take things too quickly. We want you well and strong once again. Your sparrows have been missing you."

Simona managed a half smile. Unbidden, a tear slipped down her cheek. She hastily wiped it away.

"While you are up, I will tidy your hair a bit."

Una was very gentle. Little by little she worked her way through Simona's tangled strands of long, dark hair. When she was done, she laid the comb aside and pinned the hair away from the girl's face.

"That's better," she said with satisfaction. "Now, that is enough for this time. I am going to wipe your face and hands and then we will call for Ira to remove the cushions so that you can lay down again."

Simona wished to protest. She had only been half-sitting for a few minutes. Surely a little more time would not hurt! But she knew that Una had reason for her decisions, so she said nothing.

A gentle rustle of bells summoned Ira. Without comment he eased the two cushions from behind her and Una tenderly laid her down.

Simona could not stop herself from whispering, "Thank you, Ira," as he turned from the room. It seemed likely the first time that Ira had ever been thanked for performing such a mundane duty of a servant. He almost jerked to a stop, then caught himself and, with a nod, departed.

Day by day, Simona began to gain some strength. Una stayed true to her word and would only allow a bit more freedom at a time. It seemed slow progress to Simona who wished to hurry forward—but it was steady progress. The day finally came when Una announced that she would be allowed to sit on a chair to take her meal.

After a few more days Una offered to help her dress once again. The sleeping gowns would be put aside for nighttime only. Simona rejoiced with each new freedom she was allowed. And then came the morning when Una asked her if she felt strong enough to walk to the small courtyard.

With Simona's eager reply, Una signaled for assistance again and brought Ira to walk at her other side—just in case he was needed. Simona was able to make the short walk with only the arm of Una as her support.

It was so good to be out in fresh air again. The hottest part of the summer was over and the morning air was not yet sultry. Simona breathed deeply—and smiled when the sparrows, who seemed to remember, flew in close hoping for some breadcrumbs.

Una had thought of that, too, and handed Simona a small container with a few crusts for her pets. Simona smiled, a full, delighted smile. The first one for a very long time.

Simona was surprised to learn that Enos had been in and out of the home the entire time she had been recovering. He had not come to her room nor, apparently, checked with the staff to see how she was doing. Nor did he come to her room now that she was well enough to be up again. There were no comments made by staff members. They were taught to serve, not to question.

Simona felt that she deserved a few answers so she dared to prod. "Has the master not been sent back out with the Pharisees?"

"No, he has not."

"Was my illness what has kept him at home?"

"No, I do not think so, Lady Simona."

"How is he? Is he well?"

There was silence for several minutes. It seemed to stretch on and on to Simona. At length Una spoke, very carefully, searching and trying each word. "I think he is—well—of body. Perhaps not so well of spirit."

Simona's eyebrows lifted. How could she get more information without Una feeling she was breaking confidence? "Did he not get reassigned?"

There was a hesitancy, but Una did answer. "I understand . . . not."

"Was he—was he terribly disappointed?"

"Definitely!" The word seemed to slip out before Una had time to guard it.

Simona fell silent. She had pushed enough. The one emphatic word had said a lot. Enos would not only be disappointed. He would be angry. He felt strongly that the man from the Galilee had to be stopped. Though Simona did not share his opinion, she could understand his disappointment, his hurt—perhaps his shame. He would feel rejected. No wonder he held himself apart.

Her thoughts turned to her own feelings. She, too, had failed Enos. She had lost his child. Was it carelessness on her part? Was it something she had unknowingly done? Or something she had neglected to do? She had hurt her husband deeply at a time when he was already struggling. No wonder he did not wish to see her.

"I think I should go back to bed now," she said to Una.

And the woman was instantly on her feet. "Have we tired you?" she asked, anxiously.

"No. No. It's just that I think I could use a little nap. I am fine."

Una escorted her back to her room and tucked her into her bed. "Would you like the shades drawn, Lady Simona?"

"That would be good. Please."

The chambermaid fussed with the draperies to be sure that no stray rays of sunlight dared to enter the room. She was silently exiting when Simona stopped her.

"Did you hear who—who replaced Enos—with the Pharisees who went . . . ?"

Una stopped and thought, rubbing her hands together as though thinking through what she would say. Then she nodded slightly. "I understand it was someone by the name of—Judah, I think—from Antioch."

Simona was surprised when Enos suddenly appeared in her room. Neither spoke as a few seconds ticked by. Simona had no idea what to say and Enos appeared to be equally struggling.

It was Simona who found her voice first. "How are you?"

"How am I? It is you who has been ailing."

She nodded. What could she say? She switched her gaze to the toes of her sandals.

He decided to speak. "You heard they took me off the team to hunt the pretend Messiah?"

So that was what they were calling him now. She nodded. She could not say she was sorry. She was not. As far as she was concerned no one should be hunting the man down like he was a common criminal. She knew of nothing yet that he had done wrong. In fact, he had healed a number of people—free of charge. That did not sound like a man intent on crime.

She roused enough to ask, "What will you do now? Can you go back to your classes?"

"I am back in class. They could hardly take that privilege from me. Since they did not have a crime of which to accuse me, they could not come up with some other trumped-up scheme." He sounded very bitter.

Simona was having a hard time thinking of something to say. She did not wish to speak of their lost child unless her husband decided to broach the subject. She was afraid that her fragile emotions would still bring tears. She wished he would just leave. He didn't.

"What is the news—from your . . ." What should she call them? "The ones still following—tailing—the rabbi?" Immediately she knew that it was not the right question to ask.

"Stupidity! They just talk. They never act. Have you heard about his latest spectacle? They claim he has given sight to a man who was born blind. Had never been able to see anything from birth—eyes didn't even open up—yet they all get together and make up their stories about this incredible miracle. Even his parents got bribed to take part in it. Foolishness, utter foolishness. And all they do is to put the family out of the synagogue! They did nothing to the fake rabbi. He keeps on with his deceit. They are just going to sit around and let this—this deceiver convince the masses that he is some kind of demigod. I cannot believe how stupid some people can be that—"

Pounding on the outside door stopped his flow of angry words.

Simona wondered what was happening now. Maybe it was some more news about the Prophet. Hugo would be taking care of the door.

But in case Enos would be called away again, she felt compelled to say something while there was still time. "I am—I'm sorry about the baby," she said quickly. "I wish . . ."

He gave her a blank look as though he did not even know what she was talking about. Then he shrugged his shoulders. "We can have another one if we decide we want one." Then he turned to leave. "I'd better go see what the noise is all about."

He walked away. The noise at the door was a courier sent from Simona's family. Her father was very ill. Could she come?

The sudden news made Simona feel weak. She should be there. She should be there to help with her father. To comfort her mother. Dared she request to go?

Then Enos spoke. "Go if you like. You are really not needed here for anything."

"How could I go? It is a long way . . . And I've been . . ."

"There must be someone traveling back and forth. I will send Ira out to see what he can find out."

Ira did find someone. A caravan, Simona was told. Slow-moving camels. Plodding along, one behind the other. Simona feared she would never make it home to see her father one last time. At least she might be there to comfort her mother.

As Una helped with packing what would be needed for the journey, Simona realized that none of her present clothes were really suited for traveling on a camel. There was nothing to do but to pick the least fancy garments and some solid veils to keep out the wind and dust.

In just two days' time, Hugo delivered her to the market square where the caravan was preparing for the journey. It did not look like a comfortable way to travel—nor a fast way.

Enos had left his regrets that he could not be there to bid her farewell as there was an important meeting he must attend. It had been Hiram who had handed her a small bundle of dried fruits and some cheeses gathered from the kitchen. Ira was the one who slipped a few of his hoarded coins into Simona's hand so she might purchase whatever she needed on the trail. And it was Una who told Simona that she would be praying for a safe trip. Then Simona was aided to the small saddle on the back of a complaining camel, clutching it desperately as it teetered to its feet. Una stood and watched until the small caravan left the enclosure.

Enos returned to a silent house. There was no need now for Una to stay. Enos dismissed her without ceremony. The man from the kitchen and his young helper had already returned to their homes at day's end. Hugo and Ira remained, ready to serve as Enos ordered. But he did not require their help and did not desire their company. He greeted them gruffly and passed on by.

Why, he asked himself, did the house seem empty? It wasn't like he and his wife had common interests—or even conversations. The entire marriage had turned out to be a failure. He had wanted a beautiful woman, and he had been more than pleased with her appearance. But with everything that was going on with this false prophet Jesus, all attention had been focused on how to get rid of him without getting the Roman army stirred up.

There had not been any gala events where he could display Simona's beauty. And then this unexpected pregnancy occurred. He was not sorry that he had dealt with the untimely child, but he had come unexpectedly near to losing his wife as well. And, he reasoned, he may as well have lost her. She still had not fully recovered. She was much better, but he wondered if she would ever have her first glow—the flash of light in her dark eyes, the look of vigor and excitement with life that she had once had. The special, mysterious something that set her apart from other women seemed to be gone. It was what had caught the envious eyes of other men.

The whole thing had seemed to turn on him. She had been too young, he decided. Too young to understand what it meant to be a woman of charm and charisma. She had never responded to him in the way he had hoped and dreamed. He had wanted her to realize how privileged she was to be married to a Pharisee. Her deep devotion to him would have impressed those around him. That had never happened. She was submissive and agreeable, but he had to admit that, though he may have purchased her body, he had never won her heart. He should not have been in such a hurry just because she was beautiful. And to think of the price he had paid for her!

CHAPTER TWENTY-ONE

The Reunion

SIMONA FELT THAT THE JOURNEY to her former home would never end. The rocking gait of the camel she rode made her ache all over. There was constant noise and dust and cries from the drivers. It made her realize that the small cart that had taken her from her home to Jerusalem had been pleasant by comparison.

All along their journey they stopped at small towns to make deliveries or pick up goods from the markets. Sometimes the bargaining seemed to take an excessively long time before an agreement was made and they would be able to take to the trail again.

As they traveled, Simona found herself whispering short prayers. "Please God, may my father still be living."

At last her own village appeared. She wished to climb down from the camel and run toward her house. What if she missed seeing her father again by just days, or hours, or even minutes? She had no idea of the seriousness of his illness, but she was certain that she wouldn't have been called home had his condition not been considered dire.

The little caravan pulled into the local market and Simona nudged her camel to kneel. By now, she and the camel she rode seemed to be able to understand one another. With a groan of complaint, the camel complied and Simona was able to free herself from the seat that she had occupied for much too long.

She wondered if her legs would still work as she reached a sandaled foot toward the dusty ground. Her eagerness made her impatient. She knew the way home from here. She wanted to just lift her cumbersome skirt and run the short distance.

She did not do so. The caravan master was immediately at her side. His orders, upon accepting her as a passenger, were to have Simona delivered to her home in safety. He would do that—but first he had other things that he needed to care for. She must wait.

She was directed to a rather shabby tent, which she was to occupy until he was free to accompany her. Simona wanted to weep. She had waited so long. She wished to go to her father *now*.

She lifted the piece of worn curtain that formed the door of the small shelter, protecting her from the afternoon sun, and stepped into a stuffy and unpleasant-smelling interior. She almost backed out again but forced herself to continue instead. She had not been there long when she realized that the odor was quite familiar. She had just forgotten the smells of sheepskin and healing oils. She would need to get used to them again. It was a part of her village.

There was one small cross-legged stool in the tent and Simona settled on it. At least she was no longer rocking with every step of the camel. It felt strange to be still.

Finally the caravan master stuck his head in the opening and waved with his hand that he was ready to go. She was quickly on her feet. From somewhere he had obtained a conveyance of a kind—a two-wheeled cart, pulled by a wizened old donkey.

Simona would have preferred to walk but the man insisted on helping her up onto the seat. The donkey's steps were slow and measured, one weary foot being placed in front of the other.

And then they rounded the corner and Simona saw her familiar street. Had she been on her own she could have used a shortcut that would have taken half the time. There was her house. She was almost home.

The man motioned for her to stay seated until he went to the door and announced her safe arrival. He wanted no opportunity for anyone to say he had not properly completed his task.

Simona could hardly sit.

But it was not her mother who opened the door. Nor was it anyone she knew. There was a long exchange of questions and explanations. Simona was feeling frantic and wished to jump down from the cart and find out what was happening. Just as she could stand it no longer the man turned and came back.

"They have moved," he explained, agitation strengthening his words.

"Moved? Where?"

"The woman said that when their daughter married they had no need to stay in such a humble home. They moved!"

"Moved, where?"

"To the other side of town. The better homes look out toward the water."

Simona could not hold back the tears. She should have known. Her mother had always looked with envy at those residences. But how would they find her parents? She had no idea which home may have been available.

"She said it is next to an olive grove," the man went on.

The olive grove? Yes, Simona knew where the olive grove was. "I will direct you," she informed the man, and they set out again, with Simona telling him which streets to take and where to turn.

When they finally arrived, the man again bid Simona to stay on the seat, but she could no longer stand the tension. She hopped down and led the way to the courtyard gate. The man tagged along behind her, determined to be present should there be any extra remuneration for safely delivering their daughter.

It was all Simona could do to await the answer to her rap on the gate. When it opened, it was her mother who appeared. Simona threw herself into the welcoming arms and wept. Her mother wept along with her, exclaiming over and over, "You are here. You're home. Thank our God you have come."

The caravan driver finally turned away, returning to his donkey and cart. It had been a long enough day for all.

When Simona pulled back, she tried to ask the question that was burning in her soul, but the words would not come.

Her mother answered the pleading in her eyes. "He will be so glad you have come."

Simona began to cry again. She had made it in time.

Mother turned, drawing Simona with her, and reached out to close the courtyard gate. With a bit of a nod toward a window in the house, she indicated to Simona where she would be able to find her father.

Simona laid aside the small bundle she was still carrying and moved quickly into the dimly lit house. Her father was sleeping, drawing small breaths that lifted his chest in rasping intakes of air. He looked small in his bed, not the large man Simona remembered from her childhood. Had it really been that long since she had seen him?

No, not long at all. In fact, it was not yet a full year since she had left home. Yet so much had changed.

She slipped over beside his bed and knelt on the floor. For a few minutes she just watched him as he lay there. His face had grown gaunt. His once strong hands lay limp on the coverlet. His beard was peppered with grey. This was not the man she remembered. Yet it was!

She reached out and took one of the flaccid hands in both of hers. He stirred, then his eyes opened slowly. He stared as though dreaming and then the hand she held tightened firmly and the hint of a smile warmed his face.

"My daughter," he managed through dried lips, "Mary—the nourisher of my heart."

Mary! She was Mary again. She lowered her head to rest upon the once familiar hand she held, and let all of her pent-up tears of pain and fear pour out of her troubled soul.

Later as Mary and her mother sat in the shade of the large olive tree in their backyard while her father rested from the excitement of the day, Mary asked some difficult questions.

How long had her father been ill? What did the herbalist say about his condition? Had there been any word from Benjamin? Did he know about their father? Might it still be possible to find Jesus of Nazareth for healing?

Her mother sighed. "I have no answers anymore. None. I have come to the end of myself. I have made many wrong choices, but I do not know how they can be corrected. Each time I look at my . . . my home that feels empty, and meaningless, I am reminded that I—I sold my daughter so that I might . . . have this. I lost Benjamin because I was not wise enough to treasure him. And now I am losing your father. I wish I could go back and start over. But I cannot. I am lost, Mary. Totally lost."

Mary reached for her mother's trembling hand and pressed it to her lips. It was hard to see her mother in such deep distress, but she had no words, no answers. Anything she could say about her own difficulties would only add to her mother's pain.

If only we had found him, her heart cried. *I am sure that Jesus could have been the answer to our sorrows.*

Her father seemed even weaker when Mary slipped into his room early the next morning. It was not fully light, but she could not sleep. Her mind was full of questions that seemed to have no answers. If her father left them what would her mother do? Could she really manage as a widow—all alone? How would they ever be able to find Benjamin to inform him of the great changes? If they did find him, would he care? He had been a faithful son and a dedicated brother—what would he be now? Was he still alive somewhere? What would happen when she had to return to Enos? By law, she must. Yet when she thought of Enos, she felt only emptiness. If only . . . If only things could have been different.

Mary struggled. There was so much pain in her world. Deep, deep down within her, she had an unquenched thirst for answers. For truth. And she kept thinking, feeling, that somehow the unknown Jesus held the answers.

And yet this Prophet was being hunted down as though he were a madman—or a criminal. Surely all the reports of his healing and teaching could not be false. Yet Enos and his fellow Pharisees saw and heard only evil. Why? She did not understand.

If only . . . If only she—they—her family, could find him—before it was too late.

CHAPTER TWENTY-TWO

The Surprise

MARY WAS LIFTING the day's bread from the outdoor oven when she felt a tap on her shoulder. It startled her and she swung around. A grinning Benjamin stood next to her. With a glad cry she lifted an arm to embrace him. Only the quickness of his hand saved the hot loaves from landing in the dust at their feet.

"Benjamin," she cried. "Where did you come from?"

As always, he could not resist teasing. "I came from where I was. And now that I am here, I am not there anymore."

She gave him a playful poke.

He embraced her in a big brotherly hug, then stepped back and studied her. "But look at you! You are all grown up."

Oh, thought Mary, *you have no idea.*

But that could wait. "Mother and I were about to enjoy our meal. She will be so surprised. We have been frantically looking—well, we have not really been *looking* looking, because we had no idea where to look, but—"

He cut in with a smile, "You sound just as foolish as I."

She nodded. "Come in the house. We have so much catching-up to do."

He looked around. "You certainly do. How did you ever get over here? I had a terrible time finding you."

She took his arm. He was still steadying the tray with the loaves.

"It's a long story."

Hulda was just as surprised to see her son as Mary had been. But she was even more emotional.

"Benjamin—my son! My son," she wept. "I feared I might never see you again."

She held him so tightly and so long as she wept that Benjamin began to show concern. *What happened to Mother?* his eyes asked Mary. Mary just shook her head. She had no answers.

When Hulda was able to wipe away her tears, Benjamin had opportunity to ask about his father. When he heard the news, he went immediately to the room where the sick man lay. Mary, who had followed, heard a sharp intake of breath. She was uncertain whether it was her father or Benjamin who was caught by surprise.

Her father managed a few husky words as he reached for the hand of his son. "My boy. My son—now we are all together. What a blessing!"

Benjamin pulled a stool up to the bed and leaned over his father. "I am home, Father. Home to stay. I should not have left. But I have some good news. Some great news."

"More good news?" queried the father. "You being here is the best news that could come. You and Mary—both—home again. I have been blessed." Then he went on. "But I am sure the journey has been long and difficult. You must be hungry and tired. I smell freshly baked loaves. You must eat before we talk. I can wait."

With one more clasp of the hand Benjamin left with a promise. "I will be right back. I am not leaving again."

His father smiled.

The three sat down at the small table to partake of a light meal. Questions and answers flew back and forth. The first ones raised by Mary's brother were concerning his father.

What had happened to his father? How long ago had he had his accident? What was the latest illness that had put him in bed? Had they tried a doctor?

Then came Benjamin's unexpected regret. "If only I had been home, I could have taken him to Jesus."

Mary's eyes widened. Jesus? Did he know where to find him? Did he know there were people who opposed him?

Yes, he knew. Benjamin claimed that he prayed daily for the Lord's protection.

He prayed? For the Prophet Jesus? What did he mean, *the Lord*?

An easy smile accompanied his response. "The promised Messiah. The long-awaited One."

Was he sure? Mary's eyes swept toward her mother. How would she react?

Benjamin was entirely sure! Mother's wide eyes were glistening with unshed tears. She seemed pleased to contemplate her son's words.

On and on they talked and Benjamin shared the story of when he had met the man Jesus. "I had heard of him," he began, "and it all sounded like stories. Stories made-up by someone who wanted to impress his listeners. But I got more and more curious when daily I was meeting people who had more stories to tell. So I decided that I wanted to see for myself. I found a group of people who were heading out to find him. Thousands of them. A great crowd. They seemed to know where they were going, so I just followed along."

Mary and Hulda hung on every word breathlessly.

"When we got there, it was just an open area, on the side of a mountain. He sat on a flat rock and taught us all day long. We spread out on the grass. He had these friends with him. The man sitting beside me said that there were twelve of them. Special disciples. Or sometimes called apostles—chosen ones. He told us all about God, whom he called his *Father*, and how he had been sent to bring freedom from sin to people. The death penalty for man's sin could be eliminated if they believed in him. Believed that he was really who he claimed to be. The Messiah. The One sent from God."

Mary shifted in her chair uneasily. These words seemed impossible to comprehend. She dropped her eyes to the table as she imagined what Enos would say if he were here.

Benjamin was not finished. "He did miracles, too. Healed people, right there before our eyes. There was a father who brought a young son who had a demon. The Christ drove out the demon and the son was healed. The man wept like a child when he saw his son made whole again. He wept for joy."

Mary felt her own eyes fill with fearful tears. She turned to her brother. "Did you know that the Pharisees are determined to kill him?"

He looked startled. "You are sure of this?"

She nodded and swallowed hard.

"I know there are rumors. He is aware of it too. That is why he keeps changing locations. But how do you know?"

Her answer seemed impossible to utter. "Because—because I am married to a Pharisee. Because he talks of nothing else."

"You?"

She nodded, shaking loose the tears from her eyes, releasing them to slide down her cheeks. She lifted a hand to wipe them away.

Benjamin looked from one face to the other. "When? How did this happen?"

Mary and her mother shared the telling of the story of how Mary had ended up in the home of a Pharisee.

"If I had been here that need not have happened," Benjamin grieved.

"No. No, that is not right. You could not have stopped it."

"Well, I may have been able to keep Father from his accident had I stayed to help him. Then there would have been no need."

Mary leaned closer and shook her head emphatically. "Don't blame yourself. So many things happened that none of us could control. It is what it is. Now we just need to try to make good come from all the bad."

"Good? How can one make good come from—?"

Mary laid a hand on his to stop his flow of words. "You found Jesus! We were looking for Jesus, for Father's sake, but we never found him. But now—through you—we will all be able to find him. Don't you see? Prayers have been answered. Prayers we were not wise enough to pray. I believe you. I believe he is the Messiah, the One sent from God to redeem his people. It must be so!"

Mary felt a tug on her arm. It was her mother's grasp that drew her attention. "That is what I need. That is *who* I need. Forgiveness from the only One who is able to forgive sins. I was lost! I had no answers. If I had let your father go on to Jerusalem we might have found the Lord earlier. Your father might have been healed. I was selfish and—"

"Mother, please stop," said Mary gently, reaching for her mother's hand. "We all make mistakes. We all need forgiveness. But now we know where to find it. We need to share this with Father."

Mary reached her other hand to catch her brother's. "I am so glad you came home—in time."

They gathered around the bed of the ill man. Benjamin was the first to speak. "Father, I am so sorry that I was not here when you needed me. But I am here now. And I will stay. I hear you started for Jerusalem in search of Jesus from Nazareth. I am sorry you didn't find him. I found him—but not in Jerusalem. On a hillside by the Sea of Galilee. He is who he claims to be, the long-awaited Messiah of our people. The Promised One. And he does heal. I have seen it happen. Perhaps there is still time to get you to him."

Amos was shaking his head. "No, no, there isn't time. It is too late. I could no longer stand a journey."

"Then perhaps I need to go and find him—to present our request. I have heard of healings where he was not even with the afflicted. He spoke and they were healed."

Amos continued to shake his head.

Mary spoke up. "The great news, Father, is that he is not only the Healer, but the Savior we have long awaited. Our Redeemer. The Messiah."

Her father's face showed surprise. Then again he shook his head. "That could not be," he said slowly. "If the Messiah had come, the Temple priests would have known and they would have shared it with the people."

It was a logical response. The Temple priests, the biblical scholars, should surely be the very ones to first recognize the Messiah when he made his appearance.

"But they have missed it, Father. For some reason, their eyes are blinded to the truth."

"You confuse me," went on Amos. "Why would the people I have trusted since I was a boy not be right about something so important? They have the Scriptures and study them carefully."

"If you could see him, if you could hear him speak, I am sure you would be persuaded," said Benjamin.

Amos shook his head, very slowly. "I need to think about this," he said. "But I am tired. Now I need to rest. We will talk again in the morning."

Reluctantly, the family bid him good night and filed from the room, each one determined to pray. Each one trying to think of a way to present the truth so that it would be understood and embraced.

Mary was the last to leave. "I love you so much, Father. I believe—I believe with my whole heart that Jesus is the long-awaited One. The One we all need for the forgiveness of our sin. The One sent to be our Messiah."

He patted her hand. "Mary, my little faithful one. I have missed you so. I am so glad you have come home."

"So am I, Father. I love you so much."

She leaned over and kissed the familiar brow.

"Good night, my restorer of joy," he whispered.

"Have a good sleep, Father. I will see you in the morning and we will talk again."

But they did not speak again in the morning.

Benjamin was the first to rise. He filled a cup with a refreshing drink and carried it to his father. He realized immediately that it was too late to speak again. The man they all loved had already left them.

The next days all seemed to blur together. They were days of planning, days of doing, days of mourning and burial. Painful days. Days when Mary dreaded waking up in the morning, that haunted her sleep when she went to bed at night. She would never see her father again. She could not bear the thought. He was a good man. A good father. He followed carefully all the laws and regulations of the way he had been taught. But he had rejected the Savior, who had come to bring forgiveness. There was no way to describe her grief, no way to bring comfort to her heart. She felt like a child again—lost and alone, and weeping for her father.

CHAPTER TWENTY-THREE

The Talk

"I DON'T KNOW WHAT TO DO. I can't leave Mother here all alone. Yet I do need to go back to—to my home. It is almost time for the Passover. I was told that I must be home in time for proper remembrance."

"You must be anxious. Your husband must be a patient man to allow you to be gone for so long."

Mary sighed but made no reply.

Mary and Benjamin were sitting in the shade of the olive tree. The late afternoon was still hot, but without the direct sun overhead, it was gradually cooling.

"You must really miss—"

"I miss Una," Mary broke in.

He leaned forward. "Who is Una?"

Mary stirred on her wooden stool. She had not meant to voice her thoughts. She turned toward her brother. "My—my maid."

He smiled in a teasing way. "I had forgotten that my sister is a lady of leisure—and has a maid now."

But Mary did not return the smile.

Benjamin studied her for a moment. "Am I missing something?" he asked softly. "I have noticed a deep sadness in your eyes, even before we lost Father. Is something wrong?"

Mary did not speak because the proper words would not come. Slowly a trickle of a teardrop slipped from beneath her lashes and dampened her cheek. He reached a hand toward her and she responded by placing her trembling hand in his. But she still did not speak.

"What is it? You know you can talk to me. We have never kept secrets. Remember?"

"My home—with servants—it is . . . it is not like you think. Not what another might envy. My marriage is filled with sorrow. My husband . . . I do not think he is at all happy with me. I don't think he is happy with himself. With life. He is—is restless and angry. And most angry with Jesus. He sees him as an imposter. A fraud."

"Then he has never seen him. Heard him speak. Seen his miracles."

"But he has. Enos was one of the Pharisees sent to follow him, to challenge him, to expose him. Enos saw—and he heard—but it just made him more angry. I think he . . . he fears this man. Sees Jesus taking away his own position of authority and honor. Enos gets so angry just thinking about Jesus that he—he utterly trembles with rage."

"Is he—is he ever—abusive to you?"

Mary turned slightly in her chair so they could speak face to face. "No, not really. But I hardly ever see him. He is gone—away—to his classes or—or—I don't know where. But he is seldom home."

"Maybe that's good."

"No—no, it is not good," she was quick to respond. "We have been husband and wife for almost a year and I do not even know him. When he does come home, he just orders me to—whatever he wishes. We don't talk about things. Life."

There was silence as Benjamin pondered the words his sister had just spoken. "I would call that abuse," he stated. "Is that what it feels like?"

She sighed deeply. "I don't know. I am so confused. I no longer have any idea what a—a normal marriage should be. I used to feel hurt when Mother nattered at Father. I didn't think it was fair, but now—now I think that silence may be even worse. Harder to live with." She stopped to wipe her eyes on her sleeve. "I thought the baby would change . . ."

"Baby? What baby? You have a baby?"

It was too late to take back the words. Mary had told herself that the baby she had lost would remain her secret. She still felt guilty whenever she thought of the infant that she could not save.

"No. No, I do not have the baby. I wasn't able to carry the child. I lost him. I—"

"What did he do?"

"No, he didn't do anything to the baby. He wasn't even there—when I lost him. He did not—he was not happy. I don't think he was prepared to—to be a father."

"Why do you think that?"

"He seemed angry—he left . . ." She hesitated and then went on. "I got very sick—and I . . ."

Benjamin left his chair and put his arms around his sister, holding her as she wept. "It's okay," he tried to comfort her. "It wasn't your fault. Sometimes—sometimes things just go wrong."

"Please," she begged him. "Don't tell Mother. She has enough grief to bear. I didn't mean to tell you—it just . . ."

"I'm glad you did."

Mary pushed herself away. "I do need to get back to him. He's still my husband. It is still my home."

"I understand. I'll go to the market in the morning and see if any caravans are going that way. It seems they leave every few days."

"I don't like to leave Mother."

"I'll be with her. I am staying now. See if I can get Father's shop producing again. I think it has been missed in the village."

"You'll be okay? Living back here again? Just you and Mother?"

"You are worrying about me now?" He smiled.

"Maybe it's just a bad habit," she teased. Then she turned serious. "When you went away, all three of us worried. Mother often made remarks. And even though Father didn't say so, I could read the worry in his eyes. For the first several days I would catch him looking down the road—watching for you. And then he had that terrible accident . . . We all hoped that you'd come home—we knew you would if you heard—but we had no idea where you were."

Benjamin remained silent. Deep in thought.

She turned to look at him. "Where were you? What did you do?"

He stirred and smiled his teasing smile. "I learned a lot."

"Like?"

"Grass doesn't really taste good. It takes a lot of wheat kernels to fill your stomach. Dogs do not like to share their food."

"You're teasing, I hope."

"Yes, I am teasing. I got a job—as a shepherd."

"You don't like sheep!"

"I do now. I got to understand them. Actually, they make very good friends."

Mary leaned back in her chair and took a deep breath. The evening air was pleasant, almost cool.

"We've changed, have we not?" she mused.

"They say that is what life does to one. Changes. Grows. Teaches. I was rather slow in learning, I fear."

"Maybe we all are, looking back," she agreed.

"I wish I had come home sooner. That's my one regret."

"I wish you would have, too. I missed you. Every day."

"I missed you, too, little Mary."

"I'd forgotten that was what you used to call me. Little Mary. Sometimes it made me upset. I didn't want to be little anymore."

"I know. And I did not want you to grow up too fast. I *liked* you little."

"I have a new name now. Did you know that?"

"A new name? Why?"

"I'm told that Enos thought Mary too common."

"So, who are you now?"

"Simona."

"Simona?"

She nodded.

He repeated the new name a few times. She could see his lips moving as though he were tasting it. "Actually, I rather like it. I think it suits you. Simona! He chose well."

"I became comfortable with it." She shrugged. "He certainly could have done worse."

They both chuckled. Then sobered. It had been so good to just sit and chat.

"I suppose we should get some sleep. If you find a caravan leaving soon, I'll need to be ready."

But neither of them stirred. The time had become too short. Too precious.

"And you'll stay with Mother?"

"Strange, is it not? I left home because of Mother. I thought I was too big, too old, too wise to listen to her constant—what did you say, *nattering*? That describes it well. Yet, here I am, actually volunteering to be the only one left in the home with her. And I'm neither dreading nor fearing it. I would say God is a God of miracles!"

Mary turned to her brother. "She has really changed, hasn't she? I've found myself thinking how much I would just love to bundle her up and take her back with me. Having her with me would make my life so . . . so different."

"Oh, no—you can't have her. I need her here. I'm counting on her to get my meals and wash my—"

"Oh, stop it!" But Mary laughed. It was the first time she remembered laughing for a very long time. It made her feel like weeping. "I know she's going to be very lonely without Father. I—I hear her weeping—at night—when the house is quiet."

"She'll miss him. And perhaps she has regrets."

"Regrets? I guess we all have regrets."

"You, too?" he asked. "I keep asking myself over and over if—if I should have insisted that—that I should not have walked out of Father's room until he listened to—to truth. Until he understood the importance of—of putting his faith in Jesus—as the Messiah, the Promised One. The Savior." By the time he finished voicing his regrets, tears were freely running down his cheeks.

Mary cried with him. They sat in silence.

At last Benjamin spoke. "Have you ever wondered if perhaps . . . perhaps he woke up and thought about it in the night, and decided that—that Jesus—is—is who he claims to be? What if he was given another chance?"

"You've wondered about that, too?"

"Over and over. And then I ask myself, did I say enough? Did I make it plain—clear—that our Faith of old was just to sustain us, to prepare us for when he came? It is no longer enough, since the Christ has revealed himself. We either accept him, or we reject him. We cannot be undecided. There is not a third option. No middle of the road."

"It's frightening—and beautiful—to think we're living at the very time he is here. So many have waited for so long. Have hoped and dreamed and prayed—and here we are, at the very time he fulfilled the Promise. And yet, I feel . . . feel sad that I haven't yet seen him," Mary said. "Just like Father, I had hoped to—to see a miracle, to be healed, in whatever way the healing is needed."

"I understand. I don't think one can totally understand it until you see him. Hear him. Sense his power. Taste of the loaves, if you will. I don't know how anyone could be with him and not find Truth. It's like a . . . a heart magnet, drawing you to him. You know . . . you know he is just who he claims to be. The Promised One."

"Oh, I wish Father had been with you."

"So do I. I feel so blessed to have been one of those who sat and listened to his words. So many . . . so many have. But so many still have not. Like Father—and you."

"Perhaps there is still time—for me."

"I pray that will be so. Jesus will soon be traveling to Jerusalem again. For the Passover. Maybe you'll be able—"

She shook her head. "Enos does not think it proper for the wife of a Pharisee to be seen out in the streets."

It was another reminder that Mary—Simona—would soon be back in her own home once more.

CHAPTER TWENTY-FOUR

The Return

Benjamin found a caravan. It would be leaving for Jerusalem in three days. Hulda instantly began fretting when she heard the news. It was too hot to be traveling. Mary was too fragile to be riding a camel all the way to the ancient city. Who knew what kind of men would be in charge? What if there was a robbery? How would they know when and if she arrived safely?

On and on she went with one reason to worry after another. Mary hoped she would soon run out of bad possibilities. At the same time, Mary understood it was just a mother's love that was causing the anxiety.

It was nice to feel loved.

Enos felt adrift. Disconnected. But from what? He wasn't sure. It felt like his whole life had been derailed. He didn't know where he fit—or even where he wished to fit. He'd been cut off from the little group who were monitoring the Nazarene. And that meant he was also cut off from the remuneration that had been a part of it. He missed the funds. They had been more than reasonable. However, he was permitted to return to gathering the Temple fees, which were taken to the priests for counting and recording each day. But the few coins pilfered, in no way compensated for the loss of the traveling money he previously earned.

His friend—or foe—Judah from Antioch was not there to help him with the daily collection process, and the new coworker was uninteresting and small of stature. He was sure the man was also dull of thinking. Enos didn't even bother trying to start a conversation. And if the new man did, Enos was quick to cut him off.

One thing did concern him. The young man, Seth, seemed to have hawk eyes. Enos felt the sharp gaze studying his every move. He didn't care much for Seth. But he seemed to be the only option. Not many of the young scholars were interested in spending time in the hectic outer courtyard and the rule was they must always work in pairs.

Enos knew he had to be careful. With Seth watching, it was not as easy to separate the larger coins when collecting from the frenzied merchants and adding the proceeds into the money bags that were provided. It cut into the daily take that Enos had come to depend upon.

Seth was also uneasy whenever Enos exerted particular pressure on a vendor, whereas it was the part of the experience that Enos enjoyed most—the challenge to raise the fees as high as possible for these Gentiles.

And Simona was still away. He had no idea why she needed so much time just to bury her father. He shouldn't have let her go. It wasn't that he was used to her companionship or conversation—but it did feel strange to come home to a house with only two elderly servants on hand.

He grumbled under his breath. The whole bride thing had turned him sour. He was not sure what he had expected, but the need to keep watch on the false Messiah had ruined a lot of things. It seemed that all of the pleasures of life had been stolen from him. No banquets. No celebrations. No acknowledgments in the streets. Even the Temple did not seem to have the appeal it once had. He did hope that the upcoming Passover would bring more life back to the city. At least the visiting *commoners* who crowded the city over the Passover season could be counted on to view the Pharisees with admiration and a bit of envy. That had been missing for far too long.

But the Passover was close at hand. It would be the first Passover at which Enos would be able to present Simona as his wife. She may have lost some of her glow since the loss of the baby, but she was still a beautiful woman. In fact, he felt that she had matured in an agreeable manner once she'd begun to gain her health again. She was more woman now than girl. He was sure that there would be many envious glances. The thought pleased him. He must see that she had a new and luxurious robe for the occasion.

That thought reminded him that his funds were low. But, with the Passover crowd soon pushing its way into the city, the busy Temple court was sure to produce additional fees so that collections would be sure to increase. He could likewise grow bolder in what he extracted for his own use.

When Simona had left, he'd given her strict orders that she was to be home in time for the Passover week. That was fast approaching. Surely, she wouldn't dare to ignore his stipulations when she left to see her father. There had been no word from her since the caravan master had reported that he'd delivered Simona safely to her destination.

Life could get so complicated! It was not easy being a Pharisee who was determined to reach the top rung of the leadership ladder. The more he struggled to get noticed, the more he seemed to be ignored. And Simona had not served to speed his advancement as he'd hoped she would.

The long trip back to Jerusalem by caravan was even more challenging than the trip away had been. All the roads were crowded with pilgrims heading toward Jerusalem for the Passover event. Simona had never seen such throngs since her younger years and had forgotten what it was like to fall in step with them. Once her father had been so seriously afflicted by his accident, the family had not attended the feast.

And the previous year the event had just been completed before her marriage was arranged. Now she understood why Enos had said that he wanted the city cleared of all the "riffraff" before he presented her as his bride.

The riffraff? Was that how the Pharisees saw the faithful pilgrims who made the long, arduous journey to the sacred city to pay their Temple dues and add generous contributions to the Temple treasury? It didn't seem right to judge them so harshly.

As she neared the city and the crowd swelled in both number and noise, she felt the press of bodies was about to suffocate her. The dust from the camels and donkeys, and the many pairs of weary feet, seemed to hang in the air, stifling her breathing. She would be so relieved to get home. Back to the familiar. Back to Una and her generous care. She could not wait for a bath that would be both refreshing and relaxing.

She would even be pleased to see Enos again. Her hope—her prayer—was that they would find some way to build a home of love and unity, like her father and mother had given her.

Certainly, her mother had been a constant complainer over the years. But her father had always responded with love, keeping the home a place of reasonable harmony. Simona still grieved that her parents had never been able to build together on the peace and joy that her mother had found in her new faith. Her father had deserved to share life with a woman who offered love in place of discontent. If only . . .

The last leg of the journey, through the gates onto the narrow city streets, was even noisier and more chaotic than it had been earlier. Simona had never seen such crowds. She could not imagine what the days ahead would hold once the festivities had actually begun.

She did hope Una would have plenty of warm water for a thorough washing away of road dust and sweat.

There was no one to meet Simona when she finally arrived. She spent the last of the funds that Benjamin had given her to find a man with a donkey to take her to her home. She let herself in and looked about for Hugo, who under normal conditions never left his post.

It was Ira whom she first encountered. He looked surprised to see her and bowed low to show his respect—and to seek her forgiveness for not being on duty.

He looked shamefaced, and since she knew a servant was never allowed an excuse for being negligent, even if the reason were a valid one, she was quick to speak. "I do apologize that I had no way to let you know when I would be arriving. Would you please let Una know that I'm home?"

Ira looked even more distraught. "I'm sorry, Lady Simona. Una is not here."

"When will she be back?"

Ira fairly squirmed. "Una was dismissed as soon as you left, my lady. I'm sorry that I do not know the arrangements for what is to be done upon your return."

Simona tried to process the words. "Of course," she replied. "There was no need for my chambermaid while I was away. Thank you, Ira."

"May I be of assistance to you, my lady?"

For a moment Simona frowned. What help to her could Ira possibly be? Then she smiled. "Would you place my belongings in my room, please? And let Hiram know that I would like a light refreshment. Then I believe I will retire. It has been a long and arduous journey."

She expected a bow and a curt "Yes, Lady Simona," but there was only silence and a strange look on the face of the servant.

"Is something . . . amiss?"

Ira was wringing his hands, betraying the level of his distress. "It is just that—there have been many changes, my lady, since you were last with us. I am afraid that Hiram is no longer in the kitchen."

Simona frowned. "Then, just tell whoever *is* in the kitchen that I would like a bowl of broth and some bread, please."

"Yes, Lady Simona."

He picked up her cases and headed to her bed chamber. Simona followed. After depositing the items in her room, he stepped back and apologized with a bow. "I am sorry that there is no one to help with your bath and preparations for retiring."

"That is fine. I am used to caring for myself."

He bowed himself out and Simona turned with a tired sigh to unpack and put away her own belongings.

It wasn't long until there was a knock on the door. Without even turning to the door, Simona called out permission for entry. When she lifted her head, it was Ira who was placing a small tray on her table.

"Are you in the kitchen as well?" she quizzed.

He bowed in reply.

"Are you alone? The only staff left?"

Another silent bow.

"Ira, what has happened?"

"The master has decided that it is not necessary to have staff for an empty house since he is rarely home."

"So now that I am back will the other servants resume their jobs again?"

Ira hesitated. "I do not know, Lady Simona. Hiram has returned home to the Galilee. He said he didn't care much for the noisy city anyway. He took the boy Edim, who is his nephew, with him. I don't know about Una. We did not discuss such things, my lady."

"I see."

He looked embarrassed. And frightened. At last, he dared to speak unprompted. "You realize, Lady Simona, that it is improper for me to be in my lady's chamber. I must never return again. So . . . so you and the master will need to work out the arrangements for your future care." He nodded toward the tray he had delivered.

Simona put her hands to her face in embarrassment. "I am so sorry. I've just come from my home, where we all live and share together. I will not—not endanger you by asking you for any more favors. Is it—can I—go to the kitchen, myself?"

"It is your home, my lady."

"Yes, but—but it does not feel like my home."

He gave a small jerk of a nod. He understood.

"Thank you, Ira." She motioned toward the door. "You are dismissed."

With another bow, he hurried out.

Simona sat down on the room's only chair. What had happened? Would she be able to learn the new rules? The circumstances?

Was Enos angry? Or poor? What was going to happen when he arrived home and found that she had returned?

The tray of food was left untouched. Simona went to bed and tried to sleep.

There was a knock on her door the next morning and Simona awoke to find herself still wearing her traveling clothes. She hastened to her feet and tried with anxious hands to put herself into some kind of orderliness.

Enos strode in. "I heard you have returned" was his greeting. "Good. We have much to do to be ready for Passover."

She blinked. She had no idea how to prepare for Passover. Her father and mother had cared for all the preparations.

He looked at her, his eyes running up and down her crumpled, slept-in robe. "For one thing," he said, "you will need a new robe. I will look after that."

Why—why does he always leave me tongue-tied? She could never read his thoughts or know his desires—so she just gazed back blankly when he spoke to her.

He paused, seeming to study her. Then he nodded. She wondered why. But he did not seem angry. For that she was thankful.

"We will have a banquet in two nights' time. An important event. And I do hope you will be rested by then and looking your best. I will have Ira find someone to come in and help you prepare. I will see to the robe and jewelry."

He looked toward the door and she understood that he had said all he had come to say. There were no questions asked concerning her family or her long journey.

He started to leave and then hesitated, "Oh, yes, we will be attending a number of Passover events, as well. You are to go to the widow Mary for all the instructions. Ira will see that you get there."

He moved toward the door again, and then stopped once more. "We no longer have kitchen staff, so you are free to use the kitchen as you wish. I am taking my meals with the other trainees now. If you need supplies leave a note for Ira and he will go to the market."

He reached for the door's handle and then swung around to face her, a shadow having crossed his face. "Under no circumstances are you to go to the market yourself," he commanded. Now, he did sound angry. He left, slamming the door behind him.

He had not even given Simona a chance to speak. Well, at least he had offered her a bit of freedom. She picked up the tray that still held the food from the night before. Olives. It had lots of olives. She had never learned to care for olives. She would see if the kitchen had anything with more promise.

When Simona reached the small kitchen, she was not pleased with what she found. It had not been cared for since Hiram had left, she was sure. The first thing she did was to find a large apron and wrap it around her slender body. At least she could keep her day gown from becoming soiled by her housework. Then she looked for cleaning tools. They were adequate. She needed water—plenty of water. Hot water. There was no fire for heating the water, so preparing the fire was the next task to be done.

She did a survey to determine how to tackle the chore ahead, then began to sort and organize what she found. By the time the water had heated she was ready to go.

It took her the morning hours to complete the task but by the time she was done she was well satisfied with her accomplishment. The kitchen, though small, was now neat and tidy. She sat down on a high stool and, on a shard of pottery, made a careful list for Ira of what was needed from the market. She wrote his name on it and left it on the counter.

It was then that she remembered that she had forgotten to eat. She placed a few items on a tray and without even removing the large apron she carried the tray out to the small courtyard. She was pleased to see that the fountain was still spraying silvery water heavenward. She had just settled herself on the bench when a sparrow appeared. She smiled her greeting.

"Have you missed me?" she asked the small bird, and it dipped its head to the side. The bright, dark eyes were still attentive. "Of course, you did," she answered for him. "Here—here are some crumbs."

Two more sparrows joined the first, coaxing with little chirps. She tossed them crumbs as well, talking to them as she ate her simple lunch. In her dark and troubled world, they brought her comfort.

Simona lingered for a while after she had finished eating. There was no reason to hurry. There was nothing else that she could do with her day. At length she stood and lifted her tray, dreading the thought of having the whole afternoon before her with nothing to do.

She was just turning toward the entrance door when she spotted a bit of color tucked against the corner of the bench. She went back and reached for it, puzzled as to what it was.

At first her mind refused to make sense of it. She turned the item this way and that as she studied it. Obviously, it was incomplete, whatever it was. It looked like . . .

And then she stopped with a little gasp. It was the beginnings of an infant's foot covering. She remembered—she had been working on it before she had become ill—and lost her baby. How did it get here? It must have fallen from her basket on the day that she chatted with Una. And now, there would never be a tiny foot that needed its warmth. She clutched it to her bosom and began to let the tears fall unchecked.

CHAPTER TWENTY-FIVE

The Preparation

Simona was happy to have her own kitchen. The preparation of her own meals helped to fill her day. She was looking forward to trying new things and chatting with Ira about what he was finding in the market at this time of the year. Perhaps there were special dishes that she could prepare for them.

But it was a short-lived fantasy. The very next day she was escorted to the home of the widow Mary for her lessons concerning Passover and all of the various events and customs that went along with the occasion.

Simona looked forward to seeing her previous mentor once again. She knew that she could not really call her a friend. But she was not an enemy, and in Simona's world every positive relationship was someone to treasure.

She was ushered into the familiar study and took the extra chair that had been placed to indicate where she would sit. She tried to still her racing heart as she waited for the elderly woman to make her appearance.

When the widow Mary came into the room, it seemed to Simona that she had aged. She was using a cane now. Simona could not remember a cane before—and less than a year had passed since they had resided together.

The older woman nodded as she took her seat and sighed with appreciation as she settled on the familiar padded chair.

"How have you been, my dear?"

The gentle query caught Simona off guard. She had not expected to be greeted in such a warm fashion. So she was slow with an answer and the elderly woman turned slightly to study her.

"I see a shadow in your eyes. Has something difficult happened?"

All at once Simona recalled other times when the woman had seemed able to read her mind. Still she did not know how to answer the question. She mentally reached for the first thing that she felt safe to discuss. "I have just returned from burying my father," she managed to say.

The widow showed immediate compassion. She reached for Simona's hand and gently gave it a pat, her own eyes now clouding. "I am so sorry," she said softly, and Simona knew that the words were sincere.

"Did you—have a moment for a farewell?" the woman then asked.

Simona looked away. How much could she say? She had been there—in time. But the conversation with her father had not been a satisfactory parting. Her father had not understood about the need to believe. The entire family had grieved, not only because of his parting but also because he had not prepared to meet his God. He had not understood that Jesus was the Promised One. That one must believe. Repent.

But how could she speak all these thoughts to this woman who spent her time in Temple worship and training young women to be equally devout? Surely, she would not understand.

"You hesitate," the mentor went on to say. "Is it still so painful?"

Simona could only nod. "I am not sure you would—understand," she whispered.

The older woman hesitated, and then she spoke again. "You have impressed me, Simona. And you have been much on my mind and in my prayers since you spent time with me before. You are young and sweet, and humble and honest. I admire that in one so young. You can trust me with your confidences. I may not understand, but I will not judge. And I do hope that I may be able to comfort."

Dared she share her soul? Her secrets? Again, she hesitated. There were so many things that troubled her. She was being asked to share her pain.

"I—I also lost a baby." Tears came easily.

The woman's eyes opened wide. There was silence. Then she spoke softly.

"I know the pain. The questions. I, too, lost a baby. Many, many years ago."

"I'm sorry," whispered Simona.

"I am sorry, too," the older woman said as she reached for Simona's hand again. A pause. "And your husband, how did he respond?"

Could she be so truthful? "He's rarely home. I seldom see him. He is a student, you know. With the Pharisees. He is very committed. Very diligent." Had she said enough?

"But . . . ?" quizzed the older woman, her eyes on Simona's face.

"He said—he said—we could have another one—if we decided we wanted one."

There was silence, while each woman sorted out her painful thoughts.

"Are there other things on your husband's mind right now that would cause him to be . . . disconnected?"

Simona thought about the question. Perhaps that was the answer. She knew that Enos was deeply bothered at present. She leaned forward and lowered her voice. "He—he is very upset about Jesus of Nazareth," she said. "He was put on a committee to follow him about and try to—to expose him as an imposter. But they took him off that committee because they feared he was so passionate and uncontrolled he might stir up the Romans. I know he's angry and frustrated. He thinks Jesus is a fraud and an imposter, pretending to be the Messiah. He calls him evil and wicked. He doesn't understand that he is—" Simona stopped short. What had she just said to this woman from the Temple courts?

"I see," said the older woman, sitting up straighter in her chair. "I do remember that you said your father—who was crippled—had been searching for the man Jesus, hoping to be healed. Correct?"

Simona nodded.

"Did he ever find him?"

"No, he never did."

"So, your father was still crippled when he died?"

"Yes."

"How do you feel about that?"

"I—I feel very sad. But that is not what makes me weep when I think of him. My father had been willing to believe that this Prophet could make him well, but—but he was not willing to believe that he was—*is*—really the Messiah we have waited for."

"And you believe that?"

Simona hesitated. She shut her eyes for a quick prayer for wisdom and courage. It was dangerous to make such a public statement. But she could not deny her newfound faith. "Yes. I believe that. With all my heart." Her lips trembled but her eyes held strong conviction.

"I see!" said the mentor. "And if I asked you why?"

"My brother saw him. Listened to him speak. Ate from the miracle bread that he produced for the crowd. He believes with all his heart. So does my mother—now. It has changed her."

"Does your husband—Enos—know your new beliefs?"

"No," she admitted. "He does not. We have not talked since I have come home."

"I see."

Silence. The widow seemed to be sorting her thoughts. Options. When she spoke again, her voice was gentle, quiet. "We are now moving into Passover. The holiest part of our year—our Faith. We think about God's great deliverance of his people from the tyranny of Egypt. The lamb's blood on the doorpost that meant salvation for the oldest son of the home. But it is even more than that. It is also looking forward to the coming of our Deliverer of the future. Our Holy Scriptures speak much of him. We have waited for many years. Many centuries. And still we wait. The fullness of time has not yet come. There are prophesies still unfulfilled. We wait. Patiently. Prayerfully. The holy scribes and priests are watching the Scriptures, longing for the fulfillment of the promises."

The widow Mary stopped and looked into the face of the young woman before her. Her voice seemed to demand careful attention to the words she was about to speak. "Don't you think, if this Nazarene were really the Messiah, they would know?"

For one moment Simona's faith wavered. It made so much sense. Of course, those who studied the Scriptures should know.

And then she remembered the glow in her brother's eyes as he spoke of Jesus and shared his words and his promises. She remembered the change in her mother, a woman who for years had lived with discontent and anger, and who was now compassionate and loving. And most of all, she remembered the comfort to her own troubled soul when she had whispered a prayer, accepting this

Jesus from the Galilee as her own Lord and Savior—the One they had waited for. Her new and fragile faith was restored.

"They should know, but they—they have been blinded."

The woman shook her head. She shuffled some of the loose papyrus scraps on her desk. Without looking up she spoke. "So, what is he like—this Jesus?"

Simona felt her face flush. "I don't know."

The widow Mary raised her head. "So, you have not seen him?"

"No—no, I have not seen him." Simona placed her hands over her heart. "But I—I have felt him."

The woman shook her head. "Faith is not a matter of feeling, my dear. It is a matter of fact."

"But—but once you find Jesus—you just know they are one and the same. You know."

The woman's eyes looked damp with unshed tears. She swallowed, and played with her pages again. When she did speak again, her voice was soft and gentle. "You do know that it could cost you. Your relationship with your husband. The right to worship in the Temple. In extreme circumstances, your very life."

"Yes. Yes, I know. I have thought about that." Her head dropped, and she took a deep breath before she could go on. "But what it could cost me to believe him is little compared to what it could cost me to deny him."

The woman again shifted uncomfortably in her chair. "We must get on with your lessons," she said. "Your husband will expect you to be prepared."

So saying, the widow Mary began a study of the Passover celebrations. The *do*s and *do not*s, the meaning of each event, each symbol used in the services, the procedures, and the gatherings. Simona felt her faith grow as she listened to all that God had done for his people. What a rich and blessed heritage, her heart responded. And now Jesus!

When the lesson was completed, the mentor looked at the young woman before her whose eyes shone in appreciation and anticipation. She paused and seemed to search her own soul. Then she spoke again. "I am going to give you a bit of advice that I have never given another woman before. And I struggle to give it even now—but under the circumstances I feel I must."

Simona felt her heart begin to tremble.

"You are young, you are passionate, and you still have not experienced much of the harshness of life." She sighed. "I have observed your young husband. He, too, is passionate—extremely so—but you are now on opposite sides. My concern—my advice . . ." She stopped to carefully explain her position. "I will not ask you to deny your newfound faith. I choose to cling to the God I know—the God I understand. Your faith is between you and God."

She took a deep breath. "However . . ." The very word sounded heavy with meaning. "However, unless you are backed into a corner where you must state your position, keep your new faith . . . personal, for now. Until after Passover. This is always a time of fervor, of excitement and—yes—passion, but I have a feeling that this year is going to be . . . even more so. A turning point. A collision of the old and the new. I do not speculate as to what will happen, but I think a lot of lives will change. A lot of our world will change. Be sure that what you feel you have found is worth living for—worth dying for. Because there may be a high cost. A cost that will change everything. Everything!"

The widow Mary rose slowly from her chair and surprised Simona by holding out her arms. The young trainee was only too glad to accept the warm embrace.

"God go with you, my daughter," her spiritual mentor whispered, before releasing her.

CHAPTER TWENTY-SIX

The Passover

It had begun even before Passover.

Stories about this same Jesus had buzzed in the streets of the city for weeks as the celebration days approached. Whispered versions of the tales had reached all the way to the classroom where Enos had been attempting to concentrate on the writings of the prophets. He had pretended not to listen as Judah of Antioch related one of the most jarring stories to Seth.

First there had been an illness. A wealthy man named Lazarus of Bethany had fallen ill. His friends had been eager to support the family in any way they could. His sudden death was a shock. Folks who had known him reported that he had always seemed to be a man of vigor, who worked hard and spent wisely. A number of friends traveled the short distance from Jerusalem to support the family on the day of his burial, and many stayed for the extended time of grieving with the sisters—even those who were not professional mourners. Such was the community's love of their brother.

Lazarus had been considered a good man, a faithful attender of the Temple and a charitable neighbor. His death had touched the entire community. There was concern that the sisters would find it difficult to support themselves without the strong back of Lazarus to work on their behalf.

Enos rolled his eyes as Judah continued. For then the man from Nazareth had woven himself into the narrative.

The family was still in mourning when this Jesus had shown up with some of his followers a short time later. It was no surprise to the people who had been watching—waiting—that the self-proclaimed Messiah would travel south around the time of the yearly Passover celebration. He was, after all, a devout Jew. But it seemed like a bad time to impose himself on the grieving sisters.

With emphasis, Judah repeated the next portion of the tale. It was claimed that by the time Jesus arrived, Lazarus had already been in the tomb for four days. They had all been taught that a man's soul, by this time, was prepared to wing its way to the afterlife, abandoning its vigil beside his corpse.

Even Judah had admitted that the story got a mite cloudy and confusing as it passed from lips to lips, but the ending could not be mistaken. The same people who had been there, and seen Lazarus put in the tomb, watched again as Jesus called and the dead man came forth, still bundled in his graveclothes. He was returned to the weeping Martha and Mary, alive and well.

The news had spread like wildfire. The fire lit the tinder of Enos's rage. For one thing, the village of Bethany was close enough that any curious resident of Jerusalem could simply make the walk to see for himself.

At least he was comforted by the fact that the entire episode was of particular alarm to the Temple officials. How would they ever stop this self-proclaimed prophet now? The miracles that had been attributed to him previously were of little concern compared to bringing someone back from the dead. Enos would be proven correct in his warnings. Perhaps now they would appreciate his foresight regarding this imposter.

Enos was biding his time, anticipating the feast and half expecting the Nazarene to slink back into the wilderness until the raging cooled. Some alleged that this is just what he'd done.

However, as though the rumors were not bad enough, on the very first day of the Passover Week, an impromptu crowd had quickly formed, waving palm branches and declaring him to be a king. *The* King.

No one was more enraged at the sight than Enos. This common man was setting himself up, acting out the prophecies that he had apparently researched in Scripture, and was determined to fabricate an image that made it appear he was fulfilling them.

They were just on the brink of their Passover celebrations when Enos brought the word home to Simona. "The banquet we were going to attend this evening had to be canceled. Instead, we are having a gathering to decide how to apprehend and arrest this Jesus. Finally! Finally, someone is willing to listen to reason! He must be stopped. I don't care how we do it but it must be done—now!"

"Wh-What do you mean, arrest him?" Simona stammered. "What did he do?"

"He lied, for starters. He is no more the King than I am the King." There was such hatred in his voice. His eyes.

"Will they . . . imprison him?" she dared to ask.

"No. He does not deserve prison. Death. We will ask Rome for death. Surely we can make them see that he has so violated our Faith, we have no alternative but to eradicate him."

Simona could not even speak.

Enos spun on his heel and called back as he left, "Do not wait up for me. This could take all night!"

As soon as she heard the door slam shut, Simona crumpled onto her bed, trembling, and began to pray.

Simona did not see her husband again until the end of the week. It had been an odd day, one that had frightened her. At its highest point in the sky, the sun had totally disappeared. Simona could see no dark clouds that had caused it. It was strange and eerie and made her fearful. She wished Enos was home with some kind of reasonable explanation for the strangeness. Surely he would know what was happening.

Instead, she had retreated to her bed chamber and closed her door, shivering under a heavy blanket. In the midst of the darkness the earth shook. She had heard of earthquakes but had never experienced one before. She wept alone in fear that something else, even worse, might happen next.

At last the sun returned and the earth seemed to be stable once again, but Simona still did not leave her bed.

When Enos finally did come home he came directly to Simona's room. He looked disheveled and weary, but he wore an exaggerated smile.

"We did it," he bragged loudly.

Simona did not speak.

"Took all night running back and forth, but Pilate, that weak-livered Roman, finally took action."

Simona did not dare to ask what that action was.

"Well—the whole mess has about ruined Passover events for us. Not much but Temple services from now on. But it was worth it. Now the world might turn back to some kind of normal once again. I was right. They'll have to give me credit now."

Then he picked up a totally different line of thought. "Sorry about the special banquets. I was looking forward to being able to socialize once again. You did not even get to show off that new robe. I thought the color perfect for you."

Then just as quickly, he cut back again to his previous thoughts. "Quite a crowd gathered today. I heard folks saying they never remember a crucifixion bringing out that many people."

"What . . . crucifixion?" Simona dared to ask.

"That prophet! Well, he was not a real prophet, but he had a lot of people fooled. What did you think I've been talking about?" He did not wait for an answer. "Well, he won't be around to make fools out of people anymore. Finally, we will have some peace, and things will get back to normal."

Simona felt physically ill. She would have excused herself had she been able to speak. She could not. They had actually killed the One sent from God. On a heinous Roman cross. How could they have done such a thing? Why had God allowed it to happen? Surely, he could have stopped them.

But Enos was continuing. "Well, all is not lost. There are still a couple lesser events coming up. You can use the robe for the Temple gathering tomorrow."

"I—I am not feeling at all well," Simona managed to say.

"What now?" he sounded very angry. Simona dared not answer.

Enos swung around and surprised her by asking, "What is available in the kitchen? I'm famished. I haven't eaten in two days, it seems."

"You will need to ask Ira," Simona managed to respond. "He goes to the market."

"Where is he? I did not even see him when I came in."

Simona frowned. She had not thought of it, but she had not seen Ira either. A thorough search revealed that neither Ira, nor anything that belonged to him, was now present in the home.

Simona found a simple note beneath her pillow when she retired. It bore only one short message. "I am sorry, Lady Simona."

The Passover became a disjointed, somber event. Many people feared to take part. Those who had traveled for many miles, at great personal expense, felt robbed of the religious renewal that they had been anticipating. Many contemplated putting as many miles as possible between themselves and the ugly events that had just transpired. But they could not travel on the Holy Sabbath, as much as they longed to be gone. Who knew when Rome might decide to get involved in the fracas? And if they did, where would they stop?

Even the very devout who lived in the sacred city decided to simply lock their doors and stay in the safety of their homes rather than venture out into the streets.

There was grumbling. Why couldn't the religious hierarchy have chosen a different time of the calendar to rid themselves of a nuisance man who wished to call himself a prophet? They had certainly chosen unwisely. Passover was a sacred event and their eagerness to dispose of a false rabbi, no matter his following, should not have interfered with God's ordained gathering of his people. The entire city and surrounding area seemed on edge with the disappointment and inconvenience.

Merchants, who saw Passover as the time to fill their coffers, placed unsold celebration merchandise in back storage rooms. Market stalls discarded extra produce that had been purchased to serve during feasting of out-of-town visitors to the event. Even the Temple merchants had way too many sheep, doves, and expensive scents left over with no immediate way for them to profitably eliminate the oversupply. The distraction over the Nazarene had proven costly.

It seemed that the whole world had been the loser when Jesus of Nazareth was placed on the Roman cross.

Simona stirred from her bed and went to the kitchen. The Sabbath day had ended and she was free to prepare food for herself. She hoped she could find something still on the shelves to sustain her, even though she was quite sure there would be nothing remaining. She had already used up what had been left behind by Hiram. No one had been to market. There was no back garden to draw from.

She had not seen Enos since he had brought the news of the Messiah's crucifixion. Simona had spent the night weeping and praying by turn. She had been so sure that he was the One they had waited for—but if he had succumbed to death on a cross, they must have been wrong.

Yet her heart refused to accept that fact. There was something wrong with this whole event. He was doing only good deeds, healings, exorcisms, feeding, encouraging. Why were they foolish enough to kill him? She did not understand. Her mother and her brother would be so crushed. They, too, had believed. They had been so sure. Now she was confused. Broken. Left hopeless. How could this be?

And also she was left alone, no husband, no food, no hope. And she had declared to the widow Mary that she was a believer. How foolish that seemed now!

Without even thinking she began to pray as she walked, "Lord Jesus, I don't know what to do. Where to go for help? I have had nothing to eat today—and very little yesterday—and the Sabbath has just ended. What should I do, Lord? May there be something—something left in the kitchen, even though I found nothing when I looked last night."

She pushed aside the inner curtain just as the door from the outside entrance opened, as well. It startled her and she jerked to a stop. Enos never used the back entrance.

But it was Ira who entered. In his hand he carried a pot and under his arm she could see a wrapped loaf.

He was as surprised as Simona, bowing quickly. Then he hurried to apologize. "I am sorry, Lady Simona. The—the master was no longer supplying money for the market. I could not shop. So, I left. But then I remembered that you would have nothing to eat. I have brought a stew and bread."

Simona stood and stared. Then she began to weep. The words may not have made sense to the former servant, but for Simona they put her upside-down world back together again. "He is real! He answered my prayer. I must believe. I do not understand—but I must believe!"

Ira stared. "Is my lady—?"

"I am fine." She cut in. "And I do thank you for the—for coming, and for the food, and for being such a caring friend." She wiped away her tears.

Ira looked ill at ease. "You—you know that I cannot stay, Lady Simona. With no money for supplies I cannot prepare food or care for the household."

"I understand."

"What will you do, my lady?"

She replied honestly. "I don't know. But—but I am sure now that God will provide—something, some way."

"Can you go home, to your family?"

"I cannot leave my husband."

"But he does not come home. He eats with the Pharisees. He does not supply the kitchen . . ."

"I know. But perhaps things will change. Now that he is no longer trying to—to destroy the Prophet—maybe he will . . . I don't know."

"I am sorry, Lady Simona, that I cannot help."

"I'll be fine. God will—somehow . . ." She could not finish her brave words. She had no idea what she would do.

The man bowed and turned to the dark doorway, a worried frown still wrinkling his brow.

Enos was still agitated. They had finally, finally, taken action regarding Jesus of Nazareth—who would no longer be walking back and forth across the land gathering duped followers into thinking he was the Promised One—the Son of God. Such rubbish. Well, they were finally done with all that. He just hoped that all of the so-called disciples and devotees would leave the city soon. All they did was stir up trouble.

He headed to the room where the evening meal was being served. The Passover celebrations had ended but the city was still throbbing with tension. He had not attended any of the usual activities. He filled his bowl and took a seat off by himself, not in the mood for idle chatter.

Enos was still struggling. The partner he had in gathering the Temple fees watched him like a hawk. It was as though he expected him to be pilfering coins. The previous fellow, Judah of Antioch, had never been so suspicious. It had been no challenge to feel out a larger coin while counting out the money from the vendors and slip it into his hidden pocket under his sash. Now with the sharp eyes constantly on him, he needed to be extra cautious.

And he had foolishly paid way too much for the robe Simona was to have worn to the Passover week feasting. Way too much. And then the banquet had not even taken place and the merchant would not return his money.

Enos was still working on his problem when he looked up to see Judah, the young man from Antioch, on the other side of the room. Judah! He hadn't seen him since he had returned from spying on the prophet. There was his answer! He would team up with Judah again in gathering the fees.

Enos left his unfinished bowl of food and hurried across the room.

"Judah!" he said, holding out a hand toward the man. "Good to see you. Great job! Great job! Now we will have some peace."

Judah made little response to his greeting. He merely gave a bit of a nod.

"Now that things will get back to normal, I am hoping that you will join me again in gathering the Temple fees each day. I have missed . . ."

But the young man was already shaking his head, and then he indicated the bundles in his hands. "I am leaving," he said curtly.

"Leaving? When?"

"I will be on my way as soon as travel is allowed."

"But—you have not yet finished your training. You cannot be a Pharisee without finishing the studies."

"That is true."

They stood and studied one another in silence. Then Judah dared to speak. "I cannot be a Pharisee," he said firmly. "I do not agree with them."

"Think what you're losing, man. Surely you would not throw away all of the privileges of belonging to such an elite—"

"I prefer to think of what I am gaining. Jesus—the Nazarene—was not an imposter. He should not have been placed on a Roman cross."

Enos cut in. "There was no alternative. You know that. Only Rome has the authority to give what was the acceptable death penalty."

The young man's eyes darkened. He looked alarmingly broken. At last, he could speak. "I think you know, just as I do, that no death penalty was deserved. It was a fraud. On trumped-up charges. Even Pilate knew that. But he did not grant justice. He broke that Roman code of law and allowed a mob—a hired and coerced mob—in order to please the hierarchy by calling for an innocent man's death. No, I have no desire to be a part of something of which I am so ashamed. And I am not the only Pharisee to question the extreme action that has been taken."

"Don't you realize that such words could get you stoned?" hissed Enos.

"And you would be there to throw the first stone, wouldn't you?"

Enos was so offended by the remark that he could not even respond.

"Goodbye, Enos," said Judah. "May God have mercy—on all of you."

Enos's rage prevented him from trying to stop Judah. He stood trembling in place, watching him go. But in his thoughts a promise was forming. *You will pay for those words, if I have to see to it myself.*

His eyes squeezed closed. He had no desire to speak to anyone. The room had begun to spin. He had to leave—now. And the only place to go was home. He had not been there for a while, because there had been no reason to bother.

As he let himself in, Enos made no attempt to be quiet. He knew that Hugo had left, as had Hiram—and then Ira. There was no one left to serve him.

He headed for Simona's chamber, walking straight in with no respectful rap. She had already retired for the night, but she was not sleeping. She sat up as he entered.

"At least *you* are still here!"

"Yes," she replied simply. "I am."

He noted that her voice quivered slightly. It pleased him. At least someone still had some respect for his authority.

"Who is to care for the kitchen?"

"I believe that is a decision for the master of the home." She said it with so little fear that it unnerved Enos.

"And if I say I wish some food, what then? You are the mistress—and you have knowledge of a kitchen, I understand."

"Yes, my lord. I do. But there are no supplies in the kitchen."

"Why?"

"There has been no one to go to the market."

"Why?"

"There were no funds for purchases."

He hesitated for only a moment. "So what am I to do?" he bellowed.

"I do not know, my lord."

Silence followed. There was nothing more to say. So Enos left the room, still in a rage, his thoughts already searching for a way to absolve any personal blame. His mind went to Simona.

It was all her fault. If he had not paid the heavy bride price and brought her to his home things would have never escalated to such a difficult circumstance. He'd had servants, a man to go to the market, another in his kitchen, food to eat whenever he asked for it, another servant to care for his home and garments. What did he have now? A woman? A woman whom he could not even put on display. A woman with no more sense than to weep over a fraudulent prophet.

He stopped.

Somehow, all of this was interconnected. He hadn't yet worked out how—but all of his grief and worry started with the two of them. The man called Jesus and his wife. Well—he had taken care of the prophet, but what could he do about her?

CHAPTER TWENTY-SEVEN

The Impossible

SIMONA KNEW WITHOUT CHECKING that Enos was already gone when she awoke the next morning. She did not pretend that she was disappointed. She rose and dressed and headed to the kitchen, knowing full well that there would be nothing there.

Enos was likely enjoying a meal with the other students.

As to her own meal, she wondered if she might have left a bit of the bread that Ira had brought. She was quite sure that she had sopped up every drop of the mutton stew.

How long could she go without food, she wondered. She was not sure if she really cared. She just hoped that the process of expiring was not too long and pain filled. She recalled the terrible suffering when she had lost her unborn child. Would the pain of starvation be equal to that? She shuddered.

There was no food. She would need to conserve every bit of energy. She was returning to her bed when she heard a commotion from outside, and before she could even wonder what was happening, Enos burst through the door.

"There is a crazy rumor going around," he almost shouted at her. "They say that the prophet is not in the tomb."

"What—what happened?" she managed.

"That is what I plan to find out. We are having another meeting. We'll get to the bottom of it. Rumors must travel with lightning speed. It is already all over the city. Some are so stupid as to claim he was seen alive. Impossible! We made good and sure that he was dead when he was taken off the cross. Do they think we're fools? That we don't know death? But the masses are so gullible—so stupid—they will believe anything."

He was about to go out the door when he turned back to her. "Maybe you should go and stay with the widow Mary until we get this worked out. The whole city is going crazy again. Do you know the way?"

Simona had no idea if she could find her way across the city. She had traveled by cart before. The curtains had been pulled. She hadn't even seen which of the maze of streets they had traveled.

Enos must have seen her puzzled look. "Stay here if you want. I have no idea how long this will take. Perhaps a servant girl can bring you something."

And he was gone.

Simona felt weak. A chair was nearby and she took it. She felt dizzy. What had happened to Jesus? Why would anyone take his body? Doubts began to push against reason again. Maybe he was not the . . . ? But she had been so sure. Her very heart had claimed him as her Messiah. Her Deliverer. And now . . . ?

Would this nightmare ever be over?

Simona spent the day in her room again. There was nothing to eat. There was nothing to do. There was no one to talk to. She was sure that she would never be able to find her way to the widow

Mary. Nor did she know anyone else in the city. What did people do when they had no one? Nothing? She had never been in that situation before.

A new thought came to mind. *I can pray.* Surely it was an answer to her prayer that Ira had brought her food. Perhaps Jesus would hear her, would give her wisdom.

She knelt beside her bed, her face turned upward and her cheeks streaked with falling tears.

"Lord," she prayed, "I don't know what to do. Where to go. I need wisdom. I need help. I wish to leave—but I have a husband and have promised to be faithful to him. I must . . ."

A loud clamoring at the door stopped her prayer. It was Enos who burst into her room. She had never seen him so angry.

"You!" he screamed at her. "I just realized that you have—have believed him. You have been grieving for him. You, with the rest of the foolish—the misguided . . ." In his anger even his words seemed difficult to form. He reached out and jerked her arm. "It is true, is it not? Say it! Say you think this Jesus is—is who he claimed to be. You are as . . ."

She had managed to rise to her feet. Trembling, she took a deep breath. "Yes," she managed in almost a whisper. But her voice grew stronger. "Yes—I believe."

He slapped her so hard she almost lost her balance. "You, the wife of a Pharisee, dare to mock me by being one of his—his . . ."

"Followers," she said with confidence.

He could not find the words. He shoved a sheet of parchment toward her.

"It is a writ of divorce. I will not be disgraced by sharing my home with a woman who has such poor judgment—such disregard of religious commitment. I cannot believe how you could disgrace a Pharisee in such . . ." The ferocity of his words spewed saliva into the air around him. He was shaking with anger as he shoved the parchment toward her again.

Simona's hand trembled as she accepted the legal document. "What am I to do?"

He wiped a hand over his face. His eyes were still flaming. "Now why would I care? Just get out of here—and take all evidence of your presence with you." He turned from her and reached for the door handle. "And never come back—ever," he added. "I never want to see you again."

The door opened and then slammed shut with such force that Simona felt the whole room shudder.

She stood trembling. What had just happened? She looked down at the document she held in her trembling hand. One word seemed to jump from the page. *Adultery?* She had been charged with adultery. She was not an adulteress, could not have possibly . . . What did he mean?

Collapsing on her bed, Simona's body shook with each wave of tears. She was alone, abandoned, in a city she did not know, with no place to go, and no idea how she could ever get back to her former home. And not a coin to her name.

Gradually, a thought brought unexpected calm. She straightened. She had prayed. Was this an answer? Certainly, it was nothing like the answer she had prayed for—or expected.

She whispered aloud another brief prayer. "Show me, Jesus. Please, God, show me what to do."

The first thing to be done was to obey the final words of her former husband. She was to leave, and to take everything that was hers with her.

She turned to her dressing room. Such fancy robes hung from the hooks. What was she to do with them? They were not garments that were worn on the streets. Yet, she could not leave them as *evidence* of her existence. She looked for some type of container in which to carry them. Perhaps there was a bag of some type in the kitchen.

The house seemed quiet but the last thing she wished was to confront Enos in the hall. Opening her door slowly, she tipped her head to catch any sound of movement. She heard nothing, so she dared to make her way to the kitchen. There was nothing suitable.

So Simona went back to her room and pulled a blanket from her bed. Then she began to methodically fold each garment and stack them together. They made a clumsy, heavy package. It would be all but impossible to carry. Would she be able to manage them?

If not, she reasoned, she would discard them, one by one, as she traveled. She tidied the room as much as she was able. She could not bear to leave it in disarray. She took one last look about the room that had been hers, knowing that she had never been happy here. But at times she had felt safe. She was about to raise her bundle when she thought of her little friends.

She wished she had some crumbs—but she did not. At least she could bid them farewell. They had been good company. Their fluttering and chirping had brightened many of her days.

Simona entered the small courtyard. There were two birds drinking from the fountain. She stood quietly and reached out to them. Though her hand held none of the crumbs that she normally brought, soon one of the sparrows lit lightly on her upturned hand.

"Little friend," she whispered softly, "I am sorry to disappoint you. I have no food. Our world has turned upside down—both yours and mine. I will miss you."

The second sparrow fluttered in to find room on her hand. For a moment there was a scramble of wings until they both were settled. They tipped their heads and looked up at her. One chirped.

It was then her tears fell. "I am so sorry," she whispered. "If I had even a crumb it would be yours. I'll miss you." And with the words, she gave a little wave of her hand that sent the birds into the air once again.

Returning to the room that she had counted as her own, Simona hoisted the heavy bundle to her shoulder. Quietly she entered the hall, moved to the main door, and left the building. She was now on her own. She had often felt much like a prisoner during the time she'd spent in the small home, but as she left it she felt fear rather than release. What would she do now? Where would she go? She was on a busy street with many homes, much like the one she had just left. Where were the main streets of the city? She had no idea.

"Which way, Lord?" she whispered as she began to walk.

She did not actually choose a path. She just walked in the direction she was facing, with no idea where it would take her.

Reason suggested that she needed to find the center of the city. It would soon be dark and the streets would be deserted—or inhabited by people she didn't wish to meet. Perhaps she would be wise to seek out some type of off-street shelter for the night and do her searching in the morning.

Her stomach reminded her that she had not had a meal of any kind all day. And there was no water near to trick her stomach into feeling it had been nourished. So for the moment there was nothing she would be able to do about that. Walking forward a step at a time seemed the only option.

It was a long, uncomfortable night. Simona crouched behind some shrubbery in an alley off an unknown street. The night was dark, thick clouds blanketing the full Passover moon and all of the stars. The alley, too, was unlit by any surrounding buildings. And it was cool. She dared not take advantage of her one blanket, knowing if she did, the garments she had wrapped in it would be unprotected and loose to any wind that might blow as she slept.

Her stomach had not ceased to demand food. She had nothing. She assumed that if she had to go without for many days she would get used to the feeling to the point where it would not be as bothersome.

She did not rest. She was much too aware of her circumstances. What would happen if she were found? She had no idea if night patrols might consider a lone woman on the street after dark to be an offense that required punishment. Or if the people of the night would feel she was fair game and would be prone to robbery or abuse. She really knew nothing of city streets.

She tried to quiet her mind enough to sleep, but sleep would not come. Every now and then she would hear stirrings from somewhere. Was it man or beast moving about in the nearby alley? She dared not try to find out, lest she herself would be discovered.

The first appearance of softening darkness brought her much relief. Soon she would be free to start another attempt at progress. The increasing glow also gave her a sense of direction. The morning sunrise would first appear to her right—east. If she remembered correctly, that would mean that the bulk of the city would be straight ahead. Was that the direction she should take?

By the early light she unrolled her heavy bundle and sorted through her garments. She divided them between fancy and expensive or simpler everyday wear. She was about to shove the first bundle deep into the bushes, and then she noticed the very expensive robe that she had never had a chance to wear. Might she be able to get a few coins for it? Surely there was someone in the city who would look with pleasure on such attire. She switched it over into the pile of the plainer robes and pushed the fancier pile back into the bushes as far as she could force them. Then she re-bundled what she planned to take with her. It was much smaller and lighter now. It would be easier to carry.

By the time she felt ready to go, the morning sun was just peeking over the tops of the city walls. She heard an early morning rooster crow from somewhere nearby. The sound pleased her. It seemed so ordinary. Like a reminder that the real, solid and sensible world was still there, somewhere, just waiting to be discovered again. She lifted her bundle to her shoulder, then said a quick prayer before moving out into the street.

Enos had settled enough to wonder if he had acted rashly. Had it been a wise move to banish Simona from his home? She was still a very beautiful woman. Things should settle down once again now that the fake prophet had been cared for.

Everything should have been concluded neatly by now had it not been for the ridiculous rumor about his missing body. Enos pressed his way into every assembly he could find to hear what was being said about the debacle. He felt confident that the mystery would be quickly solved. How difficult could it be to produce the mangled corpse? To end the speculation immediately?

Still, it had caused quite a stir among the higher officials, with each group of administrators pointing fingers at another. Who made the error? Certainly, someone must be to blame for such an oversight to happen. And then slowly the truth came to light. For the grave—the well-guarded grave—was without a body.

They had used a heavy stone to seal the entrance. They had placed guards on duty through the days and nights. It should have been foolproof.

The most puzzling aspect to what Enos learned was the wild

story that the guards swore to be true. There had been bright lights. And voices. They declared that they were unable to move—or even to speak.

It was all so strange and disturbing. And rumor had it that the hierarchy had paid the guards hush money and sent them out of the city—somewhere. Of course, they promptly denied doing so.

The popular theory was that some of the false Messiah's followers had managed to sneak in, overcome the guards, move the heavy stone, and get away with the body.

It seemed very strange, even to Enos, that the graveclothes, which included the head wrap, were all still in the tomb. In fact, the headpiece had been carefully folded and left behind. Why would thieves do that? Was it in mockery? Was it to insult the careless guards who swore they had never left their position nor slept through the night?

The other oddity was the guards themselves. Enos had watched them from far down a corridor. They shook with fear. Still later he'd heard one of them testify. They'd seen something. Experienced something. They could not properly describe it. Did not want to discuss it. These men, familiar with the horrors of war, danger, and deception were still clearly anxious and unnerved.

There was a reasonable explanation, Enos was sure of it. But until it was disclosed, there would still be the false rumors being passed from tongue to tongue. He was tired of it. Until it was settled, life would be disrupted.

He turned his thoughts back to the present. He needed funds. Badly! With Simona now gone, he would need to get his home back in order once again. If he didn't, he might lose that also. And that also meant that he needed money to replace his servants. The ones he'd had were likely already working for other masters. He did not wish them back anyway. They had pampered Simona. He was still angry with them.

And he had neglected his studies as well. He would never rise to the top until his full training had been completed. But it all required money. The only possibility that Enos could see was the Temple fee collection.

Judah. Judah! The very name made him angry. How could he desert his calling and foolishly side with the false prophet from Nazareth? Had he learned nothing? The true Messiah was to come as a king—not a companion of fishermen.

Yet, though Enos wished to be indignant with Judah for deserting his training, he knew the real reason he was upset was that, by leaving, Judah was no longer available to help with the daily gathering of the Temple fees. Enos didn't care for his present partner. He would never be able to pilfer enough funds to get back to his proper way of living with the hawk forever at his elbow. Enos cursed aloud. Life had become so unfair.

CHAPTER TWENTY-EIGHT

The Seeker

Ezra the scribe pulled his tangle of keys from the pocket tucked in his robe and reached to place the one selected in the heavy vaulted door lock. It was really too early to be up. He wondered why he had felt stirred to leave his bed so early in the morning.

It was just that everything seemed upside-down and topsy-turvy in the world at present. Passover had come and gone—if indeed one could refer to the events of the past week as Passover. Nothing about it felt normal—or even real. In the past he had always come away from Passover week feeling refreshed, rejuvenated. Not this year. He didn't suppose that anyone had felt the renewal normally brought by celebrating the familiar rituals that had drawn his people together year after year over the centuries. This year, it had been confusion, and even darkness. He had never felt anything like it before.

Certainly, there had been bad times, depressing times, even times of danger and tumult over the years but this—the past week—had been different. He still had not sorted it out in his thinking. He was just glad it was over. At least, he hoped it was over.

To his surprise the lock did not accept his key. The room was already open. He didn't understand it. This protected space where the archives of Holy Scripture were kept was never to be opened to public admission. Never!

He entered cautiously. Who could be trespassing on sacred ground?

He noted a flicker of light coming from one of the alcoves where the most official of the priests, with rights and responsibilities, were allowed—no, *bidden*—to pour over the sacred writings year by year to keep the words fresh in their minds and hearts. But who would be there now, at this hour of the morning?

He walked forward cautiously, ready to defend himself if necessary. But it was the grey head of Justus, one of the elderly scholars, that was bent over the scroll that Ezra recognized as the writings of Isaiah.

It surprised him. Justus knew the words of Isaiah as well as anyone possibly could. He could recite the entire book. Why would he feel the need to be up early in the morning to peruse it again? The elderly man did not even lift his head. Ezra supposed his entrance had been undetected until the man spoke without even lifting his eyes from the place he was reading.

"Good morning, Ezra. Did you lock the door behind you? I believe I forgot to do so when I entered. I was too intent on my mission."

Ezra faltered from lowering himself to the room's one extra chair. He had not locked the door. He had feared he might need to escape from some intruder. He turned in relief and went back to spin the key in the lock. Then he shook the handle slightly to be sure the lock was secure. He dropped the key back in his protected pocket and returned to the elderly man who was still bent over the scroll before him.

At last, he dared to speak. "So, what has brought you from your bed so early in the morning?"

"Actually, I came last evening."

"You've been here all night?"

There was a slight nod of the head.

"Why?"

Justus raised his eyes and sighed. "This—this whole troubling mess we've created . . ."

"You think *we* created it? It was none of our doing. We . . ."

"Well, we did little to prevent it."

Ezra frowned. "You think we should have? What could we have done?"

Justus rubbed a shaky hand over his greyed beard. "That is the answer I have been seeking."

"In Isaiah?"

He reached out and moved the scroll back a little, one hand lingering on its edge as though protecting it. "Isaiah . . . and Joel and a few of the others."

"Why?" Ezra repeated.

Again, Justus lifted his head. His eyes were shadowed with fatigue—and something more. It was plain to see that he was deeply troubled. "There are so many of the sacred Scriptures where . . . where he fits."

"The Nazarene?"

"Well, he wasn't really a—a Nazarene. Not really. At the time of the Roman census, Joseph—his father—had to return to Bethlehem. Did you know that?"

"I believe I did, yes."

"He went to Bethlehem—David's city—because he was in direct line back to King David. Did you know that?"

Ezra pulled the second chair closer and lowered himself onto it before answering. "I—I guess I never really thought about it."

"No. And I think there were way too many others who didn't think about it. Under our laws, he could have actually laid claim to the throne." Justus pushed up from the desk and scooted his chair back a bit. "And there are so many other prophecies that fit."

"That's easy to explain. He was shrewd. We know that. He made sure that he fulfilled the prophecies from the sacred writings."

"A number of them were done *to* him, not *by* him. Especially concerning the crucifixion. How could he have managed that?"

Ezra had no answer. Instead, he switched to another common argument he had heard repeated many times. "But if—and I say *if*—he was really the Son of God, the Promised One, as he claimed, how could he—as God—break the Commandments that he, himself, gave to his people? It doesn't make any sense."

Justus passed a hand over his wrinkled face. "Such as?" he queried again.

Ezra knew this was one of the habits of Justus that his students had often resented. He was always turning their questions back toward them again. "Such as—the Sabbath—keeping it holy. And sinners—not keeping company with those who did not keep the laws. He broke those rules numerous times."

"You may have answered your own question."

"What do you mean?"

"He made the rules. He established the Law. He could decide when and how those rules did, or did not, apply to him. To this new order."

"I would say that is rather a roundabout way of coming to a conclusion. That is not what we've been teaching in our classes. We are to stay strictly with the Scriptures—not our own, new interpretation."

"I taught you and all the others that this practice was so because we are human. We are not God. We did not make the rules—nor do we decide when the old rules will change because the times have changed."

He stopped and rubbed his beard again.

"And as well—perhaps he did not change the rules. Perhaps our interpretation of those rules was a—a bit misunderstood."

Ezra kept his eyes from rolling out of respect for his teacher. "Like . . . ?"

"The Sabbath. We had always been taught to—to rescue an animal that had fallen into a pit, for example. He was rescuing a man from the pit of disease. He did not use the Sabbath for his own comfort or convenience—as we surely would have done."

Ezra hated to concede the point. He pressed further. "And the sinners . . . ?"

"Only God knows the heart. Perhaps that man, whose outer appearance was sinful, had a heart open and ready to accept the forgiveness of God. He just had not had the knowledge up until he met the Master. Jesus knew who would respond to truth, once he heard what truth was. We cannot judge."

Ezra left his chair in agitation. It seemed that his elderly, respected teacher was pushing things a bit far.

But Justus wasn't finished. "And the miracles. The healings. The exorcisms. Who could doubt those things done before our very eyes?"

"The evil one, too, has power," replied Ezra.

"That is true," responded the elderly scribe. "But it is not used for the glory of God. Only for the destruction of man."

Ezra could not let the remark go unchallenged. "Perhaps by bringing *apparent* healing, or even true healing, to someone, he is bringing others to destruction by leading them astray. They become worshippers of the wrong source. In their ignorance, they switch their allegiance to the wrong power."

The older man thoughtfully pondered the words. That was one of the attributes his students had always respected. He listened well and responded only after careful consideration, not passing quick judgment on their arguments even though others in the class might feel the statement was presumptive—or even foolish.

"I suppose, on occasion, that could happen—for a time. But the truth would be brought to light eventually, should one be searching for truth. That is another reason for us to be constantly on guard and seeking truth." He motioned to the scroll on the table before him. "That is why I am here. I am searching for truth."

"And have you found it?"

There was a pause. "I feel I am getting closer." Another pause. He seemed to lift his shoulders and his chin jutted, just a bit. "But in this case, close is not sufficient. It must be fact. Assurance!"

"Assurance?" quizzed Ezra. "If I understand the word, that leaves no doubt."

The older man leaned forward. It was the first time that Ezra had noted how lean his shoulders were under his tunic. "He aligns with so many of the prophecies. Even his death—his resurrection . . ."

Ezra was quick to respond. "You believe he was resurrected?"

The steely eyes fixed on the younger man. "You have a better explanation?"

Ezra drew back without giving an answer. The truth was that he had no explanation at all. They had already listened to all the weak arguments. The guards had failed, fallen asleep at their task, drank too much to get them through their grizzly task of crucifixion, or left before they should have. The tomb had not been properly sealed. The huge stone was not heavy enough. So his disciples, or grave robbers, or even an animal had stolen his body. He had only swooned on the cross and was able to somehow push aside the weighty stone and free himself—and that, in spite of his serious injuries and loss of blood. The guards had not noticed, nor heard, any commotion or grinding as the stone was rolled back.

Ezra sighed to himself. When you put them all together, they did sound rather preposterous. Ezra had no reply. He was merely grateful that Justus had not bothered running through the list of rumors aloud.

Instead, the thin lips of the elderly man uttered one word. "Lazarus?"

Ezra knew the stories that were going around about that man. That dead man.

"Too many witnesses to ignore. And the crowds that day? Their words." Justus tapped the reports concerning Lazarus that lay before him, reports that Ezra himself had written up after a thorough investigation.

"It's all in here," Justus said simply. "All of it."

Ezra's reply was not strong—nor confident. Still, he voiced it. "I have always thought there was something strange about all that."

"What do you mean?"

Ezra squirmed, like a child being caught in a misdeed. "I don't know. But some . . . strange . . . magical powers, maybe. I don't know. But it just—it doesn't seem real. Does not seem . . . right."

"Have you met Lazarus? Heard him give his account?"

"No, of course not. The Sanhedrin feared it might conflict with the truth we were seeking."

"Well, I have! I have talked with his two sisters, too. Devout! All three of them. They would not make up such a story. The women had grieved—for days—over their dead brother. And then Jesus merely spoke the words, and—"

"I know," cut in Ezra. "We have been over and over the whole thing. I was on the team that was sent to check it out. Our conclusion was that we found no proof—one way or the other."

Justus was slow in responding but when he spoke there was

strength in his voice. "I am inclined to believe they are telling the truth. Every word of it."

Ezra had a quick response. "I would need more proof. If we accept this—this story about Lazarus—then—then it throws off—so much of what we believe, what we have been taught through the years. Our entire belief system would need to be—be revised or—"

Justus stopped him. "Not at all. It all fits."

"Not about the Sabbath. Not about the sinners," argued the younger man.

"Taught? Or added?"

"What do you mean?"

"You are as aware as I, about the many little sidebars, if you will, that the Pharisees—meaning we ourselves—have added from time to time, to give the laws more *clarity* and *direction*, so the masses may be able to follow them more completely."

"Our predecessors have added some directives, yes. Filled in some holes that do not fully explain . . ."

"As though we, as mere men, have all the answers. That we could be wiser and clearer than God himself has been. As if we know God—his plans, his workings, his purposes. It is already there, I tell you. In words that we do not, cannot change."

"You think they've changed?" asked Ezra.

"No, *they* have not changed. I think we may—in our own limited knowledge—have made them into what we think we can understand. Or even what we wish them to say."

"Surely you don't think . . ."

"I think we are men. Limited. And he is God!"

There was a long pause as each man seemed to be reviewing his own thoughts.

Ezra broke into the silence. "Let me understand this. You can actually believe that there is the possibility that this—man, was the promised Messiah?"

"I am conflicted," admitted Justus, his head bowed. "I have gone over it and over it in my thinking, my research . . ."

"But?"

The grey head lifted up. Ezra saw the deep eyes still with doubts. Then his thin shoulders lifted once again. "But I confess, I am leaning more and more toward believing that this man Jesus—whom we just allowed to be crucified on a Roman cross, who disappeared from the tomb—was telling the truth. It all fits!"

Ezra looked around the room. Were they still alone? "Be careful what you say, master—what you even think," he cautioned the older man. "Walls have ears. There is no compromising in this matter. Either you are in line with the courts, or you are out."

Justus took a moment to ponder the words. "Yes—yes," he finally answered. "You are quite right. And your words have just convinced me. My heart—my soul—tells me—I need—I must—accept my deep convictions. I believe . . . and I am not alone in this—there are others also of the priesthood who are asking themselves the same question—I believe he is who he has claimed to be, the Son of God, the long-awaited One. The Promised Messiah."

Ezra leapt to his feet. "You are talking foolishly! Do you not realize what those words could cost you?"

Justus sat silently. His shoulders slumped. When at last he spoke, his voice was strong. Resolute. "Yes. Yes, I believe I do."

Then his head lifted and his shoulders straightened. "But it is a cost I must be willing to bear. To deny it would cost me far more."

CHAPTER TWENTY-NINE

The Challenge

Wandering the city streets, Simona knew she was getting farther and farther from her former home. What was Enos doing now? Had his anger cooled with the coming of a new day? Would he be able to go back to his classes to prepare himself for the prestigious position he so desired?

What was happening in the city around her? Had they recovered the stolen body of Jesus? Who would steal a body from a tomb—the place where the deceased should rest in peace? The place considered by most to be sacred? And what would anyone do with a body?

Her thoughts went further. Why did Jesus die? If he was the Messiah—and she had been so sure in her heart that he was—why did the Lord God allow him to die with his mission incomplete?

She was not a scholar, but bits and pieces of her brother Benjamin's recited lessons niggled at the back of her mind. Were there not prophetic Scriptures about what was to happen with the coming of the new king? She searched her memory for them but she was unable to put the pieces together. Something about someone coming first to prepare the way. Was he to be a prophet? Simona did not know of anyone heralded as such a person.

There had been stories about a man who was baptizing in the Jordan, but he had been killed by wicked King Herod. There was also something about someone entering the city on a donkey. Both Benjamin and she had laughed at that story. It did not seem like the proper way for a king to arrive to begin his reign. Surely a king would ride in on a warhorse. Simona was sure there were other pieces to the puzzle but she couldn't remember them or put them in context. She would need to ask Benjamin.

Benjamin! Oh, if only she had some way to make the journey home to her mother and brother. She longed for them with her whole heart.

But her return would be in shame, head bowed low. She'd been rejected. Divorced! Accused of adultery. There was so much shame involved in her present situation. Could she really go home again under the circumstances? Her mother would be so angry. Would she still claim her? Take her back? Likely not.

It would be better to stay in this strange city and see if she could eke out her way, perhaps as a servant for someone. She did know how to do household chores. Her own mother had taught her. But how did one make connections? Where did one go to find employment? Simona had no idea. She wished she had someone to ask. If only she could find the widow Mary, she was certain she could get some answers.

But even as those thoughts came, she realized that the widow Mary might not wish to have a divorcee in her home either. Not one charged with adultery. Simona could not prove her innocence. She felt branded. Tarnished. An outcast. There were ways for widows to find help and support. Not so for those charged with adultery.

She pulled her shawl more closely about her face. She did not wish to be seen, to be recognized. Who would want to have any association with her now? She was on her own in a strange city that felt foreign and unfriendly. It was not like the small village in which she'd grown up. She did not know how to navigate her way to meet her own needs.

Her first need was nourishment. She'd had nothing to eat or drink for many hours and her body was demanding food and water. Already she felt dizzy and weak. Where did one find help in a city this size? She staggered on.

It was a simple trough for watering animals. She saw a man lead his donkey away from it, drips of water still falling off its muzzle. Simona did not hesitate. She walked directly to the channel and dipped in her hands. It felt warm to her touch—but it was wet. Water. She cupped her hands and lifted them to her lips, then cupped and drank again.

She must remember where she found it. Her eyes lifted to study the street, the surrounding buildings. She saw nothing familiar but took note of what was around her.

She was not in the best area of the city, she was sure. The buildings looked old and unkempt. The people who crowded the streets were not well-dressed. Two women walked together, their faces hidden by plain, unadorned shawls.

Another scruffy-looking man with a donkey was making his way toward the trough. Simona knew that she should move on. She dipped her hands once more, turned her back to the man, and drank the tepid water. Then she pulled her shawl closely about her face and continued on down the street.

It was already getting hot. The sun had climbed steadily into the sky as Simona wandered through the streets. She was still lost.

Uncertain and desperately needing nourishment. What should she do? What could she do? Her options were limited.

"I haven't prayed," she scolded herself, and she stepped aside and pressed close against a raw brick building. It was not a long prayer, but a desperate one.

Do not panic, said the voice within her. *Stop and think.*

Simona withdrew, as much as she could under the circumstances, for the street was now busy with scurrying bodies.

Think! What resources do I have? The question seemed moot. She had nothing. Not a coin in her possession nor a skill that was usable in her present circumstances.

And then she remembered the costly robe that she had bundled in her blanket. Nearby, to her left, a path led from the street to—the sound of movement. She wasn't sure what she'd find, but she decided to take the path.

She hadn't traveled far when she began to recognize the sounds of many voices. A market? She was quite sure that it must be. She moved toward it. Where there was a market there were people. Not people hurrying along a busy street, anxious to get somewhere—but people who sold and purchased wares. Would anyone there be interested in her robe?

She had no idea of its worth or the amount of coin it had taken Enos to pay for it. She did not expect to get its full value, but even if she could gain enough to put some food in her hungry stomach, it would be of help. Her steps quickened.

The closer she got, the louder the voices became, and as she rounded the last corner, there was the market to her right, stretched out before her like a sea of color and noise and shifting parts.

She stood and looked. Her eyes passed over it front to back, end to end. The stalls seemed to stretch on and on. She could smell sweat and dust and animal droppings. She wrinkled her nose. A market was not really a pleasant place to be.

But she could also smell food. She moved toward the aroma. Was it roasting fish? A stew? She wasn't sure.

She was eager to find out. But first, she needed to see if there was a vendor interested in her very expensive robe.

The pilfering of the fees had not been going well for Enos. His present partner kept him on edge, preventing him from any bold moves in selecting coins to slip into his little belt pouch. He had long since come to realize that words, meant to be distractions, would not work with this young man. It seemed that his eyes never left the hands of Enos.

Only now and then could he manage to slip a coin into his belt container. Most often, they were the smaller coins. They did little to help Enos with his present living conditions. As a Pharisee in training, he still kept his small home. But he occupied the home alone. Not even one servant was on hand to help him with his daily care or comforts. He was free to take meals with the other trainees, but they were simple meals. Not at all pleasing to his palate. He longed for the tastier dishes that he had been accustomed to when Hiram had been in his kitchen. Hiram had been expert in making even simple ingredients into a mouth-pleasing dish. How Enos longed to have him back again.

He had no idea where Hiram had gone. But even had he known, there was no hope of tempting him back with the few coins Enos managed to add to his stash week by week. He was getting nowhere.

For this reason he was in a sour mood when he arrived to join his partner for the daily collection. He might as well just tell his superiors that his studies were taking more of his time and he would need to withdraw from the daily gathering of Temple fees. But he hated to lose even the little that he'd been gleaning daily.

Seth greeted him in the same colorless manner that he always did. Enos had not yet figured out this young man. He seemed shy and withdrawn and rather short of energy and wits. Yet according to reports he was doing well in his studies. More than well. He often topped Enos in the lessons.

This, too, rankled Enos. How could one who appeared so void of intelligent thought do so well in his studies? Had he found some way to cheat his way through? No, that could not be. Seth didn't have enough faculties to match wits with their Pharisee teachers. They closely watched the students they were mentoring.

Now, Enos returned the nod offered by Seth as they picked up the empty coin bags and proceeded to the first vendor. Enos did not try to engage the young man. He had already found that he got little vocal response.

Enos muttered the fee to the nearest Gentile merchant, held out his open palm, raised his eyes to meet Seth's, and then dropped all the coins he'd collected into the bag that Seth held out to him. He hadn't felt safe in flipping a single coin into his own pocket. Seth's eyes had been firmly fixed on the process.

The next transaction was much the same. Enos reached out, closed his hungry fingers around the money. But once again, knew he was being watched. Each coin was dropped into the bag that they would take to the priests. They moved on.

The third vendor managed the largest table of goods for sale. His fee was double what the other men were charged. Here Enos always hoped for at least one coin of higher value. To his delight he spied one particularly large coin among the cluster.

This was his moment. Enos closed his hand slowly around the payment and let his fist fall to his side where it was hidden from Seth. He pressed his thumb into the cupped palm and carefully flicked one of the small coins away. It worked perfectly. The little mite clinked on the stone pavers, tumbled for a moment, and then rolled across the courtyard a short distance. All eyes followed the mite, giving Enos one stolen moment to lift the valuable coin from the center of his fist and secret it away.

Once more he dropped the remaining contents of his hand into the bag. Seth seemed none the wiser. "Sorry," Enos smiled. "Guess I need to be more careful not to drop any."

As usual, Seth just shrugged a careless shoulder. Though he added the stray that he'd turned his back to retrieve from the ground. It fell with a high-pitched clink.

Seth gave the bag he held a bit of a shake, a habit that had always irked Enos. Whether it was to rearrange the weight at the bottom of the bag or just to hear the jingle of the coins, Enos didn't know. But it was annoying.

They moved on down the row of vendors. They were almost done for another day. It was soon time for the evening meal to be served. Enos pretended to be hungry, but in fact he was in a hurry to get to a place of privacy so he could study the worth on the large coin in his belt.

Excusing himself as soon as he and Seth returned to the common halls, Enos headed for his own private quarters. As the outer door banged shut behind him his hand reached into his private pouch and withdrew the heavy coin. Even Enos was surprised at the potential worth of the gold he held in his hand. Now the problem was going to be how to get it exchanged so that he would be able to use lesser coins in daily life. But that was a pleasant problem to have, one he was pleased to contemplate.

He went to his small stash, withdrew a few smaller coins that would easily pay for a generous meal at his favorite city eatery. Then, leaving the gold coin and burying the small bag deep within its place of hiding, he left. His mood had just changed for the better.

Strangely, for just a moment, he wished Simona was still with him so he would be able to boast about his new wealth.

Simona approached the market stall timidly. What did she know about the value of goods? Yet even if the robe provided her with enough so she might feed her empty stomach, it would be of more worth to her than the garment she now held. She noted that the man had looked up as she approached and his eyes had dropped to the robe.

"May I help you?" he queried, his eyes still on the garment.

Simona took courage. "I find it necessary to sell this robe," she said without preamble.

"Is it your property?" was the first question from the doubter.

Simona's reply was heavy with reproach. "Of course, it is mine! Would I sell something that belonged to another?"

The man's eyes told her that indeed he thought she might.

"It was a gift to me—from my husband." That claim sounded strange, even to Simona's ears.

"My—my former—husband. He has now—now departed."

Well, it was true. Sort of. She had not claimed that he had died—but she didn't correct the man when he came to that conclusion. If she were totally honest, she would need to admit that she was the one who had been forced to depart.

"My sympathy," said the stall owner. Simona felt that his sympathy was no closer to the truth than her own words had been.

But the man had turned back to the robe. Simona saw his eyes light up. Sympathy for a needy widow or not, she was sure that he was already figuring in his mind the money he would make in purchasing the fine robe and then returning it to the seller's market. "I may be able to help you."

Simona was not experienced in dealings, but she recognized the words as those used by one who wished to make a sizable profit.

He named a price. Still, he had not looked up at her. She felt certain the robe was worth much more than that.

Simona felt a nudge at her elbow and turned to see that the man from the next stall had wandered nearer. He too reached out a hand to judge the worth of the robe on the table. Without even being invited to join the bidding, he jumped in. "I would up that by ten percent."

The head of the first man jerked up. He had not expected to have competition. He frowned in annoyance. "I do not believe the lady was speaking to you," he hissed.

Simona quickly took advantage of the situation. "I am needing to sell this valuable, never-worn garment—and I am quite willing to sell to the highest bidder." She turned to the man at her elbow. "Of course, you are invited to be included in the transaction." She used the word she'd heard Father use in his shop, looking straight into the eyes of the angry man who had made the first ridiculously low offer. "I know it is of far greater value than I have just been offered. I will seek another vendor if neither of you is serious about paying a reasonable price."

The competing vendors stood for a moment and frowned at one another. Simona wondered if, being side by side, they often competed.

Simona laid her hand back on the robe. She wanted the two vendors to realize that she was the owner of the item at hand. Neither would possess it unless she accepted the offered price. She had no idea what that price should be, but until one or the other stopped bidding, she would claim the garment as her own.

As the bidding war went on Simona's eyes widened. Was the robe really worth that much? She had hoped for a few coins so that she might purchase a meal or two while she sorted out what she could do to care for her future needs. What she was hearing now may even buy her transportation to get home to her own village—and still have leftover coins to help her family.

At last the bidding stopped. The two men glared at one another. The second vendor, who had joined in uninvited, was the winner.

"And I will watch you—carefully—as you count out the coins, to be sure that you actually pay this woman what you have just promised," the first man muttered to his rival.

Simona felt relief. She might not have noticed if the buyer had chosen to short her of the offered price. Though she was comfortable adding long columns of numbers, she had rarely handled coins before. Father had not allowed it.

Both men seemed to distrust one another as the coins were counted out. Simona watched them watching one another. She was confident that the proper price had been paid. The coins made a neat little stack on the table. Simona realized that she had no purse or any type of bag to carry them. She felt her face reddening.

She turned to the first vendor and nodded. "I see you have small bags for sale. I will take one please." The price for the bag was clearly posted.

Simona counted out the proper coins. Just as the man reached out to claim them, Simona looked up and nodded again and tossed another small coin into the pile as her thank you.

Then she scooped her coins into the purse, gave a quick dip of her head to both men, and left the market.

As she walked away, her thoughts turned to prayers of thanks. Her Lord had provided. She was now able to face the difficult days before her. The first thing she would do would be to purchase something for her empty stomach. She headed toward the smell of cooking food.

CHAPTER THIRTY

The Change

Simona still felt the heavy weight of the killing of Jesus, whom she had learned to trust. He was to have delivered her broken world from all its tumult and her subjected people from the hands of the Roman masters. And now he was gone. It still did not seem real, nor did it align with the feelings in her heart.

She could think of little else as she stumbled back across the market square after purchasing and consuming a serving of fish, a loaf of bread, and a refreshing drink of water. Her strength began to return, and her head began to clear as she walked. What was her next step? She still didn't know anyone in the city who would be able to help her.

As she reached the street and turned to her left, she saw people shifting this way and that, obviously trying to make way for someone coming from the other direction.

As her gaze moved over the crowd, she saw flashy robes and confident strides. Pharisees! The last people she wished to meet were Pharisees. She turned and retreated the way she'd just come. Scurrying to keep ahead of them, she took the first street that was an exit from the one she'd been traveling. She prayed it would not be the one on which they would continue their journey. But just in case it might be, she hurried forward, checking over her shoulder every now and then.

They didn't come her way. She breathed a sigh of relief and began to look around her. Where was she? Nothing she was seeing was familiar.

She was still wandering and wondering how to find her way when she heard someone among the crowd call out, "Simona?"

It was a woman's voice, and when Simona looked up to see who had called her by name, she was surprised to see Esther, the maid who had cared for her when she'd been at the widow Mary's. "Esther! I cannot believe—"

But she got no further. Esther interrupted, "What are you doing here?"

"I am—am on my own now. I'm looking for a place I can stay."

"On your own? Whatever do you mean?"

"It's a long story."

Esther shook her head. "You're really alone?"

Simona nodded her head. "Yes," she replied. "I am entirely alone."

"You must come home with me. It—I—don't have much—but it is shelter. The sun will soon be going down. You must get off the streets."

Simona made no reply but fell into step with the older woman.

They walked in silence, quick steps taking them to the safety of Esther's residence. By the time they climbed a small knoll and entered a plain wooden door at the back of a larger house, Simona was out of breath. "You live here? In this small lean-to?"

Esther had told the truth. It wasn't much. But it was shelter.

Simona was thankful to lay aside her blanket-wrapped bundle. It had become heavy as they hurried through the streets.

Esther threw aside her shawl and took a deep breath. "Now, you must tell me what you are doing out on the backstreets of Jerusalem."

Simona spilled it all out in one quick, long breath. She'd been put out. Divorced. Sent away. She had not done what she'd been accused of doing, yet her Pharisee husband had been angry because she'd believed the Prophet was the true Messiah. "And now—what does it matter?" Simona ended her discourse. "They've killed him on a cross and have stolen away his body." Tears threatened to roll down her cheeks.

"You haven't heard?" Esther sat up and leaned forward.

"They *have* found his body?" Simona asked hopefully.

"No—no—they have found *him*—or rather he has found *them. Us.*" Esther was smiling even as she said the words.

"What are you saying?" asked Simona, shaking her head. She had no idea what the woman was talking about.

"He is *alive*! Oh, I have not seen him myself. But he came to a gathering of the disciples. He talked to them—ate bread with them. They didn't find him in the tomb because he has risen. It's true. He *is risen*."

Both women were weeping tears of joy by the conclusion of her words.

Was it possible? Could it be? Simona was still shaking her head, needing assurance. "You're certain?"

"I am sure. He is as alive as you or me. One of the former Temple priests who knows the widow Mary has gone back to the Scriptures and put all the pieces of the prophets of old together. We should have known. Should have realized! It's all there. All fulfilled."

"Then they'll accept him. As real. The leaders? And priests? We'll all be able to . . ."

But Esther was shaking her head. "Sadly, no. Most of them still refuse to believe. Many of the true believers have needed to go into hiding. Most of the Pharisees and Sadducees and many of the Sanhedrin strongly deny that it is so. They still maintain that someone is playing tricks on them. That Jesus is still dead and his body has been hidden away."

"But who would do that—hide a body?"

Esther shook her head. "No one who is a true believer."

Simona wished to hear more. Who had seen the Master? When? What had he said?

Esther shared all the information that she'd heard from fellow believers but there was still so much that they didn't know, especially the answers to Simona's questions about the future.

"When can we see him?" Simona could feel her throat tighten at the thought. "I want to meet him." It was little more than a whisper.

"I don't know. He comes—then leaves again."

"Where does he go?"

"He doesn't say."

"So what are we to do?"

"We wait. We wait for his instructions. He'll tell us what we are to do when he's ready."

Wait? Hadn't she already done that for so many months? It seemed impossible to one who longed to see him.

Enos had talked to one of the money changers at the Temple. This was a man with whom he'd had previous dealings. He was a man that Enos believed would be able to keep their business private.

But first he must be tested. So Enos pretended interest in the world of coin. The man had previously enjoyed any chance to show off his knowledge of foreign currency and was more than happy to share with Enos even more than he wanted to know.

So, it was revealed easily that the coin he'd garnered was a Roman gold coin. Many Jews from Rome came back for the Passover celebration so that news was not surprising. It was a bit harder to get information about the value of the coin without arousing suspicion. The donor who had spent it must have been a wealthy tradesman anxious to prove to God his great devotion by the size of the sacrificial animal he'd purchased. Enos did not dare to get too specific but gathered from what the man said that this coin would be worth a year's wages. It was hard for Enos to refrain from showing his delight.

"Where would one be able to convert to common use such a large sum?" was his next question.

"Well, that's a bit much for a table like mine. But the Temple treasury is often able to manage something of that value," the good man responded. "They have coinage from many foreign countries—from the smallest to the greatest values. They have ways to work with the governments of most of the countries where the tradespeople also travel. Coin is converted back and forth via the trade ships or caravans, depending on the nearness of the country where it originated."

Enos had no idea the Temple was so involved in foreign exchange. He thanked the man for his informative chat and left for home. He knew that the Temple would be of no assistance to him, however. He'd never dare to show up with a coin of such value. Any story he concocted would immediately be suspect.

But the information had been helpful. He had a coin of great worth. It pleased him just to know it was in his possession even though it was beyond his use for the present. It was gold. It would not go down in value.

He left for home earlier than usual, wishing to have another look at the impressive coin. As he reached to open his door a peculiar feeling went all through his body. It stopped him short, hand still on the door pull.

Nonsense, he told himself. *It's just because I'm still not used to coming home to a house that is totally devoid of other occupants. Once I'm able to convert the coin, I'll hire staff again.* He opened the door and stepped in.

There they sat. Five of them—a mix of priests and Pharisees—at his table with his bag of stashed coins spilled out before them on his table. And in the very middle of the pile was the Roman gold piece.

Fear washed through him, followed quickly by raging anger. "What is the meaning of this?" he barked. "Why have you dared to invade my private quarters?"

The man of highest rank merely pointed to the display of coins.

"Am I not allowed private funds? Coins to pay for what I need?" Enos hissed.

"Not this one," said his superior. "You see, this one . . ." He pinched the gold piece between thick fingers. "This one I placed with my own hand at the table of Lucius the dove seller this morning. It has been marked you see, right here, so there is no mistaking it. Two of my fellow priests were with me at the time and can verify my story."

So, Seth had been a *plant.* They'd been watching Enos.

The large man in his colored robe spoke again. "So, what did you hope to gain by stealing from the Lord? Surely you would know that we do not take the treasury of our Temple lightly. These are gifts meant to care for the House of the Lord and the work that has been entrusted to us. As you can imagine, we, your superiors, are most disappointed in your conduct. Never has one been so brazen as to try to take from the Temple what is not his—nor ours—but God's."

"It was taken from a vendor," Enos choked.

"It was to go into the treasury—directly into the Temple resources."

Enos cast a sideways glance toward his door. The man at the table noticed the slight movement of his head.

"There is no use trying to run. We have guards just outside the door. They carry spears with tips that were newly sharpened just this morning. And they are trained to use them well. You may as well sit down, young man. At least a sincere confession may take some of the weight of guilt from your soul."

Enos did not respond. Nor did he take a seat. He was far too busy mentally searching for a way out of his dilemma. At the present all his brain was telling him was just how much he hated the young man Seth.

To suggest that the coin must have caught on his long sleeves as he'd faltered to recover one that had fallen to the pavement, that he hadn't noticed it until he was home and was planning to bring it back directly in the morning, would be sheer foolishness. In fact, anything that he could say would be foolishness.

He nodded silently and took the offered chair. Even as he sat, he wondered if there was some way that he could switch the blame to Simona. But no, that would also be foolish. Simona had never set foot on Temple premises.

"We're calling together a full assembly in the first hour of the day tomorrow. The crime will be judged by an official committee and the sentence passed down. It will be decided whether you will be given another chance, once your time of punishment is completed, or if you will be removed from all contact with the community of the Pharisees—or worse."

He need not explain what the *worse* would be. Enos knew that some crimes were punishable by stoning.

The man nodded his head and all of the entourage stood with him. "We are assuming," said the man in charge, "that all of the coins in this bag have been stolen in the same way—so we are removing them all and placing them back in our coffers where they belong." He cleared his throat and looked down toward Enos once more. "As the first hour begins, precisely. Be there!"

Enos watched as all of his monetary wealth was swished into the cloth bag and carried out with the departing officials. Once the door closed and the sound of their many sandals flapping along the pavers faded, Enos stood again to his feet, banged his fist on the table and released his rage in a torrent of angry curses.

Then he spun on his heel. There was no way he would remain come morning. No way. He would devise a plan that would take him far from the city. He had the entire night to make his escape. Thought by thought the gears of his mind worked toward a solution.

But what if they had posted a watch at his door? He would use the window from Simona's room. They all knew that he now lived alone. Hopefully, they would not think about the rear window.

He had little time for preparation. But there was little to prepare. He had no money, no weapon, no food in his home, and few clothes except the garb of a Pharisee. He could hardly travel in the flowing, colorful robes. The few things he would take with him could be gathered in five minutes. He did snatch up his Pharisee belt with the hidden pouch. Who knew if it might come in handy somewhere along the trail?

Stealthily he entered Simona's vacated bed chamber and crossed, without light to the room's one window. He stood for several minutes, studying the outside darkness for movement within the deep shadows. He could make out the small fountain, now devoid of the sparrows Simona had pampered. They had long since learned that there would be no more crumbs.

After some minutes, he lifted the lattice screen aside carefully, eased his body out and dropped the short distance to the ground. A barrel in the corner of the courtyard provided him with a way to scale the wall.

He dropped into the alley, then cautiously started down the backstreet that held the deepest shadows. By the time the rising sun touched the city, he planned to be many miles away.

CHAPTER THIRTY-ONE

The Hardship

THE LITTLE LEAN-TO WAS neither roomy nor warm. Esther shared what she had, but Simona found herself thinking of the heavy robe she'd just sold at the local market. It would have felt so good to be able to spread it over her to hold back the chill of the night.

She was nudged awake by a hand on her arm. It was Esther urging her to rise. "I'm going to join others for a prayer time," she said in a quiet voice. "Would you like to come?"

Simona didn't need a second invitation. She would have agreed fervently had Esther not cautioned her with a finger lifted to her lips. "If we wake the rooster he makes one awful racket," she whispered.

Simona nodded. She looked forward to meeting the rooster in the daylight. They left as stealthily as they could, Esther casting nervous glances toward a small shed at the back of the property that served as a coop.

The sun had not yet made an appearance, nor was the world

in total darkness as they hurried down the street together. When Simona felt they were far enough away she dared to whisper, "Where are we going?"

"Several of us meet at the back of the baker's shop. There are many small groups that spend time in prayer each morning before we start our day. We can't do so openly, so we have organized small groups scattered throughout the city. Some of the disciples have a much larger group that shares a residence and its courtyard. But there's no place where we could all fit together—except the Temple. Few of us are that brave. So we share. And we exchange messengers back and forth so that we can keep up with the news of Jesus. We're very cautious because the Pharisees and the Temple leaders still reject Jesus as the Messiah."

"Would they make trouble if they knew you were meeting like this?"

"We expect they would. There have been threats."

They walked in silence for some time. Simona was thankful that Esther seemed confident as they weaved in and out of streets and back alleys.

"We're almost there," she turned to whisper. "How do you wish to be introduced?"

The question caught Simona by surprise. She was about to reply, "Simona," when she realized that her name now came with complications. She was no longer Simona, wife of Enos. Nor did she dare to shame her father by calling herself Simona, the daughter of Amos.

Who was she? She certainly did not wish to be introduced as Simona, divorcee of . .

It suddenly hit her that she didn't need to be Simona any longer at all. She could be Mary again now.

"Can you just say . . . Mary?"

"I suppose. But there are several Marys among our large group."

It was true. There would always be other women with the name of Mary. So how could she be identified? Many were known by their occupation. At the present time she had no occupation. Her home village was so small and unknown that its name would be meaningless to any of those living in Jerusalem.

Esther spoke again, "For now I'll just say *Mary*. We'll figure out what it will be later."

Mary nodded. It would be nice to be Mary again. Still, it did remind her that she would need to find some type of work so that she could have a place of worth and identity within her new community.

Esther had cautioned that the group practiced quietness. Even as they prayed together their voices were not much more than whispers. They scattered about the limited space in groups of two to four and shared softly with one another. As they came and went, they did so quietly, by twos or threes, leaving in different directions, at different times, so that they never appeared as a single group on the street.

Mary was introduced to the individual attendees in hushed tones and welcomed with smiles and nods. It was enough.

Never had she realized before how special it was to be part of a body who shared beliefs. She was no longer alone. She had community now. Even though the relationship was guarded and secret, it was there. It was real. It was special in a way that nothing in her young life had ever been.

How she wished that her mother and Benjamin could share the experience with her. And, her father—oh, if only her father had accepted that Jesus was the Promised Messiah of their people.

Tears rolled down her cheeks as she thought again of the father that she'd loved dearly, who had decided that he didn't need a Savior. The old way in which he'd lived his life was enough. Why would he change? If the Messiah came, as promised, the priests would let the people know.

But the priests, who should have seen the fulfillment of the long-held promises, did not let the people know. They closed their eyes to truth and carried on. Only a few, here and there, reached out to embrace the one called Jesus—and for doing so, were stripped of their positions of prestige within the Jewish community of worship.

By joining with the cluster of believers, Mary also found employment. She was offered work in the same bakery where her small group met. The baker supplied stalls in three downtown markets with daily bread. They, in turn, sold loaves to the public.

Mary not only worked over the ovens but also wrapped packages for delivery. She counted out the quantity in each bundle and marked the price on its tag. She even marked the number of coins that the couriers would need to collect for each of the parcels since many of them were young boys who hadn't been allowed the privilege of education.

So life moved on, week by needy week. But Mary no longer felt alone. This situation might be difficult, she might return at the end of a busy day feeling weary and still confused by the world in which she lived, but there was hope.

Jesus was alive. The number of believers was continuing to grow. Like many others in her new community of believers, Mary hoped each day that she might be one of the blessed who would be able to serve her Master when the time came for him to establish his earthly Kingdom.

Enos had no funds, no direction, no transportation, so he kept to the fields, the shadows, the unworn paths. He was hungry and tired by the end of each day, but there was little food and little sleep. He wished he had at least pulled a blanket from his bed. The nights were cold and his present garment was not meant for warmth. He wrapped it as closely as he could about his curled position and tried to get some rest. But his body would not cooperate. He was not used to going without. He'd never needed to do so.

He decided to get up and take to the dirt trail again. There was enough brightness from the moon for him to feel some confidence. No honest citizen chose to travel by night, so Enos would take advantage of the well-worn paths until the sun ushered them into another morning. At least the activity might serve to keep his body reasonably warm.

As light dawned, he left the well-traveled roads and again chose his own way through the hills. He was wandering deeper and deeper into unknown and uninhabited territory. He found a small stream. The shallow water was a bit overwarm, not as refreshing as he wished, but it was needed. He also found some low bushes with some kind of berry not familiar to him. He stood, watching birds come and go. If the birds fed upon them, he considered them safe for human consumption and hastened to take advantage of what remained. It did little to ease his hunger but did revive his energy to some extent. He continued on, deciding to keep watch in the tufts of growth as he traveled, hoping to find more berries along the way.

He was soon deep into the hills. This was uninhabited territory. This was what he had been warned to avoid as a boy who wished to explore the world around him.

His father had told him with great emphasis that bandits

occupied such areas and they would not hesitate to take advantage of whatever possessions a small boy might be carrying.

They were evil, and fierce, and strong, and merciless. His father had painted such frightening word pictures that Enos and his friends never wandered toward the hills.

He found himself watching each shadow, peering toward each bush or stone outcropping. It was true that he was no longer evading but actually searching for the bandits, but he still feared them and did not wish to be caught off guard.

His intention was to join them. They were the only part of society that he felt might welcome him. After all, he was practiced in thievery, though he had to admit that his most skillful efforts had not gone well.

He was certain that he could learn if they were willing to teach him. He couldn't think of any other way to keep body and soul together now that he had offended the priests and the Pharisees. Surely, even now, they would still be searching for him in every town. Who knew what evil intent they would be planning should he be found? Enos did not wish to find out.

He found more water. It looked like a stagnant pool—but again he took advantage of it. The day was getting hot. He glanced around for shade. He needed rest. He'd been pushing forward with all his strength. The few berry bushes that he found were not enough to sustain him.

He found a spot that was shaded from the afternoon sun and settled on some sandy soil. Though it was rather uncomfortable his fatigue brought sleep within a few minutes. But not for long.

First, something jabbed at his ribs. In his semi-wakefulness he tried to push it away but it would not budge. His eyes flew open and he reached for the club he'd placed just beyond the spot where he lay. A leather-clad foot stepped firmly on his hand. His eyes switched down to whatever it was that was still hurting his ribs. It was a long weapon pinning him, and on the other end of it was a grizzled, ferocious-looking man of the hills.

Enos was barely able to squeak out the words, "I have come to join you."

Day by day, as Mary and Esther joined with other believers, they paid attention to the bits of news that got passed from mouth to mouth. They often longed for the entire story and hoped that the portion they received was factual. But they were always eager to hear more of their Messiah. Even the short reports brightened their day.

Jesus had met with two of his followers on their way to Emmaus. He'd explained many things to them, taking them back to the words of Moses and the various prophets of old.

Jesus had also met with larger gatherings of disciples on more than one occasion. The exciting thing was that he'd promised a new Spirit who would travel with them and be their daily guide and director. This Spirit would live *within* them, and so would be their constant companion and mentor. The sad part was that Jesus also said that this Spirit would be given *in place of* his physical presence. He still planned to go back to his Father. That brought grief to his followers. Jesus again reassured them.

But there was something else. It was repeated many times over that he had also promised to come back once again. Though, when he was asked when that would occur, his answer had been evasive. It was not for them to know, he'd said. Only the Father knew when that would be.

The words brought sadness to troubled hearts. Why did he plan to go back to the Father when his task on earth wasn't yet completed? They didn't wish to lose him again. They were looking for redemption—now. They felt they'd suffered long enough at the hands of the cruel Romans—and even at the hands of their own leaders. They had longed for and prayed for the Messiah-King who had been promised so many years back. And they had joyfully accepted Jesus of Nazareth as the Promised One. Why did they need to wait still longer for his earthly rule? It was hard to understand. Hard to accept.

However, the promise that he would return was something to hang on to—to hold them steady while they waited. The prayer of each heart was that it would be soon.

Neither Mary nor Esther was with the crowd that gathered in the vicinity of Bethany a few days later, but they heard the story from many witnesses, over and over. At first, those with Jesus had been unaware as they gathered that this was to be another goodbye.

The Master seemed quiet and thoughtful as they walked together, some said. When they reached the place he had in mind on the Mount of Olives, he stopped and his eyes seemed to travel from face to face. One at a time, his gaze met the eyes of each person in attendance. Some said they thought they saw tears there. There was a moment of total silence. All attention was now on his face.

When he seemed sure that they were all attentive, he lifted up his hands and blessed them. It was a touching prayer. Communal, yet in some strange way, personal. Each one felt the prayer to be a special and significant blessing for him or her.

Then, as they watched, he began to slowly rise—up and up. Their faces lifted with him. It was slow at first and then it began to pick up momentum and they realized that he really was leaving just as he'd said. Most stood in silence. A few began to weep. It was true. What they were watching was really taking place. It was not a dream. At length he seemed to merge with the clouds—then he was gone.

Into the silence, someone spoke. "It's true. He is the Messiah—just as he said." And as one, they began to testify. He was the Messiah they'd been waiting for. They could hardly wait to get back to Jerusalem to share the news. To celebrate.

The crowd began to move toward Jerusalem. Cresting the Mount of Olives they could already see the Temple complex stretched out on the hill across from them, the House of God itself shining where it rose, so close at hand. Had anyone witnessed his ascension?

Some of the men began to run. Soon they'd reached the city and headed straight for the Temple where they knew many people would be gathered. They couldn't wait to share with others what had just happened.

Those who heard the news were astonished. Some joyfully accepted that he really had been the Anointed One. Others shrugged their shoulders and whispered something about it just being one more trick to deceive gullible people. They'd grown tired of all the claims they'd heard. But the unbelieving words didn't dampen the enthusiasm of those who believed. They stayed on, celebrating and sharing the great news as others appeared. The air was filled with praises to God.

CHAPTER THIRTY-TWO

The Encounter

MARY AND ESTHER JOINED the vast crowd who gathered for Pentecost. Word had passed from one group of followers to another that they would meet across town at the residence of one of the disciples. Some thought Peter, whose name was heard frequently among the groups of believers, might address the crowd. Mary and Esther discussed that fact as they wound through the streets to get to the place of meeting.

"I've been wishing to see this man Peter," said Esther. "I hear he speaks often at the Temple court and crowds gather to listen to him. He was one of the twelve who traveled with Jesus."

"Can you imagine what it would have been like to actually know Jesus? I would have loved to have been able to listen to his teaching." Mary paused for a moment, and then went on. "My father wished to see him—for healing. He was so sure that Jesus could heal his crippled legs that we set out for Jerusalem hoping to find him."

"Did you?"

"No, we never did. He'd left the area, they said. My father was never healed."

"I'm sorry," whispered Esther as she reached to touch Mary's arm.

Mary felt the tears coming as they did each time she thought of her father. "The saddest thing is that we became believers. Benjamin, my brother first. He heard Jesus preach—even watched as Jesus fed the people with fish and bread. So Benjamin believed. Then he came home so he could share his joy with the family. My father was very ill. But Mother—Mother believed. And I—I'd come home to see my father—then I believed as well. But Father—he couldn't understand. He—he put it off that evening—but—he didn't live till morning." She could not go on.

Again, Esther reached for her arm. "I'm so sorry," she said.

The street was becoming crowded with people going their way. It assured them that they were on the right road. But as Mary looked around her, she noticed many styles of dress among the group, both of the men and of the women. And then she began to hear strange words. Words she didn't understand. Mary hadn't realized that Jews from so many different nations were living in Jerusalem.

It was hard to find a place to stand when they reached the house where the believers were gathering.

As Mary and Esther moved through the crowd, strange things began to happen. First there was a roaring sound like a mighty windstorm inside the building. Soon it became even stranger as odd shapes, appearing like flames of fire, began to land on all the heads around them. The eeriness of the moment seemed to have the attention of everyone, and then people began to speak. But it was not all one voice, or even one language. There was a general murmur throughout the entire place, but even so, one voice did not seem to interfere with the voices of others—and even though all seemed to speak at once, each voice seemed to be distinct and separate. It was not confusion or chaos. It was a message, separate and apart for all who were gathered together.

All of the commotion drew a larger crowd of curious people. They seemed to just keep coming and coming. Several men stepped forward to stand at the front of the crowd.

"That must be Peter," Mary whispered to Esther, pointing out an imposing man near the center of the group. She felt a sense of awe. He looked so big, so masterful, yet so understanding. He raised his hand to stop the murmur that ran through the mass of humanity.

He spoke to the crowd, referring back to the prophecy of the ancient prophet Joel. In his prophecy Joel spoke of a coming day when God would pour out his Spirit on all people. He spoke of sons and daughters prophesying, young men seeing visions, and older men dreaming dreams. Both men and women would share in this new experience of worship of God.

The listeners were stirred as they heard the words of Peter. "What should we do?" they began to cry.

Peter had a ready answer. "Repent of your sins and turn to God, and be baptized," he told them. And many listened to his words. Many believed and followed Peter's admonition. Mary and Esther joined the group in another step of faith and obedience. About three thousand were added to the number of baptized believers.

It was with renewed assurance of faith that Mary and Esther made their way back to their small dwelling. They still lived in an uncertain world, but God, through the sacrifice of his Son Jesus and the presence of the Holy Spirit, would be with them each day. They would endeavor to be faithful until his promise of coming again would be fulfilled.

The name of Peter had become a familiar name among the community of believers. They also heard people speak of John, Philip, Stephen, and several others who were now involved in keeping the new group of believers who worshipped together, walking and working in unity.

But it was Peter who took the leadership. It was Peter who preached at the Temple. It was Peter for whom prayer was requested when he was arrested by the Temple officials and put in prison to await trial. And it was Peter for whom there were prayers of thanks when word was passed on that he had been led from the jail by an angel of God.

Peter soon became the voice of authority—the servant of God. So, it was not surprising to any of the group of believers when Peter led the newfound church forward.

There were exciting reports of miracles and healings such as Jesus himself had performed when he had still been with them—events much beyond what could be done in human strength or wisdom. Each story of the power of God at work through the followers of Jesus caused praise to be lifted heavenward. But to the doubters—the opposition—the news of miracles, of growth, was a renewed threat to their leadership. Opposition increased.

It was a tremendous blow to the entire believing community when Stephen was stoned by an angry mob because of his faith, his preaching. Especially so when this mob was comprised of Jewish brothers rather than anxious officials of Rome. If Stephen was not safe, were any of them?

The question was on everyone's mind. Several families were already feeling persecution in daily life, and threats were becoming more and more common. Even the baker was aware of this. One of his clients sent notice that he would no longer be buying his bread since he had an infidel working for him. Apparently, the infidel he had in mind was Mary. This former vendor was busy trying to pressure other vendors to also veto the baker's goods.

Threats and pressures came in many ways. More and more of the believers were dispersing to other, more hospitable, areas. It no longer felt safe to raise their families in a city that was hostile toward them. Often their own former neighbors and friends with whom they had shared worship at the Temple were now their enemies.

In small groups or family by family, they began to leave the city. And that quickly increased when a Pharisee named Saul, a man with intent to rid the entire area of the people who claimed that Jesus was the Messiah, took to the streets of the cities and towns to bring in those believers for trial, punishment, jail, or even death.

Mary and Esther chatted until deep into the night. It was clear that it was no longer safe to stay in Jerusalem. Esther had no family left in the area. Mary's mother and brother were many miles away.

Mary still had concern regarding the impact of her divorce. Would her mother believe her innocence? Was it worth the risk? Together the women decided that it was their only choice. They would need transportation to get to the village. They must search out a caravan heading that way and arrange to hire one of their camels. They could take turns walking and riding.

Esther, knowing the city much better than Mary, took the leadership. Day by day she attended the market, watching for a caravan that would be traveling to the north. It took several trips before she found one that would accept them as travelers. They would be leaving in two days. That did not seem like enough time to say goodbye to their friends still in the city and to prepare for the journey. But they accepted the offer.

Bright and early on the day appointed they hoisted the small bundles of their belongings and left for the place where the caravans departed. The sun was just beginning to show itself on the distant horizon.

As they hurried through the gate leading away from the city the women stopped short. There beside the path was a group of men in tattered clothes—half of them with hardly any covering. They were bruised and beaten and chained to one another and then to a thick post.

The pitiful cluster was far too close to the passing pathway. For a moment Mary and Esther hesitated. Neither of them wished to travel so close to those who were obviously criminals that the Roman soldiers had brought to the outskirts of the city. This same portion of the road was well known for its Roman crosses that were used with some frequency. Most avoided passing this way.

"What should we do?" whispered Esther nervously, drawing back a step.

Mary held her ground. "We have no choice. This is the only road to the caravan. They're in chains. They won't be able to harm us. Besides they look far too spent to even move."

It was true. The criminals looked as though they had already been beaten into submission and abused all along the trail. One looked half dead as he slumped earthward, just the chains from the stout post beside him still holding his body off the ground. Others were caked with blood and dirt. Some had ugly open stripes on their bare backs and shoulders from the whips that had been used.

"Just—don't look at them. Stay as far to the side as you can—and walk briskly," insisted Esther. And she set out to lead the way.

Mary was about halfway past when she distinctly heard her name. "Simona?" A chill ran through her body. Who would know her—and by that name?

She intended to keep on walking. But the same voice, not more than a whisper, repeated her name. She stopped and took another look at the badly beaten man who hung limply, supported by his chains.

"Enos?" she asked in disbelief.

The eyes lifted. It was Enos.

"Water," was his next word, though it was garbled.

Mary looked around. The only source of water she could see was an animal trough. She laid down her bundle and hurried toward it. With nothing in which to carry water, she scooped up as much as her hands could hold and hurried back to the man she'd once known as her husband. He drank thirstily and she rushed back for another attempt. He drank this too. It seemed to soften his parched lips so that his words were clearer when he spoke again.

"Simona," he managed, and his voice seemed to rise in its urgency. "The divorce I gave you—it's a fake. It's not from a man of law. I—I wrote it out myself. Tear it up. I know you were not guilty of adultery. I needed some charge against you. I had none. Throw it away. I—I am sorry—I . . ." His voice was fading again.

Mary leaned as close to him as she dared and, knowing their time would be short, spoke plainly what mattered most. "I believe in Jesus. I follow him. He says we are to forgive. I forgive you, Enos. I forgive you. He will forgive you too, whatever you've done. If you ask him, he will forgive you. That is his promise."

Just as she finished the last words she heard the rustle of armor nearby and a very angry soldier hollered, "Get away from those prisoners if you don't want to end up on one of the crosses with them."

She jerked away from Enos, grabbed her bundle from the ground and hurried to obey. She had just enough time to call back toward him, "Ask him Enos. Ask him."

"I've been such a wicked man," she heard him say.

"Ask him," she called back as she hurried on down the path to where Esther stood waiting, anxious and afraid. She heard his words, "Jesus! Messiah! Have mercy. I am a sinner—please forgive . . ." The voice faded.

Mary was in tears.

"Did he hurt you?" asked Esther with concern when Mary caught up to her.

"Yes, he did. A long time ago. But that is forgiven—now."

She knew that Esther had no idea what she was talking about, but now was not the right time to stop and explain.

She would always grieve for the man she had just witnessed in such a shocking condition. And all the more so because it seemed he was headed for one of the ugly crosses that stood on the nearby hill. The picture brought more unchecked tears.

A new thought came to Mary. The words Enos had shared were words that released her. She was not a divorced woman. The document had been false. She could tear it up and throw it away. She would never be accused of the ugly word *adultery*.

Having heard Enos ask the Lord for forgiveness, Mary prayed, "God—Jesus—accept his prayer—and forgive him."

CHAPTER THIRTY-THREE

The Journey

THE JOURNEY WAS NOT an easy one and this particular caravan seemed to dawdle on its way. Day by day they tramped north through the dusty landscape, toward the Galilee and on to the small village that Mary had once called home. And day by day, whether hot sun or drizzling rain, she asked herself the same questions. What would she find when she got there? Was her mother still there? And Benjamin? Had he gone back to where he had tended sheep before he'd heard the voice of Jesus and accepted his message to the people on that day? She prayed the same prayer over and over. "Lord, lead me. Lead us. We need your guidance and care."

Esther struggled with the burden of the difficult travel more than Mary, who was younger. To compensate, Mary tried to give her more miles on the back of the camel while she walked—but Esther took careful note of the passing of the day and insisted that Mary get her full share on the camel's leather saddle.

Day by day they plodded on. At night they tried to rest on the sandy ground, wrapping their simple blankets close about them. It was hard to remember, in the heat of the sun, how chilled the night could become.

One day, mid-journey, the caravan master simply refused to leave camp. His lead camel had developed a limp. All day he fussed over her. Applying warm cloths, then medication taken from his bag of herbs, then cloths dipped in the nearby stream of cool water that was on its way to the Jordan River.

Over and over he applied the same routine. Those traveling paced in frustration, hid as best they could from the heat of the sun, and tried to relax in the limited shade. Even the rest of the camels seemed to be angry that they were not allowed to carry on. They kept moaning and groaning and shuffling as far as their tethers would allow them to stray.

While stroking the soft tufts of fur beneath their camel's loose lower lip, Mary wondered why the other camels didn't take advantage of their day of rest. Then she realized that she was acting in the same way. Her only desire was that they could continue on in order to get the journey over.

The realization prompted her to deny her impatient mind and allow her own body to relax enough to release some of the aches and pains from walking and riding, stretching out the various parts of her body that were suffering fatigue.

Everyone seemed to feel relief when the caravan master checked the next morning and declared that his leading camel was once again able to continue. The line of beasts fell impatiently into proper order after urging one another on with their grunts and head butts.

It was Esther's turn in the saddle and Mary was thankful that she was the one who would walk. She needed some way to work off her impatience. At a frustratingly slow pace they were getting closer to her village and she could not wait to see what they would find.

But still, her thoughts returned to what she'd left behind. Enos would have been placed on one of the crosses. Such a cruel and unthinkable way to die. She again thanked God that Enos had taken advantage of Christ's open invitation to each sinner and had asked for forgiveness for his sins. She had no idea what all those sins might have been, nor did she wish to know. God was the one who kept the account. He was the one who cleaned the slate, erased the record of wrongdoing—for Enos, and for all those who asked for his mercy.

As the caravan drew to the side of the trail for their midmorning stop, Mary moved up beside Esther in case she needed help dismounting.

Though Esther looked fatigued, she managed a smile. "Are you seeing familiar landmarks?" she asked.

Regretfully, there was nothing yet that brought back memories. However, one of the drivers assured her that they would arrive at her small village before nightfall. There were still two more market stops on the way, but these shouldn't take long. It was just a matter of unloading some cargo and perhaps picking up items to carry forward.

As they moved on it was Mary's turn to ride but she begged off. She would walk alongside Esther, she told the driver, and let the animal have a bit of rest. For some reason that Mary could not comprehend, the camel seemed to know that the usual routine had been broken. At first it balked, refusing to leave without a passenger. Then it would not fall into proper line as the caravan prepared to continue.

The driver grinned. "Camels!" he quipped, "they are more honorable than men. They accept their duty and carry their load.

But do not try to overload them. No! They will refuse to take a step. You must treat them with honor as well."

Mary moved up beside the camel to make the creature content that she was fulfilling her duty and not leaving her passenger behind. She ran her hand over the shaggy neck. "Come, Bella, we're ready to move on now."

Without hesitation, the camel fell into proper line. But the animal's strides were much longer than Mary could manage and she found that she and Esther dropped farther and farther back in the line of forward-moving travelers. Bella accepted the fact. She seemed to believe that she'd offered her services and if her former passengers preferred to lag behind and eat trail dust, that was up to them. She was anxious to reach the place where refreshing water awaited the caravan.

It was just as the master had said. Both stops were cared for in quick order and the group moved on again. This time Esther was happy to take her place in the saddle once again. Mary was eager to walk on. Her own village was just beyond the next group of hills. She was so anxious to arrive that she knew she would never be able to sit aboard the camel's back. She needed to be free to set her own pace.

Once they disengaged themselves from the caravan and hoisted their small bundles of belongings, Mary could not wait to hurry through the streets to the family she hadn't seen since she'd been home to visit her ailing father.

The familiar questions returned. Were those who remained still okay? Had Benjamin stayed to care for her mother as he'd promised? Had he been successful in opening up her father's business once again? Were they still growing in their faith in the Messiah? Did they know what was happening to the believers in Jerusalem?

She had so many questions that she longed to pick up her dust-covered skirt and hurry toward their home. Only her respect for her culture and her concern for her traveling companion kept her from doing so. She would not leave Esther on her own.

But just up the street and around the bend was home. Mary grew more anxious with each step she took. What would she find when she knocked at the house?

Her mother opened the door. "Mary?" It was a question rather than a greeting.

Mary answered by throwing herself into her mother's arms and clinging tightly. She knew that her mother had received her answer from the way Mary's arms tightened about her, drawing her close. Tears flowed on cheeks but neither knew to whom they belonged.

"You're home! I've been praying. We heard such awful things about what is happening in Jerusalem. I feared for you—each day. And now you're here. Benjamin will be so relieved. He didn't know whether to go to Jerusalem and look for you, or stay home and care for me. We were so worried—but we took some assurance from the fact that you are married to a Pharisee. I reminded him that surely the mobs will not harm the wife of a Pharisee."

Mary eased herself back a step and reversed the direction of the conversation. "How are you, Mother?" she asked, lifting a hand to the woman's cheek.

Her mother grasped at Mary's hands. She managed a tight smile. "I am fine. Just fine—now that I know you are okay. And you? Why are you here—all alone?"

Mary managed a little laugh. "Well, I am not really all alone. My friend Esther is with me. She waits patiently just outside the door. She said she'd like to give us a few minutes to greet one another."

"Esther? I don't recall you mentioning Esther . . ."

"No, I don't suppose I did. She was my maid when I first went to Jerusalem—while I spent time training with the widow Mary—my mentor. Then we lost touch for some time. But God caused us to find one another again. We've been sharing Esther's rather small accommodation and working for the same baker."

Her mother's eyes showed surprise. "Working? Why? Where is your husband, the Pharisee Enos?"

Mary lowered her eyes and took a deep breath. "I am a widow, Mother. I've been on my own for the last several months." Mary hurried on before her mother could start asking questions. "Esther and I have been a part of the exciting group of followers in the city. The number has grown and grown since Peter has taken the leadership. There are . . ."

Her mother cut in. "We've heard there is persecution—that . . ."

"That's true. Many are leaving the city and going to safer places to share their new faith. Peter says that it's the way the Lord is building his church."

"Oh my!" Suddenly her mother released her hands. "You say you have a friend with you and here we stand and . . ."

It was a reminder to Mary as well. "I'll call her. She was resting on the side bench in the shade. It's been so warm for walking."

"You walked?" cried Mother as Mary passed through the door.

"No," Mary called back. "We rode a camel too—we took turns."

"Oh, my!" the woman repeated.

True to Esther's word she was resting on the side bench, which was still shaded from the afternoon sun.

"I'm sorry . . ." began Mary, "to leave you alone for so long. We . . ."

"I've been enjoying it. The sparrows have been entertaining me."

The sparrows. Mary thought of the hours that she'd spent with the sparrows while she'd lived with Enos. Indeed, they were entertaining. They had helped her through many lonely hours. She wondered who was looking after her sparrows now.

Esther stood and stretched. "I have aches in places I didn't know I had muscles," she admitted.

Mary smiled. She felt the same way and her body was much younger than her friend's. "I expect Mother is in the kitchen making tea," she said. "That's the first thing she does when her routine is interrupted."

Mary was right. When they entered the house, they could already smell the tang of freshly brewing tea. "Esther, this is my mother Hulda. Mother, this is my friend Esther. Had it not been for her I don't know what I would have done when I was left alone. She took me in and found me a job and has been like a sister to me ever since."

That brought a chuckle from Esther. "A much *older* sister as you can see."

But Hulda greeted the woman with a warm embrace. "I do thank you. I was so worried with all the reports regarding the situation in Jerusalem. But perhaps those reports have been exaggerated as they have traveled over the miles."

"No," Esther admitted truthfully. "I don't expect they have. Jerusalem is no longer a safe city for all who wish to follow our Master. And it seems to get more violent every day."

"Why?" asked Hulda. "I don't understand why there is such opposition. Why can't they see the fulfillment of the prophesies, at least? Everything is just as had been promised. He's come. At last, he has come! How can they not . . . ?"

"Blindness," cut in Esther. "The enemy has blinded them. Not only their eyes, but also their hearts."

There was another excited celebration when Benjamin returned home. He too could hardly believe that his sister was back safely with them once again.

After the requisite description of how they'd traveled, and a welcoming of their new guest, Benjamin accepted a cup of tea and sat down beside Mary. "Why are you here? Did your husband feel you needed a change of scenery or did he think the city was no longer safe?"

Mary knew she owed them some explanations—but now did not feel like the right time to share from her heart. "I'm alone," she said simply. "A widow. As such I've been living with Esther and worshipping with the followers of Jesus. We had a strong, growing community of believers, but it is now being persecuted by the Jewish leadership who still cannot accept that Jesus is the true Messiah for whom we've waited. Esther and I were advised to leave the city. Many others have fled as well. And I'm afraid that the days ahead will see many more moving to a safer place to protect their families."

It had been a long, hurried speech. Mary wished to get it all said so they could move on to other things. But the words brought back the emotion of it all. She stopped, shaking her head. "Jerusalem is in turmoil," she finished simply. "I have no idea what will happen in the future—but for now . . ." She sighed, unable to finish.

This time her brother's words held no trace of teasing. "I've heard such reports. Word comes with the caravans and with other travelers. Many don't feel safe to even go to the yearly feasts anymore—after the events of Passover and the commotion at Pentecost. Others claim that if you're still true to the teachings of Moses you're still safe in the city. You won't be persecuted."

Esther smiled. "Strange, isn't it? We as the followers of the Way are also true to the teachings of Moses. In fact, we're the ones who have accepted *all* of the teachings of Moses. We find in his writings and those of other prophets the very things that have been fulfilled in the coming of the Messiah—Jesus. We're the true believers."

CHAPTER THIRTY-FOUR

The Announcement

THE DAYS PASSED one by one. Each morning when Mary arose from her makeshift bed she pushed back the curtain and looked south in the direction of Jerusalem. Would this be the day they were all waiting for—when Jesus would return as he'd gone into heaven, in the sky above the Mount of Olives? Each evening came again with a shadow of disappointment.

It seemed that she grieved just a bit more with each day that took her further from the Lord's ascension and promise to return. "When, Lord?" she prayed again. "You said you'll be back. But when?"

Stories of oppression in Jerusalem increased. A steady flow of believers passed through their area, heading even further away from the hotbed of persecution.

News came with the caravans. Saul of Tarsus, the dreaded persecutor of believers, was heading north now. He was chasing down noteworthy witnesses for Jesus—all the way to the Sea of

Galilee and beyond. He was rumored to have permits given by the Sanhedrin itself to make arrests and to conduct prisoners back to their courts to be put on trial.

But these accounts could not be compared to the astonishment that followed. A believer returning from the far north made the whispered claim that this same Saul had actually converted and was now counted among the fellowship. Stories about how this had occurred varied widely, but the thread running through them all was that he was on a trip to Damascus to arrest those who had believed. There had been a turn of events when a voice from heaven spoke to Saul, striking him down in the road and leaving him blind. He was led by the hand for the rest of the journey and remained blind for three days, until God sent someone to pray for him. Through the experience, he became a believer.

There were also accounts of Saul's own flight. It was told that he'd had difficulty in getting accepted by those who felt certain his claim to be a follower of Christ was just one more trick to get access to their community of faith, to gather additional names to add to his scroll.

Mary's community discussed the rumors often when they met together. Could someone as violently against belief in Jesus change? Was it possible? Benjamin spoke out in favor. Mother was less convinced.

Gradually word came that this Saul truly was a changed man. In fact, his name had also been changed to Paul—by God himself.

Mary gasped at the words that followed. The woman who related this news went on to say that, as Paul, he'd been commissioned to go to foreign areas to take the words of Jesus to Gentiles.

It was too much to absorb. Mary's mind whirled with the implications of such a suggestion. "Oh, Lord Jesus," she pleaded, "have we been too slow in accepting you? Have you skipped past my people—your people—and offered your salvation to *them,* those pagan Gentiles? Our *enemies*?"

Mary found other stories far more pleasing, those that told of the continued ministry of Peter, and of John, and of Philip. More and more messengers were branching out from Jerusalem, and more and more believers were added to the new gatherings. And to her continued amazement, more and more affirmed the idea that the privilege of salvation, through Jesus, now extended to all who would believe—both Jews and Gentiles.

And still Christ had not returned.

Mary slipped out of her simple robe and slid under her covers for the close of another day. It was the first evening that she hadn't paused to look south before retiring to bed. A single tear slid down her cheek.

They had expected that his return would be soon. It was this single thought that helped them live from one day to the next, rarely making plans for the future. Gradually the unwelcome thought had become impossible to refuse. It might be a longer wait than they had anticipated. They needed to start to plan ahead.

The small house that had been occupied by Hulda and Benjamin was stretched to its limits with Esther and Mary joining them. At first, they accepted the crowded condition. It wouldn't be for long, they reasoned. But a day came when they decided they must talk about the situation.

Benjamin led the discussion. "There's an available house at the end of the street that I've been watching. It is now for sale and I've placed my offer on it. The elderly couple is going to live with a son in Damascus. I figured that my absence will free up the room I've been using. Esther can keep the storeroom upstairs that she's been using as a bedroom. Mary can take my bedroom, though it's small. And that will leave Mother in her own room. I realize that each chamber is small—but they'll be private."

The women had all been holding their breath. Now Hulda spoke. "Will you break bread with us? Daily?"

He shrugged. "I hadn't thought of that. But, yes. I'd enjoy sharing my meals with you—for now." He grinned again.

Mary, who thought she knew her brother well, recognized the grin. There was something he wasn't yet saying. "What does the *for now* mean?" she dared to ask.

"The home I plan to buy needs a bit of repair. But as soon as I have it ready . . ." He paused and grinned again. "I plan to make arrangements for my marriage."

"Your marriage? You haven't said . . ." There were too many questions bursting from Mary that needed to be asked all at once. "How much work will it take? Can I help . . . ?"

He waved a hand, leaned back in his seat, and smiled.

"You still haven't told us who it is that will be joining our family," Mary went on.

"It's Judith, the baker's daughter."

"I love Judith," said Mary.

"She'll fit very well into our family." There was relief in Hulda's voice and a smile in her eyes.

The days passed quickly. Benjamin spent many hours working on the repairs to his new home. Mary pretended she was helping by taking him fresh drinks of water or clumps of ripe grapes. The improvements added much to the small dwelling. She was sure that Judith would love it.

Things were also very busy at Judith's home. Her family too was excited about the coming wedding. One day soon they'd hear the village trumpeters make the announcement. Then they'd look out to see the groom being conducted to the home of Judith's parents to collect his bride.

Mary thought back to the elaborate setting for her own wedding to Enos the Pharisee. It all seemed so many years ago. This wedding would be different. There would be no bedecked cart with prancing horses, no elaborate banquet with rich wines and fancy delicacies, no wedding garment that cost a year's wages. Mary, looking back, knew that none of those things had resulted in a satisfying marriage.

Benjamin's planning produced a lovely wedding on a cooler day that allowed guests comfort as they watched the exchange of the promises. Mary noted that her brother's eyes could hardly leave the face of his glowing bride.

And Judith? Mary hoped and prayed that Judith would feel more comfortable in becoming Benjamin's bride than she had felt when taking up her position as a wife. Her brother and new sister-in-law certainly looked happy together—and they even looked relaxed as they took their position at the head of the banquet table after the ceremonies had ended.

Mary wiped at a tear that threatened to fall. She loved her big brother. He deserved every happiness that life could bring him. And Judith looked like the perfect woman to do just that.

For some reason the small home, still shared by three, seemed empty and quiet without Benjamin. Mary was very conscious that he had been the one with the positive outlook that had kept the home in good spirits. The three women who shared the home were prone to being introspective, serious, and concerned with the needs of each passing day.

At least she could still continue her work in Benjamin's shop. Esther had taken over most of the kitchen duties of the home. Hulda, who was having problems with a hip that caused pain and frustration, gave opinions and advice from her padded seat in a chair that her son Benjamin had built—just for her. She protected it with the ferocity of a den mother. Even when neighborhood guests dropped by, Hulda welcomed them warmly but claimed her own special seat.

The household managed to run smoothly. And the family felt complete again whenever they met with the few believing villagers who gathered for prayer and singing. Always the theme of their words was *Come, Lord Jesus. Rescue us from this world of sin.*

Months went by and the hills around them moved again from the heat of summer into the coolness of another autumn. Mary began to realize that they might actually usher in another series of fall celebrations before the Lord returned again. It seemed so long to wait—and wait.

Winter came. They got through its dreariness. Spring, as promised, followed. The news they received really had not changed. The church continued to grow. Persecution still happened. New leaders were added. Dear friends passed on. Another martyr was grieved. Still the world went on.

One early morning, Mary arose to the reminder that they were well into another spring. The sparrows were nesting nearby and feeding from the daily supply that Mary left for them. Again, her thoughts went back to the feathered friends she'd left behind in the yard of Enos. Was anyone caring for them?

For some reason she felt old. Weary. She knew that wasn't the case—nor was her age the reason for her heart's weariness. But she didn't understand why her thoughts gave such a slump to her still-young shoulders. Her mother and Esther were having a rare disagreement about the shopping list for the local market. She didn't wish to listen and she didn't wish to take sides. Instead, she slipped out the door while each was still expressing their personal point of view.

The streets were almost empty as Mary began her short journey. She lifted her eyes toward Jerusalem. "Today, Lord?" Again, she neither heard nor felt a reply.

She got to the building where Benjamin worked and let herself in to the back room. There would be no one in the shop. The workday had not yet begun.

She'd just taken her place and reached for a ledger when she heard a stirring in the room next to hers. Was someone there? Benjamin never came in so early. The day was always long enough, he'd told her. Why add to it by being there before one needed to be?

She moved quietly toward the sound. The door was open just a bit and she cautiously peeked inside. It was Benjamin. He was busy with tools. The one he held in his hands at present was for sanding smooth boards. What could Benjamin be building?

She was about to slip away quietly when he glanced up and saw her. He motioned her in. "You caught me," he said. There was a big smile on his face.

She looked down at the half-finished project on the near table. It looked like a baby cradle, and she turned her gaze to her brother. He was still grinning. "Are—is . . . ?"

He laughed outright. "Yes," he answered with a great deal of enthusiasm. "But don't tell Judith. She doesn't know yet."

"She doesn't know about the baby?"

"Not the baby, silly one. The cradle. She's quite aware of the baby. He's kept her stomach upset for weeks."

Mary smiled. She remembered her own upset stomach. The

thought brought terror rising in her eyes. She'd also been sick—for days and weeks. And she had lost her baby.

Would that happen to Judith? *Oh, God, please no. Please, please take care of Judith—and the baby.*

The news of the upcoming birth brought excitement to them all. On some days, Mary even forgot to look to the skies for the coming of her Lord. She refused to admit it, even to herself, but she did hope that she would get to meet this new little someone first.

Hulda was beside herself in her anticipation. As she sat in her special seat, handheld tools clicking as she made baby garments, Mary saw the gentle smile that seemed to light up her entire face. She had sent Esther to the market for the softest, purest, lightest wool that was available. She used it now and Mary knew that as she worked she also offered up prayers.

The baby was not due until September. And in a way, that made the summer limp along on slowly moving feet. On the other hand, the coming blessing helped each of the women to have hopes and dreams—and courage—once again. God was still a God of renewal.

Mary was at work when a young neighbor boy rushed in with a message for Benjamin. He was wanted at home. It was now mid-September, and Benjamin had been getting more fidgety with each day. Now he looked about to explode—or faint. Mary was not sure which. He tossed the board he'd been working on to Mary. She was glad it was small and that she'd been able to catch it. She had no idea why he threw it to her, or what she was to do with it. She laid it aside.

"What can I do?" she asked.

Benjamin seemed to be coming back to conscious thought. "The midwife—we need the midwife."

"She's already there," spoke up the young boy. "I was sent to get her first."

They started out together. Benjamin's longer strides had Mary struggling to keep up. She tried to distract him with meaningless discussion but he didn't seem to be listening. Her normally calm and relaxed brother was uptight and distracted.

When they arrived at his home it was Mary who went in to speak to the midwife. She was assured that things were progressing well. Judith asked to speak to her husband and Mary went to get him. At first he was hesitant but when Mary assured him that the midwife had given her permission, Judith was comfortable and the labor was just beginning, he followed her into the bed chamber.

Cautiously he approached his wife. She was not moaning and groaning as he'd been led to believe she would be. She even smiled as she reached for his hand. He responded, but he looked about to weep. Mary gave them a few minutes together, then seeing Judith's face begin to tighten as another birth pain began, she reached for her brother's arm, nodded to the midwife, and hurried Benjamin from the room. They retreated into the courtyard, where there was ample room to walk off his nerves.

It was well into the afternoon when Mary heard the cry of an infant. Benjamin stopped midstep and looked at his sister. Mary gave a slight nod. She saw Benjamin's locked fingers lift, even as his eyes lifted to the sky, and she knew that he was offering a prayer of thanks.

As difficult as it was for her to walk, Hulda was determined to see her new granddaughter. With Benjamin on one side and Mary on the other, they helped the older woman slowly down the street and into Benjamin's home. Esther, who had been invited to join the celebration, walked along with them.

A smiling Judith greeted them from her bed, where the new little one slept soundly on her arm. Benjamin lovingly lifted the baby and carried her to the chair where her new grandmother was waiting to be introduced.

Hulda was in tears. "There was a time—a long time—when I never expected to be so blessed," she whispered as she held the baby close.

Benjamin grinned. Now that the birthing was over and the mother and baby were both doing fine, his easy smile had returned.

Proudly he uncovered the tiny little feet that looked so small in her father's manly hand. "See, she has all her fingers and all her toes," he announced, happily. "I've counted them—twice."

There was happy laughter. *Benjamin has to make every event into comedy,* Mary thought with a smile. It was good to see him so relaxed again.

"And her name?" prompted Hulda.

Benjamin exchanged a glance with Judith. "We want it to be a special name—for a very special little girl. We first thought of Mary. And though Mary is a lovely name and many very special ladies are called Mary, it has become a bit common, which makes it hard to keep all the Marys easily identified."

He looked at Judith again and received another slight nod.

"We did find a name we both like—and since we also know a beautiful woman, whom we both love, who carried the name well"—he turned slightly toward Mary—"with your permission, of course, we have decided that we would like to name her Simona."

Simona? Mary could not have spoken had she tried. Simona? It was a pretty name. Enos had chosen well. She'd even learned to like the name—but the name also held memories of pain. Of rejection. What if—what if she was unable to separate the two?

Would the name always take her back to the difficult years of her marriage?

She looked again at the baby, sleeping soundly and securely in her mother's arms.

No, decided Mary as her thoughts shifted. *Benjamin is right. This sweet baby girl, bearing my name, will be the last piece of healing that I need. She'll make the name beautiful again. Simona.*

And then a strange, God-thing happened. A flash of memories took her back to her final goodbye to Enos and her plea for him to ask for God's forgiveness. She realized that she too, honestly and wholeheartedly, forgave him. It wasn't just words she'd spoken to Enos. It was truth. A truth that freed her heart to be able to accept and give love again.

CHAPTER THIRTY-FIVE

The Loss

MARY HAD NEVER REALIZED how quickly babies grew and changed. It seemed no time at all until little Simona was awarding those she loved with welcoming smiles. Then it was coos and giggles. Before they thought it possible, she was trying out words. Dada and Mama were first on the list. Aunt Mary sounded more like *Annmar*, sometimes hard to distinguish from her word for Grandma. Quickly she added such things as *ook* for *look* and *bye-bye* which came with the motioning waves of her little hand. *Come* was spoken with coaxing fingers.

She was a delightful child who soaked up love from her family and returned it tenfold. Even Esther, known to the small Simona as *Esser*, was included as her family.

As expected, Benjamin was a loving father, so proud of his baby girl and so gentle with the other woman in his daily care. He was also growing in his faith. Day by day he found ways to encourage fellow believers, to give aid to those in need, to ease the burden of a stranger—all in the name of Jesus.

It would have been easy to feel that the world was a wonderful place, were it not for the news that continued to come with the caravans and other travelers. Terrible things were continually happening to good people. Usually, it was against those who had become followers of the Christ. It was difficult for those who had carefully guarded the Scriptures of the past to understand that many of the verses they'd held dear and fought to protect had, indeed, been fulfilled. There was division now among those who previously stood together. Not en masse, but one by one, there were those who left the covenant of faith they'd clung to and become *infidels* in the thinking of their former companions.

It wasn't an easy choice and often came with great sacrifice. But it was the right choice, the choice that brought comfort to their hearts even as it often brought suffering to their bodies.

And there was constant friction between the Jewish hierarchy and the Roman officials. Since the Christ-followers aligned with neither power they became easy targets for those who wished to vent frustrations and anger. They were often accused of heinous crimes they were not guilty of committing. And because they lacked legal support in the courts they were unable to prove their innocence. At other times they were attacked and disposed of with no interference, simply because there was no one who chose to defend them.

Many times in listening to the accounts, Mary thanked God that they didn't live in Jerusalem—or even close to it. Comparatively speaking, she felt quite safe in their little village. Things were not easy. But their wants were few and most of their needs were met by the work of their own hands.

Though Mary hadn't recognized it, she was studying the sky less often than she had in the past. Her life was full. Family consumed her thoughts and brought delight to her days. Benjamin and Judith added a baby boy to their home. And little Simona, at two years of age, took charge of the little one, calling him *my brudder*. The rest of the family called him Amos, after his grandfather.

But even though Mary was less anxious for the Lord to return, she did pray daily and passionately—for her family, for her neighbors, for the persecuted, and for the light to be revealed to her Jewish brothers and sisters. The Christ had come to bring freedom from sin and destruction and had promised to come again to reclaim and reward his own. Since no one knew when, the need to be constantly ready was imperative.

Mary also gathered with the other people of faith in the village for prayer, fasting, and fellowship. They continued to share reports of what was happening within the Christian community, wherever the Gospel had been shared and accepted. Sometimes these reports came in the form of a letter penned from the hand of one of the leaders in their faith. These were precious indeed.

Work at Benjamin's shop continued. The economy had dipped somewhat and the shop was not as busy as it had once been, but with careful planning and spending they were able to provide for two households.

Life was not easy. But life was still good. The youngsters Simona and Amos were their sources of joy.

Perhaps Mary should have seen it coming. But like so many things in life, it came so gradually that it wasn't noted. Her mother had been growing frailer, Mary was aware of that. But it had come on so gradually that it had been accepted. And then a fall as she moved from her chair to her bed seemed to escalate all of her frailties.

Hulda became totally bedridden and the task of her care was too much for Esther to handle on her own, even if Mary was there to assist her in the evening and early morning.

So Mary had a little chat with Benjamin, who shared her concern, and it was agreed that she should give up her job with her brother and stay at home to give full-time care to their mother.

Hulda objected when she heard the plan but Mary quieted her concerns as gently as she was able, and her mother soon settled and accepted all the help that was necessary from her daughter's hands.

It seemed that the decline advanced quickly. Daily Hulda became more and more dependent. Mary found that her days were more than filled with nursing, feeding, and general care. She now had less time to spend with young Simona and Amos but she also had less energy to give to those limited moments. All of her days and much of her nights were needed just for the care of her mother.

Judith was expecting her third child. So caring for her own family when she was already weary from the weight of the coming baby was enough for Judith to manage.

Benjamin helped at any time and in any way that he could. However, he was now the one in charge of their group that met for worship. His days, too, were full. Their little church had grown with the believers who trickled in from areas around Jerusalem because of the persecution that continued. And the newcomers were always in want because of the fact that they had always needed to flee with little chance to prepare.

It was a hard time for all. And even as the passing away of Hulda lightened their workload, it added to their grief.

Mary had not known how strange, how empty and lost, one would feel without a mother. She'd felt quite in charge of her daily circumstances. In a general way, she'd been the breadwinner, the supervisor, the decision-maker for such a long time that she'd thought that things would just carry on as they'd been. It surprised her when everything seemed to flip-flop. She felt like a child again—lost and lonely and unable to navigate her world.

It seemed to take her many days to get things moving forward on a familiar yet new path. She was thankful for Esther who seemed to run a steady course amongst all the confusion and adjustments.

Little Simona was the light and joy throughout their daily journey. Amos was still very much Benjamin's boy but Simona shared her love equally with everyone. And now also her childish advice with anyone who would listen to her chatter.

Mary was now properly and clearly *Aunt Mary*. Simona was quick to say, "Aunt Mary, I think you should . . ." or, "Aunt Mary, let me . . ." followed by a specific directive.

Mary would just smile and, as the advice of the young Simona was usually good—or perhaps acceptable, or at least harmless—Mary often agreed.

Benjamin was the constant stabilizer of the two households. Mary regretted her need to lean on him—to seek his advice—and even his physical or, on occasion, financial help. He never complained. In fact, he usually recognized the need even before Mary had realized it.

The new baby arrived. It was different this time. Mary had not even been notified until everything was over, the midwife had been sent on her way, and young Simona entered her door, cheeks flushed from her journey and the rather sharp autumn wind. She climbed up on a stool beside the table where Mary was working on a batch of bread and said, excitedly, "Guess what, Aunt Mary."

Mary knew the game. She was to now make a guess.

"The moon fell out of the sky?"

Simona shook her head, her eyes twinkling and a smile on her face. She loved the game they played together.

"Your grapevine grew some apples."

"No." Another shake of the head as Simona reached for a pinch of bread dough. Mary tapped her fingers. "Are they clean?" she asked.

Simona studied her fingers. "Almost," she said, lifting them up for her aunt to see.

"Almost is not good enough. You best run and wash them."

Simona ran to do as bidden. She was soon back and up on the stool again. "One more guess," she prompted.

"Amos grew another leg."

Simona laughed at this. "Silly."

"I give up," said Mary.

Simona flung arms out, and then clapped her hands together. "We got another baby!"

"What?"

"Mama got the baby—now." Her eyes shone. Then she sobered. "But it's not a sister. It's another brother. Like Amos."

Mary began to scurry. "Esther," she called. "Can you take over with the bread? I must go to Judith."

"Mama is still in bed." Simona informed her. "She's not sick. Just tired—from getting the baby. Amos is home—with Dada. But he has to be quiet. Dada said. So Mama can rest again."

Esther appeared, her eyes wide with concern. "Something wrong?"

Mary was already wiping her hands on a towel. "Judith had the baby. I need to . . ."

"It's a brother—again," added Simona. "Another one." She shrugged her shoulders.

Mary reached for her shawl and held out her hand to Simona so the child would follow. She must get to Judith to see if she needed her aid.

"I'll be back as soon as . . ."

"Don't hurry," Esther called after her. The door slammed and they were gone.

Both Judith and the new baby boy were well. The midwife had pronounced him a healthy and fine boy. To Mary, he was much more than that. He was another son for her brother Benjamin, who held him with pride—with a bit of help from Amos, who also crowded onto his lap. As soon as they entered Simona claimed the small space that was left.

"Well, look at you," Mary quipped. "You're going to run out of lap."

Benjamin just grinned. "I'll always find room for one more," he replied, and Mary knew it was true. Her brother loved his babies.

"How's Judith?"

"I believe she's sleeping. But she's fine. Just fine."

Mary tossed aside her shawl.

"Would you like tea?" she asked as she headed toward the small kitchen.

"Tea would be good."

"Shhh," said the young Amos. "Baby sleep."

Mary looked at her brother, his arms full of babies, a look of love filling his eyes. She left for the kitchen before the tears would reveal her deep emotion.

The news of persecution continued to arrive with each traveler that came to their village. It seemed that the more they heard, the closer the events seemed to be to their own area.

Mary found it hard not to ask her brother if he felt they were in any danger. Would they, too, need to flee in the dark of some night, taking what little they could carry on their shoulders? They didn't even own a donkey. Perhaps it would be wise to purchase one—just in case . . .

But she couldn't bring up the subject. Benjamin now had three small children. How would he ever manage to transport them all?

And Judith. She hadn't seemed to gain back her strength and vigor as quickly after the birth of her last son. Mary began to feel uneasy. Again, her eyes were on the sky. *Come, Lord Jesus* was her silent cry. *Take us all from this world of sin.*

But the days ticked by—one by one—and Mary gradually began to relax again. Maybe things were not as bad as she'd feared.

However, it did not get better. Former Jewish worshippers, now known as Jesus' followers or Christians were leaving Jerusalem, as anxious fathers and mothers sought to protect their children.

The gatherings for prayer increased, both in frequency and intensity. It was obvious that their lives were in danger from a world of anger and confusion. When would it ever end?

Please, Lord Jesus. We need you now. It was not just Mary's prayer. Many were joining her.

Why was he taking so long?

CHAPTER THIRTY-SIX

The Flight

MARY WOKE TO a thumping on her door. Benjamin had recently put a large, cumbersome, and ugly-looking lock on the inside—just in case, he'd said. To Mary it was a constant reminder of the world in which they now lived. Mary knew that Benjamin had also put the same kind of lock on his own door.

"Mary," came a soft but urgent call. It was her brother's voice.

She pulled a robe over her light tunic and hurried to her door. She felt clumsy as with trembling hands she tried to get the key in the lock and the door opened.

"I'm here. I'm trying . . ." she answered loudly enough for him to hear. Had something happened to one of the children—or to Judith?

At last the lock fell open in her hands and she felt Benjamin push the door from the other side. The look in his eyes was one of panic. "You need to leave. Now. I have a cart. Bring only what is essential. Come as quickly as you can."

"What . . . ?"

"I don't have time to explain. Just come. Quickly. Get Esther."

Mary still stood, frozen with shock.

"Now!" Benjamin almost screamed at her. "Understand?"

"Yes. Yes. We'll come."

He wheeled about and was gone.

Mary closed her eyes and prayed. She wasn't sure if she used words—or simply feelings—but she reached out to God. When she opened her eyes Esther stood staring at her in confusion.

"We must go," Mary managed. "Take only what is necessary. Nothing more. We must go now—to Benjamin's. He has a cart."

In a matter of minutes they were hurrying to Benjamin's. Darkness still covered the village. The moon was pale and half-hidden by cloud cover. It was hard to be sure of one's footing. Mary wished to take Esther's arm but her hands were full of the few things that she had deemed essential.

When they reached Benjamin's they were amazed to find not just a simple cart, but a donkey and a driver. Benjamin must have been worried enough to prepare ahead. Already Benjamin had his wife and three children loaded on the cart. There was room for little else. Benjamin had stuffed blankets and food items wherever he found a vacant spot.

He was apologizing even as he continued to load. "I'm sorry—you'll need to walk—and carry your things—if you can. Later you may be able to take turns but for now—you must go."

He was placing his arms around his wife and family and planting kisses on their brows, even as he spoke. Judith was the last one he held. She clung to Benjamin, hesitant to let him go.

Mary heard the words, "God go with you." And then he nodded to the driver, slapped the dozing donkey on his rump, and stepped back.

The driver pulled on the lead rope and the cart began to roll.

It was the first that Mary realized that Benjamin did not intend to go with them. She turned to look at him.

"Go. Go quickly," he ordered.

"But—you . . ."

"Later—when I can."

He moved quickly, pulled her close looking deeply into her eyes. "Take care of them, little sister. Take care of them for me."

He kissed her forehead and released her. "Now go."

Mary heard one of the children crying, "Dada—come. Come." She still didn't understand. She heard Judith weeping and the children crying. *What was happening?*

She turned obediently and followed the cart away from their homes, out of the village. There, behind them, her brother still stood watching them go. Even in the moonlight she could see him lift his hands and raise his eyes in prayer.

They stumbled through the darkness for the rest of the night. As the sun began to bring light to their world, Mary thought that the poor donkey looked as weary as she felt.

Thankfully the children still slept, except for the baby who was nursing again, held tightly in his mother's arms. Tears still lay on Judith's cheeks. Mary wondered if she had cried for the entire night.

She changed her own pace so that she could move closer to the cart. Judith gave her a bit of a nod in greeting. "What happened?" Mary whispered so as not to waken Simona or Amos.

"Word came with the caravan. The mobs are busy gathering the leaders of the villages. Those who are encouraging the new believers. Benjamin is on their list. They're already on their way to the village to find him."

Terror struck Mary's heart. "He should have left. With us. He . . ."

"He said that if he stayed, they might spare the rest."

"But . . ." It didn't make sense to Mary.

"None of the others were prepared to flee. Benjamin has been concerned. For weeks rumors have come. He made sure he was ready . . ." Judith continued.

"But he's not here."

Judith's voice tightened. She shook her head. "He hopes by staying he can save our lives."

"He would give his life to . . . ?"

Judith nodded. "Yes," she answered.

Mary could only stagger forward. Her mind refused to understand.

Judith tried her voice again. "We talked about it. Prayed about it. He wanted us to go. He was afraid if we were there, the mob might—might do something to us—just to bring punishment to him. That he might deny his faith—to try to save . . ." She couldn't go on. Mary heard the sob she tried to control. "They've done that—in other places—to other leaders," she finally managed.

Mary felt numb.

Simona began to stir. She woke, looked around her with puzzled eyes, then back to her mother. "Where's Dada?" she asked.

"He stayed at home," Judith replied and her voice sounded almost calm. "He hopes to join us—later."

Simona lay back down and pulled her blanket closer around her shoulders. "I hope he hurries. I miss him."

It took several days of travel to reach the village that Benjamin had deemed still safe for his family. There were others there who like themselves had fled to a place of safety. Tired, destitute, broken, and confused. There was really no place to put them all. They slept wherever they found a spot, ate whatever they found to eat, wept when they hoped no one was watching—and prayed. Night and day they prayed.

They were relieved to *feel* safe, even if that were not really so. Their greatest longing was for news of what had transpired after they'd fled. Was their village still standing—or burned to the ground? Had those they left behind found safety somewhere? Would they ever see them again? What was to happen to them now?

Mary joined their ranks, though not their company. It was hard even to trust one another. Who was safe to talk to? Who might be an informer sent to expose those who were trying to hide?

Many had come with no preparation at all. Benjamin's family situation was different since he'd given their guide enough money to find them a very simple place to dwell. Mary wondered about her brother. How long had he known that they were in danger? He'd never hinted that he felt they might need to flee. Though looking back Mary remembered a few of his addresses at their gatherings for prayer when he'd suggested that people be prepared, that if possible, they seek safety elsewhere. He'd even named a few of the cities where he felt they would be accepted. But Mary had no idea that Benjamin felt the need to flee might be so close at hand.

"What a heavy burden to carry!" she thought.

And now because of his forethought they would be safe—for a time. But where was her big brother? Her protector? The husband of her sister-in-law Judith, the father of Simona, Amos, and baby John?

"Oh, Lord," she prayed aloud, "Please come—now."

They unpacked their few belongings and carried things into the little building. It was neither pretty nor clean but it did look solid and weatherproof. There was a fire pit under the protection of a little roof. And there were places to lay their mats for sleeping. It would be crowded. But it should be dry and safe from unwanted animals and desert snakes. The door looked solid and it was equipped with a heavy bar to be placed in the inside pockets for overnight.

Their driver took the cart and donkey and left for a market that he said was just across town. He came back with a few simple staples, which he passed to Mary. "I need to leave you now. I'm going to return to my home. I've done all I was paid to do." He hesitated. "You're the one named Mary?"

Mary nodded.

He reached in his cloak and withdrew a package. "I was to give this to you once we were safe."

Mary accepted the package. It was from Benjamin. She held it close. She'd open it once the man was gone.

"I must take my donkey and cart," he explained. "I need them to earn my daily bread."

"Of course," Mary nodded. "I understand."

Then he turned, climbed into the cart, and clucked to the animal. Mary watched the cart roll away. The poor animal still looked weary.

She found a spot that had a bit of shade from the afternoon sun and opened the package. There was a small bag of coins. She wept again. Her brother must have given everything he had.

She lifted the letter, recognizing the writing of her brother.

"My dear sister, Mary," it began.

I am sorry that things have come to this. What I am asking of you is unfair, I know, but you are the only one I would trust with those I love more than life itself. I know you love them also. That is why I dare to assign you such a burdensome task. Please, as best you are able, take care of my dear Judith and our three little ones. If God so wills, I will be able to join you. But according to the warnings I have received from within our community of believers that may not be possible. I have offered up many prayers for the safety of you all.

Tell the little ones that I love them dearly. Remind them of that each night as you hear their prayers, each morning as you look at the sunrise of a new day. If I cannot come to you, may the day come when, one by one, you will all come to be with me in God's place of safety and rest.

I love you, my little Mary. Pray that God will give me the strength to stand firm in my faith.

Your brother, Benjamin

Mary ignored the tears that flowed down her cheeks as she knelt on the dusty ground to pray for her older brother. She wished to scream to the heavens. "Save him, Lord! You have the power. Save him from the mob. He is a good man. A follower of your Way. Save him."

But she did not. Instead, she prayed as Benjamin had asked her to pray, "Please, God, may he be faithful to you. Keep him strong in his faith, whatever happens. As he faces his persecutors give him strength that only you can give. I love him. I will always love him. Lord—be with my big brother."

The days managed to drag by. The children asked about their father with less frequency. It was mostly at bedtime that they still wondered when he would come and why it was taking him so long. Mary wondered the same thing but she didn't voice it.

Daily she prayed the prayer that Benjamin had asked her to pray. With determination and faith, they carried on. No one would say that things returned to normal. This new life was nowhere near normal for this little family. But the days passed by and the world went on.

Mary went to the market daily. Not just for their food supply but also for any news that she could gather. Each day as she returned home, Judith's eyes held questions she dared not ask aloud. Mary's simple shake of her head was the only answer. Day by day no word came from their home village.

Mary argued with herself. Perhaps no news was good news. But she could not convince herself. Benjamin would have joined the family by now were he free to do so. He knew where they were.

Judith tried hard to present herself well for the sake of the children. She hid her tears but Mary often heard her weeping in the night. She looked pale and drained and Mary worried about her health. She coaxed her sister-in-law to eat by mentioning the baby who, too, depended on Judith for sustenance. Usually it worked, but Mary was aware that there were times when it was very difficult for the young mother to swallow what she placed in her mouth.

The children were the first to begin to adjust. They still asked for their father but with childlike faith they fully expected that he would one day join them again. In the meantime, they lived in the day that was before them, as children do.

Mary tried her hardest to lay aside her deep grief as well. Though she was losing hope that Benjamin would ever join them again, she didn't speak of it, did not even allow herself to think of it. It wasn't that she was pretending. No, she was more realistic than that. It was just that she would not allow her mind to go there, to wonder, to picture how her brother may have already died. She blocked such thoughts and whenever they became too demanding to ignore, she prayed.

And finally, after many days, there was news at the market from her own hometown. Yes—the mob had arrived. Yes—they were after the leader named Benjamin. Yes—he pleaded with them to let the others go. His arguments held them in check for a while, as they conferred with one another. If he brought them his own family, they would consider the request. But his own family was no longer a part of the fellowship of the town. Then Benjamin had no bargaining rights at all. At least let the mothers and children go, Benjamin had argued. Who would look after them?

And so it went on for the better part of the day. In the meantime, Benjamin was held in chains. They would not even allow him a drink as he stood in the heat of the sun. Men from the village tried to argue on Benjamin's behalf but were warned that their fate would be the same as his if they tried to interfere.

Suddenly, the demand changed. No one understood why. The leader turned to the large group of followers who had been rounded up and told them that the life of their leader was all that would be required. But every male from among them must attend his stoning so that they would understand what would happen to them if they continued to worship the false prophet Jesus.

When they'd arrived at the site where the stoning would take place, the leader of the group turned to Benjamin. "We are reasonable people. Far more patient than you deserve. These men you have led astray—you must tell them the truth. Tell them Jesus is not the long-awaited Messiah. You have been feeding them falsehood. Tell them."

Benjamin's head lifted as he looked out over the group of men he had been teaching truth. "Stand firm, brothers. We know . . ."

The sting of a lash whipped across Benjamin's bare back, and the blood flowed.

"Tell them he is not the Promised One!" screamed the leader.

Benjamin's voice had weakened—but it was clear. "I would be giving false testimony. Jesus . . . of Nazareth is the . . . the Promised Messiah."

The whip flashed again. Another trail of blood followed the path of the first.

"Deny him."

"Can I deny the sun? It would be foolish. Everyone sees clearly it would be a lie. So it is with Jesus—our Messiah—and Savior."

The leader stepped back. But not before he struck Benjamin across his cheek with an anger-hardened hand. He gave the signal. And the crowd was released to hurl their stones.

Mary was told that two of the followers had dared to defy the mob and tried to protect Benjamin. They, too, lost their lives. Three righteous men were stoned that day. The last words on their lips had been prayers for their murderers—and cries of triumph.

Even members of the mob were shaken. It had not unfolded like a victory at all.

CHAPTER THIRTY-SEVEN

The Longing

Gradually Mary and Esther, and Judith with her three children, began to heal. Once that had begun they were slowly able to talk and pray together about Benjamin again.

Judith began to put on some of the weight she'd lost. Mary decided to try to find a job so she might be able to earn enough to keep them fed. Esther, now growing grey with her advancing years, announced that she'd be in charge of the kitchen. Simona and Amos continued to pray for their "dada" and no one instructed them to stop. They'd been told that their father was now in heaven. So with childlike faith they directed their prayers right to Jesus whom they decided would be giving personal care to the one they'd lost and still loved.

The days ticked by. Another season changed their weather pattern. Mary's job took her to the local physician's place each day. As the days passed by, baby John continued to learn new baby tricks that pleased his brother and sister and made them squeal with laughter.

But even with the pleasant changes, a heavy cloud seemed to hover over the rather shabby little residence. Things would never, never be the same again. Benjamin, their protector and joy and light, had left them. They continued to fan the spark of hope that the Lord's coming would be soon, when they'd once again be reunited.

Not just the days but now the years had passed. The children were fast becoming adults—not yet ready to leave home but capable of helping with the daily needs of the family. Simona spent her days at the shop where wool yarns were spun and sold. Amos helped a local gardener with his fruit from the vines, and John, their youngest, was keeping a small flock of sheep for one of the widows who lived along their street. He learned to know and love each of the wooly animals almost as much as he loved his own family and spoke of them by name as he shared stories about them with his family each evening.

Mary remembered Benjamin's words about the sheep being good companions. Perhaps his young son was finding it to be true.

Esther could no longer handle the work of the kitchen but she still helped Judith with household chores. Simona also joined in wherever her hands were needed after her daily hours at the shop.

Mary continued her work in the same position she'd first found. It was rare to be a woman who could read and write and do sums at a level equal with a trained man. She was of great assistance to the man who dispensed medications and ointments. She also enjoyed the work and learned everything she could regarding the art of healing. The town had gained great respect for Mary's knowledge and encouraging aid.

The small group of believers in their village had not grown much in size but they'd grown in the fervency of their faith. Once again, they encouraged one another to watch the sky. The Master had promised to return. Perhaps this would be the day it would happen and all the pain and sorrow and clutter of the angry and deceived world would dissolve in the blink of an eye. This was their hope. Their prayer.

Every morning as Mary rose from her bed, she looked out her small window at the hills beyond and whispered the question, just as she'd done so many years ago. "Is this the day, Lord?" And the last thing she did before she reclaimed her bed at night was to bow in prayer and ask, "Could it be tonight, Lord?"

But one by one the days passed by—and he did not come.

Then word came that Jerusalem had fallen to Roman forces. The invaders not only plundered their city, but in their anger and irrepressible rage they destroyed the holy Temple. The Jewish nation might have been able to endure their cruelty—except for this act of total dominance. In destroying their Temple these pagans had defied God himself. And they'd torn out the very heart of the Jewish nation and faith. Surely, they would pay for their criminal behavior.

Many of those who'd held fast to the Jewish faith had managed to flee the broken and suffering city. How could they endure a life without their place of worship? Without God's presence? The scattered synagogues now had even more importance in their daily lives.

Esther and Mary sat in the shade, sipping cool water sweetened by pomegranate juice. It had been another busy day. They were both bone-weary. Esther was now elderly, her body fragile. She was finding it more and more difficult to be up and about on feet that swelled and ached and a back that caused suffering. Mary, too, was beginning to feel the effects of her years.

Their conversations now were often reflections of the past. So much of what had happened in their lives seemed long ago. And yet, strangely, it remained so fresh in their minds. The words *Do you remember?* were spoken often. Sometimes the memories were sweet. At other times they were filled with sharp pain. Life seemed to be such a mix of joy and grief. They realized that both the good and the bad had shaped them into who they'd become. But they also came to understand that their close relationship had been a bigger factor.

The children of Benjamin and Judith were now grown and had established homes of their own, with families that brought joy and at times suffering. Already, Judith could count five little grandchildren among them all, with two more on the way.

Judith, who'd been such an encourager to the new group of local believers, had finally consented to share the home of her own daughter Simona and her family. It had required a move all the way to Philippi.

Mary and Esther missed Judith each day. They were even more thankful that they still had one another. They spoke of her departure as they sat and reflected. "I sometimes ask myself whatever would have happened to me if I hadn't met you when I was alone on the streets of Jerusalem," Mary commented.

Esther stirred only slightly and answered with confidence. "God would have provided someone else."

Mary smiled. "I cannot imagine *someone else*. We fit so beautifully. I was so young—and so unwise about the ways of the city. The world. And you were older and wiser—and in touch with life in Jerusalem. I would have been lost."

Esther conceded but made no response.

"I've often thought of the widow Mary," the contemplation

continued. “I’ve wondered if she ever realized—believed—that Jesus really was the Messiah.”

Esther shook her head. “I don’t believe so. She passed not too long after you’d been schooled. I was still with her at the time. Oh, not with her when she died but still working in the home.”

“I didn’t know that. You’ve never said.”

“You have never asked,” replied Esther, matter-of-factly. After a few moments she went on. “It was very hard for me. I’d always felt safe in her home. When she died, I was dismissed—and frightened. I didn’t know what to do, where to go.”

Mary stirred. “Like me.”

“Then I met an older woman named Adah. She was a Jesus follower. It was she who allowed me the use of the little lean-to at the back of her house.”

“With the rooster?”

That brought a chuckle. “Yes—the rooster. He never did accept me as belonging. Always made a fuss when I came and went.”

Quiet moments passed. Esther continued. “I’d wonder what happened to Adah. She’d be gone too by now, of course. She was elderly even then. But she was kind to me. In fact, she was the one who took me to the secret meetings of the followers. That’s where I became a believer.”

“And then you took me.”

They sat in thought. “That’s how it works,” Mary said. “One finding the Savior, then sharing with another. That’s how the Kingdom has been built—one by one.”

“Sometimes,” agreed Esther. “But at other times it grows by the masses. I remember a baptism where an entire large group responded. It was amazing. I’ll never forget the—the awe—the joy of deliverance.” She shook her head.

“Like the Pentecost happening.”

"Yes—just like that." Esther sighed with satisfaction at the memory.

"And Peter shared that the Messiah had left—but he had promised to come back."

Esther nodded.

The familiar words were difficult to acknowledge. It had been so many years of waiting. Mary struggled to admit the disappointment aloud. "But he hasn't. Still, we're waiting—and waiting. And he has not come." Mary's voice sounded mournful despite her efforts to hide her emotions.

"True—he has not come—yet he has been here—with us always. Remember—he left his Spirit with us to be our guide and comforter. He hasn't deserted us."

"Of course." Mary could agree without reservation. "I don't know how I would have made it through some of the dark days without him. But I'm like a child. Impatient. I still long for him to come again."

"He will." Esther's words were simple—but filled with promise.

"When?" The one word was unintentionally sharp. "Look around us. Bad things are still happening. People are still hurting people. There is war and famine and pain and . . . When will he come?"

Esther stirred, then reached for her friend's hand and gave it a little squeeze. "We're not to know," she reminded her, "The Lord himself said that even *he* didn't know. It's all in the hands of the Father. But it will happen. Just as his first coming happened. Our forefathers, too, waited for many, many years for the fulfillment of the prophecies. The Promise. But he came. Just at the proper time. And he will come again."

"But when?" Mary's words were softer—but rich with longing.

"After," replied Esther.

"After?"

"After *all* has been completed. After *all* has been fulfilled. We don't know what's in God's plan. How many more need to hear the Word. Who is God waiting for, giving him—or her—one more day, one more opportunity to turn to him? But it could be close! So close! Maybe there's just one or two more—for whom he's patiently waiting."

Esther's voice was stirring with the emotion she felt. "Perhaps—perhaps our prayers need to change. Instead of praying that he will come, we need to pray that *they* will come to *him*. For forgiveness. For new life. This much we know, with surety, that after God's plan for his creation has been fulfilled—he, our Christ and Savior—*will* come."

Mary nodded. It was so hard to wait, but faith would sustain her. She would continue to pray for patience—and strong, courageous, faith—until the Day of Deliverance would take her home.

And she would add to her prayers those to whom the Father was still giving one more love-filled opportunity to seek forgiveness in the name of Jesus.

A Note from the Author

Two thousand years have passed—and still we wait. There have been many troublesome times. Famines, wars, plagues, and perils. Few years have been without conflict somewhere. There has also been persecution. Many of our brothers and sisters in the faith have been martyred because of their belief. And many, many others have passed on to their reward because they accepted the Savior's forgiveness and their numbered days had been fulfilled.

And still we wait.

He has not returned.

But he will come. He promised. He always keeps his promises.

But when? *After!*

After all has been fulfilled . . . After all his plans for the earthly experience of humanity are completed . . . He will return.

But for now, there is still time.

Death—or his return—will close the door of opportunity. Now is the time to ask for his forgiveness. If you have not done so, accept, in faith, his promise to forgive.

Follow it up by seeking a reliable mentor in the Truth. Find a faith community for guidance and worship. Be ready to stand firm! It may be required.

But the message is equally important for those of us who have claimed his promises and have traveled for many years as believers in the truths of his Word! Yes, the Bible has become familiar to us as we have read and studied. We have embraced his Commandments and sought to follow the Truth.

Yet it is so easy to become complacent.

Is there any need for us to check our hearts? Have we become negligent—careless in our relationship with him or with others? Need we ask ourselves if there are areas where we must seek forgiveness, work through a reconciliation, deal with a hidden sin—or just renew and refresh our appreciation for what God, through Christ his Son, has done for us?

Is there something—anything—that we should do—need to do—to be ready?

Is our faith strong enough to maintain our relationship with our Savior if persecution should come and a costly stand for our position should be required?

May we ask the hard questions, take the needed actions, and place our faith in Christ, who has done all that is necessary to take us from a sin-broken world to a glorious new heaven.

Recently I again read the book of Revelation. In spite of the fact that it is a book of mystery and tribulation, it is also a book of excitement and hope. The main takeaway is that God has his plan in place. And it will be fulfilled.

Following my study of Revelation, I went through the four Gospels. As I neared the end of John, I was impressed by the parallels of Christ's first coming and the second coming. Both events have been designed by God.

The first coming of Christ—the Baby in the manger—was God's plan. Many prophecies had been given regarding Christ's first coming. In spite of that, much had been left a mystery, testing mankind's patience and faith. Those who watched and waited spanned many generations. At God's chosen time, he sent his Son in complete fulfillment of the prophecies. Christ came, as intended, to bring salvation. His coming brought both joy and chaos. God kept his promise.

The plans for the second coming, too, have been made and promised by God. We have many prophecies and promises concerning his second coming, as well. Much has been given, yet much remains a mystery, needing patience and faith. These prophecies, as well, will all be fulfilled. Those who have been prepared and waiting have spanned many generations. It will happen according to God's time and purpose. Christ, then, will come to bring deliverance—and judgment. Again, it will bring both joy and chaos. God will keep his promise.

We must be ready.

The story you've just read is a fictional account written with the intent of making us think. The main characters exist only in the mind of the author, though a number of real characters from the Bible are referenced, including Jesus Christ whose birth, life, teachings, death, resurrection, and ascension are well documented in the Scriptures and in many other historically verified writings.

My research did not always provide the needed background information, so I used the "writer's license" in order to flesh out the characters. For instance, I found much difference of opinion as to how important it was for the women of the day to use a shawl or face covering. And I really did not discover how Pharisees-in-training lived and moved. Nor can I support the manner in which the Temple offerings and fees were gathered and documented. Much of the story's background should not be understood as historical fact. It is simply a framework to give the characters substance. Life.

Though this story was not easy to write, nor is it recommended for young readers, I pray that it brings some important reminders.

For instance, it is not always the person we would choose as *worthy* who makes the important decision of becoming a believer. God has given each individual *free will*. We deeply grieve over those we love who do not choose to repent and believe. At other times, one whom we see as the greatest sinner does seek forgiveness and God responds in mercy.

The event of Christ's coming that happened so many years ago was a dividing point in our faith—in history. Up until then, the Jewish religion, based on what we refer to as the Old Testament, documented the creation of all things, including mankind, and the religious path people were to follow. Adam and Eve sinned, bringing the penalty of death to all. God accepted the death of an animal in place of the *spiritual* death of the sinner. Through Abraham, Moses, and many faithful prophets, priests, kings, and ordinary citizens, this message from God was passed on through the centuries. People of faith, those who *believed* (both Jew and Gentile), were led by the Law, a God-given set of rules, guidelines, observances, and practices.

With the coming of Christ, the one who *fulfilled* the Law, faith switched from *actions* to *being* in a new and different way. There are still rules to follow—but salvation is not dependent on keeping *observances*, but by faith in accepting what Christ has done through his death and resurrection on our behalf. Acknowledgment of sin and admission of guilt, leading to repentance and a request for pardon, brings forgiveness and a change of heart. Because of forgiveness, the heart's desire now is to follow Christ's example by living in a way that pleases our holy God and benefits others.

Christ's second coming will be another major event. Those living at that time who have *believed* and are waiting for his coming will be transported to a new heavenly home, where they will join with the great multitude of other believers who have, over the centuries, believed and obeyed. Those who have not believed will face judgment. Only God has the authority and the knowledge to be a righteous judge, for he alone knows the human heart. God has clearly explained the steps we need to take to be ready for Christ's return:

> She [Mary] will have a son, and you are to name him Jesus, for he will save his people from their sins. (Matthew 1:21)
>
> To all who believed him and accepted him, he gave the right to become children of God. (John 1:12)
>
> This is how God loved the world: He gave his one and only Son, so that everyone who believes in him will not perish but have eternal life. (John 3:16)
>
> There is no judgment against anyone who believes in him. But anyone who does not believe in him has already been judged for not believing in God's one and only Son. (John 3:18)

Your prayer for his forgiveness does not require fancy or liturgical words but a sincere heart. Ask him—with repentance—and he will hear your prayer.

Those readers who enjoy a thrilling or at least a satisfying climax, may find it lacking in this story, for the climax of God's great plan is still in the future. But when that much anticipated Day arrives, it will be the most exciting—or terrifying—event since mankind's creation. There has been nothing like it to date nor will there be again.

For those who have *believed*, it will usher in a new beginning. All who have *believed,* since the beginning of creation and throughout the many centuries and generations following, will take their place in God's new Kingdom.

Think of it. There will no longer be pain or suffering, fear or frustration, defeat or dread—for all those things will have passed away.

That will be the ultimate climax of God's amazing plan for his Forgiven and Redeemed.

Acknowledgments

WITH DEEP GRATITUDE I wish to thank all those who have helped and encouraged in the process of taking this work from a God-whispered prompting to a finished story. A special thank you to my family who have aided in various ways. Their prayers were of major importance, and it was a blessing to us all to see God answering those prayers in unexpected ways. To all those of Tyndale House who have processed, reviewed, edited, formatted—and encouraged—making this work ready for publication, my sincere thanks. Your knowledge and expertise have been given with care and thoughtfulness. Working together has been a privilege and a blessing. Together we send out into our world a work of love and faith with the prayer that God will use something from these pages to touch hearts.

Discussion Questions

1. Which of the characters could you most relate to?
2. Would you have found it difficult to believe that Jesus was the Messiah if you had lived in that day?
3. Do you feel that some of the events of the story could happen again? In our lifetime? Do you feel that your faith is strong enough to maintain a relationship with Christ if persecution should come and a costly stand for your position should be required?
4. Do you think Mary's father's earnest desire to find Jesus so he could be healed shows an element of faith, even though he struggles with doubts?
5. If you were Mary, would you have found it difficult to forgive Enos?
6. Do you believe that Jesus will return? Could it be soon? Is there anything that you want to do to make sure you are ready?

7. Are there areas where you feel the need to seek forgiveness, work through a reconciliation, or deal with a hidden sin—or to simply renew and refresh your appreciation for what God, through Christ his Son, has done for us?

8. Near the end of the book, Esther tells Mary that perhaps instead of praying for Christ's soon return, they should pray for those who still haven't come to faith. Who are you waiting and praying for?

About the Author

BESTSELLING AUTHOR JANETTE OKE is credited with launching the modern era of inspirational fiction and is internationally celebrated for her significant contribution to the Christian book industry. Her novels have sold over 30 million copies, and nearly half of her more than 70 titles have been translated into nineteen languages. She is the recipient of the ECPA President's Award, the CBA Life Impact Award, the Gold Medallion, and the Christy Award. She met her husband, Edward, while attending Mountain View Bible College in Alberta, Canada. They were married after their graduation and enjoyed nearly 64 years of marriage, four children, and many grandchildren (and great-grandchildren) before his passing in 2022. Janette resides in Alberta, Canada.